Upstaged

BOOKS BY TEYLA BRANTON

Unbounded Series
The Change
The Cure
The Escape
The Reckoning
The Takeover

Unbounded Novellas
Ava's Revenge
Mortal Brother
Lethal Engagement
Set Ablaze

Imprints Series
First Touch (prequel)
Touch of Rain
On The Hunt
Upstaged
Under Fire
Blinded

Colony Six Series
Sketches

Other
Times Nine

UNDER THE NAME RACHEL BRANTON

Finding Home Series
Take Me Home
All That I Love
Then I Found You

Lily's House Series
House Without Lies
Tell Me No Lies
Your Eyes Don't Lie
Hearts Never Lie
Broken Lies
Cowboys Can't Lie

Noble Hearts
Royal Quest
Royal Dance

Picture Books
I Don't Want To Eat
Bugs
I Don't Want to Have
Hot Toes

Upstaged

TEYLA BRANTON

WHITE
STAR
PRESS

This is a work of fiction, and the views expressed herein are the sole responsibility of the author. Likewise, certain characters, places, and incidents are the product of the author's imagination, and any resemblance to actual persons, living or dead, or actual events or locales, is entirely coincidental.

Upstaged (Imprints Book 3)

Published by White Star Press
P.O. Box 353
American Fork, Utah 84003

Copyright © 2018 by Teyla Branton
Cover design copyright © 2018 by White Star Press
Originally published by the author under another name as *Final Call*.

Printed in the United States of America
ISBN: 978-1-939203-94-6
Year of first printing: 2018

To my daughter, Lisbon, who was the reason I wrote this entire book from bed—and who has brought to our family more blessings than I can count.

Acknowledgments

Thank you to early readers Cátia, Julie, and Gretchen, who encouraged me even while pointing out inconsistencies. You're good, ladies!

To Brent Rowley, who accepted my invitation to a concealed weapons class and who then ended up being the one to teach me about guns.

Chapter 1

I lifted the Ruger LCP .380, racked it quickly, and fired. Three shots in rapid succession—boom, boom, boom. Three more shots emptied the magazine. My target jerked repeatedly. Not unlike the jolting of my heart.

"Not bad." Detective Shannon Martin looked over my shoulder at the man-shaped paper target. Four of the rounds had hit the chest. Another went through the head. Only one was missing. "You sure you haven't done this before?" he asked.

"No," I snapped. "Just now and the last time." Truth was, I didn't want to be doing this now. My consulting position with the Portland police had led to my being imprisoned in an underground cellar, shot in the leg, and injured in numerous other ways, but carrying a gun was going too far. With my flower child upbringing, I doubted I could shoot anyone, even if my life depended on it.

"What's wrong?" Shannon's eyes went from my face to the Ruger and back again. "You aren't picking up any imprints, are you?"

We were alone inside the range, so I pushed off the earmuffs he'd insisted I wear to protect my ears—great idea, it turned out. "No imprints," I said.

Well, there was one faint feeling of satisfaction that Shannon had left when he'd shot the gun a week earlier, and even now I was probably leaving a few of resentment and maybe a little pride. Fortunately, these less vivid imprints didn't bother me.

"The older lady I bought it from said she'd shot it only a few times," he added.

"You know that if I ever actually used this on someone, I'd never be able to use it again. I'd have to relive the memory every time I touched it."

He shrugged. "I'd just find you another one."

I guess as a police detective that didn't bother him—shopping for guns, the possibility of shooting someone. All of it bothered me. I believed people had the right to defend themselves, but it was quite another thing to be the one actually pulling the trigger.

"Can we quit now?" I started to hand him the gun, barrel down, the way he'd drilled me these past few weeks.

"Not yet. You have to shoot at least a hundred rounds a month to stay in practice—and that's assuming you're hitting anything, which you are, fortunately. Now load her up again."

"A hundred? Please tell me rounds are individual bullets and not a whole clip." We'd been shooting together only once before, and I couldn't remember the terminology.

My faulty memory might have a remote—a very remote—connection to his unusual eyes. There's something about them. Something, perhaps, in the green blue color that illuminated his face. Or maybe it was the framing of his light brown lashes that made them so compelling. It was hard to think about anything else if I became caught in his gaze, so mostly I tried not to look.

"Magazine," he corrected. "It's not a clip. I know people call them that, but that's not what they are. The magazine is what holds the rounds—in this case, six rounds. And yes, rounds are individual bullets."

So six bullets went into the magazine, which in turn slid into the bottom of the gun grip, or handle as we rookies called it. Not rocket science by any stretch. Sighing internally, I pushed the magazine release button, placed the gun on the small stand in front of me, and began forcing bullets into the magazine.

Shannon stopped me when I went to put it back in. "Visually check the chamber first, just to make sure nothing's caught."

I did as he asked before proceeding to shred more of my target. Like the previous time we'd come to the range, Shannon seemed more puzzled than pleased at my success.

I didn't see what was so hard. You aimed and you shot. It was, well, rather easy. Kind of fun too, which I would never confess to Shannon. I derived a strange sort of contentment from irritating him, a trait he definitely shared when it came to me.

I shrugged. "I have good eyesight." Once again, I had to raise my voice to near yelling because of our earmuffs.

"All those herbs?" he mouthed a bit derisively, pushing the box of bullets at me.

I didn't take offense. Everyone was entitled to his opinion—even the annoying Detective Martin. My adoptive parents had been self-proclaimed hippies who owned an herb store, so naturally I'd consumed more than my share of herbs. Growing up with them had been unusual, but I wouldn't have traded it for anything—well, except maybe the opportunity to grow up with my twin, but that couldn't be changed now.

"Satisfied?" I asked when the man-shaped target finally tore in two at the chest and fell to the ground.

Shannon allowed himself a grin. "I've seen longtime police officers do worse."

Not exactly a compliment, but Shannon was careful that way. Maybe it was because he liked me far more than he wanted to. Or maybe because he'd finally started to trust both me and my weird gift of reading imprints—and begun to realize that there was nothing holding him back from his attraction to me now.

Nothing except my boyfriend, Jake, and my own reluctance to trust a man who until a few months ago thought I was mostly nuts.

Shannon was staring at me with those eyes that were probably responsible for more convictions than any detective work he'd ever done. I looked instead into his hairline. His hair, usually somewhere between brown and blond, was on the darker side now that we were in November. He needed a haircut, and the ends were beginning to curl with the length.

For a long time he didn't speak, though the air was suddenly heavy with whatever he'd left unspoken. Carefully, he began packing things away. He handed me the Ruger, zipped in a lightly padded cover.

"Keep it in your purse until I get you an ankle holster. There's an extra magazine in there, too. I've filled it with hollow points for a bigger impact."

"No way." I pushed the weapon back at him. "I don't even use a purse half the time."

"Well, you can't carry it on you without a holster."

"I'm not going to carry it at all."

"What do you think that class and all that fingerprinting was about? Your concealed-carry permit arrived in the mail, didn't it? You should have it on you at all times, whether you're carrying or not, in case you end up with a gun while working a case."

Okay, I *had* taken a class on gun safety and found it interesting. Since I'd been shot in the leg during our last adventure and had somehow ended up with the gun, albeit unloaded, I'd wanted to feel more comfortable with handguns in case such a thing ever happened again. But I wouldn't have taken the class at all if I'd known Shannon was going to insist that I carry a weapon.

"I've got the permit in my wallet, but I read that women who own guns are more likely to be shot than those who don't," I told him.

He snorted. "That's only women who aren't trained and who aren't going to practice every few weeks." He scrubbed a hand over his hair, and I followed the motion. "Speaking of which, there is a more intensive training I'd like you to attend. It's only three days. You get great target practice in a lifelike town. With popup targets and stuff."

"No, no, and no! Look, I have a niece now, and I can't have a gun around my apartment or at my store. If you make me take it, I'm just going to put it in my glove compartment."

"You don't even lock your car." The way he said *car* left me no doubt that he didn't believe my rusty Toyota hatchback was worthy of the name. He might have a point. It was always breaking down.

"Oh, right. Guess that sets me up for all kinds of liability."

"Yeah, the jail kind."

He was kind of cute when he was upset, though that was certainly not why I was arguing with him.

"Look," he continued, "your niece is only, what, three months old? It's going to be a while before she can rack and shoot a gun. By then you'll have a safe installed."

"At the department's expense?" They'd agreed to start paying me a consulting fee for reading imprints, but it wasn't a lot.

"Sure."

At this point, he'd say whatever he needed to make me take the gun, but I doubted the safe would come from the department. They didn't care if I carried a gun. They'd probably rather I didn't. But Shannon was president of the Autumn Needs to Be More Careful Club, which meant he cared about me. I wished he didn't. It made my life more complicated.

More exciting.

I took the gun and put it in my coat pocket. "There's not a bullet in the chamber, is there?"

"No. You'd have to rack it before you could shoot. But you should have checked yourself if that's the way you plan to carry it. Remember the class?"

"Oh, right." I wouldn't carry the gun with a bullet in the chamber like he did, though my permit gave me license to do so. I didn't trust it not to go off accidentally, but unless I racked it, it couldn't fire, so I was safe.

Outside it was raining. Again. The wind was also doing its thing, which made Portland bitterly cold this time of year. Shannon glanced instinctively at my feet, perhaps forgetting that during the most bitter winter months, even I usually wore something to cover my feet when I went outside. Instead of my customary winter moccasins, today I wore the boots my sister, Tawnia, had given me—no heel, fur-lined, and advertised as footwear that made you feel as if you were barefoot. They were almost like wearing thick socks, but unlike the socks I occasionally resorted to, they were waterproof. I hated not feeling a connection with the earth as I normally did in bare feet, but cold weather like this usually convinced me to use the boots or my moccasins.

I'd begun using gloves as well, something I'd occasionally done before in winter, though not for the same reason I used them now. Gloves protected me from accidentally finding random imprints and reliving experiences that weren't mine.

Of course, I wasn't prepared to wear gloves all the time. My shoe-hating, herb-loving, spirit-connected-to-the-universe upbringing wouldn't let me go that far. But sometimes after stumbling on a particularly virulent imprint, I was tempted.

Zipping my coat, I ran to Shannon's truck. Yes, a truck. I knew his house was built on an acre of land, so it made sense he might need a truck for something related to that, but I'd been so accustomed to seeing him in his white, unmarked police Mustang that when he'd come to pick me up, I'd felt a little taken aback. For some reason the blue truck made him seem more real—normal, maybe. Almost as though I'd seen a part of him that was too private to share.

It's just a truck, I told myself.

The weight of the Ruger felt heavy in my coat pocket. At least it could sit in a drawer at my antiques shop while I was working. My niece wasn't old enough even to crawl yet, much less open a drawer. Before much longer, though, it'd have to be in a safe or in a holster.

The idea of needing a gun was enough to make me seriously consider getting out of the imprint business. Except I didn't choose to read imprints. That just happened.

Psychometry was the official name of my ability to pick up scenes and emotions left on certain beloved objects or on objects involved in extremely emotional situations. I used my talent to find missing people, and the police used it through me. Some scientists believed that people like me developed part of our brains that ordinarily remained inactive. For all I knew, they were right. I suspected it was also hereditary, though because I was adopted, I wasn't sure where the ability had come from.

"Who's that?" Shannon asked.

We'd arrived outside my shop, where a bundled figure was pacing in front of my store. My employee, Thera Brinker, should be inside, but even if she wasn't and the door was still locked, all my customers knew they could reach Autumn's Antiques from the Herb Shoppe next door, owned by my friend and current boyfriend, Jake Ryan. Or I should say maybe-boyfriend, because even nearly six months into our relationship, we weren't exactly sure where things were heading.

The person outside was not a customer, then, but someone else waiting to see me.

"I don't know." I peered at the tall figure. Besides the fact that the person was likely male, I couldn't see much beyond the coat and the beanie he wore. I started to open the truck door.

"Wait. I'm coming with you."

I sighed. Shannon had been annoying before he'd stopped being so suspicious of me, but this was ridiculous. Ignoring him, I jumped from the truck and hurried toward my store. The figure stopped pacing when he saw me.

"Autumn," he said, giving me a tentative smile. "Hey, are your eyes two different colors or is it just the light?"

I'd know that smile anywhere—and the familiar greeting. My eyes were a different color, but only those who really *saw* me ever actually noticed. "Is that you, Bean Pole? Did you grow another three inches? Long time no see."

It'd been months, in fact, since I'd seen Liam Taylor. At least seven.

Liam nodded. "I need to talk to you. It's important." Before I could respond, his gaze went beyond me to Shannon, who'd finally caught up to us.

"Is he a cop?" Liam asked in an undertone.

If Liam hadn't been so serious, I might have laughed. He'd made Shannon as a cop dressed in civilian clothes on a Saturday afternoon. In the rain. That said a lot about Shannon—or about Liam. I hoped it was about Shannon and not Liam because I'd thought he'd come a long way since I first caught him shoplifting in my store.

"Why? You got something to hide?" Trust Shannon to make a comeback like that.

"Shannon's a friend," I said to Liam, throwing Shannon a glare. "What do you need to see me about?"

Liam shivered. "Can we go inside? I brought you something to, uh, see."

He meant something to read, as in imprints. A knot formed inside me. I hoped he wasn't in trouble. Either way, I had to get Shannon out of the picture.

"Okay, just a minute and we'll go inside." I turned to Shannon. "Thanks for the lesson."

"You sure you don't want me to stay?" He was using his eyes to full advantage, as if he knew their effect on me.

"I'm fine. Jake's next door if I need help."

Shannon stiffened. Wrong thing to say, but he knew my feelings for Jake, and I wasn't going to start hiding them now simply because I was also attracted to Shannon.

"Liam's harmless," I added. "He used to work for me."

Only a little bit of a stretch. I'd put Liam to work after I'd caught him shoplifting one of my antique music boxes last year. He'd seemed sincere when he said it was to send to his sister for her birthday. I hadn't simply given it to him like my father would have done—or invited him to dinner and ask if he needed a place to stay. I was too poor to go that far. But I had let him work off the music box in exchange for helping move and arrange my displays. I even gave him the music box wholesale so he wouldn't have to work more than a few days.

After that, I'd given him several more odd jobs I could barely afford whenever he was desperate, just enough to keep him honest. Then he'd graduated from high school and found a real job for the summer. He was supposed to be in college now, living on a merit scholarship and a bit of help from his parents.

"I'll call you about the safe." Shannon's eyes followed Liam, who was already opening the door to my store.

"Okay."

It was awkward leaving Shannon, though it hadn't always been. Now I never knew if I should hug him or say something to push him away. Lately, I'd really, really wanted not to push him away, but there was still Jake, and I didn't want to hurt him.

I followed Liam into my store and motioned him to wait in the back room so I could help Thera with the rush of people. Normally, I would have taken time to at least wave to Jake, but there was no chance of that now. Saturday mornings were always brisk in the antiques shop, and I had to hurry from my early morning taekwondo class to get there in time to help. The afternoons usually picked up from there. It was good for my pocketbook, though it made it hard to dart out at lunchtime for a brief shooting lesson. Unfortunately, Saturday was the only time Shannon was available during the day, and an evening seemed too much like a date to me.

"How did the lesson go?" Thera asked. As usual her white hair was swept up in an elegant knot, and she was wearing all blue, which she insisted was a calming color.

That reminded me of the weight in my coat pocket, one I couldn't rid myself of in front of my customers. "Apparently, I'm a natural."

"I thought you might be. You have good instincts."

I shrugged off the coat and set it under the counter, followed by my boots. I wiggled my freed toes and sighed with relief.

"Well, about most things," amended Thera, glancing at my feet in disapproval. She was always worried I'd catch my death of cold, even in midsummer, or contract some strange illness, no matter how many times I told her I washed my feet more than most people washed their hands—and how she touched a lot worse things on doorknobs. She didn't want to hear it.

"I hope you got a chance to grab some lunch," she added, "because it's been like this the whole time you were gone."

"I did." We'd eaten sandwiches Shannon had bought on our way to the range. I felt bad for leaving Thera on a day when it was so busy, but Shannon had been insistent. He obviously still felt responsible for the last time I'd been hurt.

When we were down to the last customer at the register and two more who were browsing, Thera turned to me, waving a blue-clad arm. "I can take care of the rest. That boy seems kind of anxious. He's poked his head out half a dozen times already."

"Thanks."

In my narrow back room, which ran the width of my store, Liam wasn't sitting in the comfortable easy chair that beckoned to me with an almost hypnotic call. He'd taken off his coat and laid it on the long worktable but was pacing from the shop door to the bathroom at the far end. He was as lanky as always—college life hadn't improved that—and his hair looked as though he hadn't combed it in a week, though it didn't seem greasy.

"So what's up?" I asked, ignoring my easy chair and going to heat water on the stove so I could make a nice soothing herbal tea. I wanted to ask if he was in trouble, but he'd come to me, and I'd let him tell me what he wanted in his own time. I took two mugs from the overhead cupboard.

"It's Rosemary, my sister."

I turned to look at him more closely. His brown eyes were worried and tinged with red that probably came from too many late nights and cram study sessions. "Is it her birthday again? Do you need a present? How about another music box?"

My attempt to lighten the mood didn't even register. "She's missing," he said.

"What makes you say that?"

He stopped pacing and pulled at the side of his hair. "She was supposed to meet me yesterday for lunch when she had a rehearsal break, but she never showed up."

"Maybe she forgot."

"She wouldn't do that. We haven't seen each other in like a year. She's not even answering her cell. I'd go to her apartment, but I don't know where she's staying. My parents say she's a flake and not to worry, but that's only because they're still mad about how she dropped out of college to tour with that theater company a couple of years ago."

I had to play devil's advocate. "What makes you think they're wrong?" I placed loose tea in the infuser. Lemon balm, Liam's favorite, with no caffeine or anything else to get him more worked up.

"She's only been back a few weeks, and she wouldn't leave without seeing me. We've talked a lot on the phone, and she was all excited about a new part she was trying out for with some other theater company. Said it was a smaller outfit but with better connections. She practiced day and night to get the part, and then she did. She was so excited. I know she wouldn't just disappear. I went over to the company, but she hadn't shown up to rehearsal yesterday." His eyes held mine. "Please, Autumn. I don't know who else can help."

"Maybe the police."

"That's why I asked if that guy was a cop. I thought I recognized him from the newspaper article about that real estate fraud business going on last summer. I was hoping he was and that you might get him to help."

Oh, I'd read that situation completely wrong. I'd been thinking Liam's problems were the kind that bordered on unlawful and that it'd be easier to convince him to make good without Shannon hovering over us menacingly.

"Well, she's an adult with a history of taking off, so the more proof we have, the better. But if your sister really is missing, we'll need to let the police search for her. They have information I don't have access to."

"Yeah, but they can't read imprints." He crossed to the

worktable and yanked a plastic grocery sack from the pocket of his coat—a deep pocket by the size of whatever was in the bag. "She had a cubby at the theater company. I took these from it when they weren't looking." Liam flushed. "It wasn't stealing."

"Of course not." I took a deep breath. Probably these imprints wouldn't tell me anything. Since the items had simply been sitting on her shelf, it wasn't likely I'd have to relive a murder or a kidnapping.

I hoped.

Liam waited, the sack extended. Before taking it, I removed the antique rings I wore to dull any unexpected imprints I might accidentally touch when I was out and about. When I wasn't wearing gloves, that is. The rings held comforting imprints that would counter any negative ones, but they would also get in the way of my perception if the imprints I wanted to read weren't very strong.

Months had passed since I'd come across a seriously evil imprint, but I remembered how it had sapped my strength. I'd wondered what might happen if someday I went too deep, if the imprint was too intense, too horrible.

There was no one to ask, so I had no clue. I'd been helping Shannon and his partner, Paige, on cases, but I suspected Shannon had deliberately kept me from consulting on the really bad ones—murders, rapes, brutal muggings. I hadn't pushed. Now I felt guilty. While I was protecting myself, how many more people had been hurt?

I reached for the grocery sack. Liam watched me intently, not pushing. He was that sort of kid. Patient, studious, dedicated to his sister. Dedicated enough to steal an antique music box for her.

Gently, I shook out the contents of the sack onto the

worktable—a worn copy of a play script, a square bag with a makeup brush peeking from one end of the zippered top, a pair of leather gloves, a brush, and a small see-through purse filled with elastics, hair clips, and bobby pins. It wasn't much, but if she'd used these objects every day, there might be imprints.

Probably not on the gloves, though they were leather and had a better chance than regular cloth. Clothes that were often washed and things easily dismissed or forgotten never evoked enough emotion to hold imprints. Fortunately, or my life would be a living nightmare. I'd have to wear gloves to buy fruit and milk at the corner grocery.

There were definitely imprints on the objects. I could feel them radiating, beckoning. What I couldn't tell without touching them was if they were positive or negative imprints. If I could figure that out, my life would be a lot simpler.

"Autumn," came a voice from the door.

I lifted my gaze to see Jake's good-looking face, framed by his black, finger-sized locs, or dreadlocks as some people called them, that always made people stop and notice. In his customary snug T-shirt, he looked strong and a little dangerous, but anyone seeing him help fragile old ladies in his herb shop would change their minds about that in a hurry. He'd been my best friend for nearly two years and a little bit more than my friend since this past summer. I'd trust him with my life.

"Hi, Jake."

His eyes took in the objects Liam had brought and the antique rings I'd set down next to them. A flash of hurt registered on his face. Once he'd been my biggest supporter where imprints were concerned, but after our summer run-in with a branch of organized crime and a crooked attorney who'd stooped to kidnapping and illegal adoption, Jake had begun to exhibit reluctance about my reading imprints.

He no longer brought in anyone who wanted imprints read, and he didn't encourage me to talk about helping people. I knew his guilt ran deep about having been unable to protect me, and nearly dying himself hadn't helped matters, but I figured that was something he would have to get over on his own. I'd finally been honest with myself about what I now saw as my calling, and I couldn't let his fear stop me, even if I knew it stemmed from love. Besides, what he didn't know wouldn't hurt him.

Or so I'd thought.

There had been a time when, if Jake had found me about to read something, he would have put his arms around me and drawn me close for a strengthening kiss—and a part of me still wished he'd do that. But he knew I wasn't sure of my feelings, and that was enough for him to back away. Not completely, though. He'd made it clear how he felt about me. Now it was my turn. He was my best friend, and I loved him, but I didn't know if I loved him enough. As much as he loved me.

"You remember Liam," I said to cover the awkwardness.

Jake dragged his eyes from the table. "Oh, yeah. Hey, Bean Pole, how you been?"

"Okay." Liam nodded a greeting but didn't elaborate, anxiousness exuding from him in waves.

I'd better hurry, or he might lose it altogether. "His sister's missing," I told Jake. "I'm going to—" I shrugged. "You know."

Jake's gaze came back to me. "You should have called me. I'd like to help."

I understood what it cost him to say that, but I wasn't sure

I wanted him to stay—though if the imprints were bad, it'd be safer for me if he did. He knew what to do.

Jake glanced out the door into the store and frowned as though remembering something.

"Did you need help in the Herb Shoppe?" I asked. He could be here only to see me, but when I'd come in, he'd had more customers than I had, so I suspected another reason.

"No." His face became more animated, but the line of concern on his brow deepened. "There's a woman in the Herb Shoppe. Her name is Suzy Olsen. She came in looking for your mom."

"For Summer?" My adoptive mother had died when I was eleven, and I was surprised one of her acquaintances hadn't heard.

"Well, she didn't want Summer. Or not exactly. She was looking for Summer only to ask her about Kendall. She says she knew her."

All at once there wasn't enough air in the room. Kendall was the almost sixteen-year-old who'd died after giving birth to my sister and then to me—twins who'd been separated by the attending physician and given to two adoptive couples. I knew little more than that, and every lead we'd researched had gone dry.

Until now.

Chapter 2

*W*hen I first learned I had a twin, I'd tried to track down my birth mother's family, but so far the only clue I had was from a former adoption agency worker, BervaDee Mendenhal, who had placed my mother with Winter and Summer Rain during her pregnancy and who later took my sister, Tawnia, to her adoptive family in Kansas. Though BervaDee and Dr. Loveridge later became romantically involved, he never confessed his secret, and she hadn't known our birth mother, Kendall, had delivered twins until we appeared on her doorstep seeking our identity.

After Dr. Loveridge's death, BervaDee found a letter in his belongings from Kendall meant for her child but opted not to forward it to Tawnia, the one baby she was aware of, because it clearly stated that Kendall had changed her mind and wanted her child to be raised by her foster family, Winter and Summer Rain, and not the couple she'd contracted with in Kansas.

In the end, Kendall received her wish, as I had been adopted by Summer and Winter. The contract with the other adoptive parents in Kansas had also been honored by Tawnia's placement. Only Tawnia and I had lost out on each other in the deal, though I wouldn't have given up my life with Summer or Winter for anything, and Tawnia felt the same about her parents.

At first I was so grateful to have found Tawnia that nothing else really mattered. Yet in the past year since my talent emerged, I found myself more and more curious about my biological family. Now I struggled with the past, while Tawnia expended her energy in caring for her husband and new baby daughter.

"Autumn?" Jake asked.

I wanted to rush out and question the woman, but Liam was staring rather desperately at the items he'd brought. "Can you ask her to wait?" I said. "I really do want to talk to her."

"Sure." Jake glanced again at the table and then at Liam. "I'll be right back."

I was going to tell him he didn't have to return because I knew he had customers, but the truth is, I was relieved. I nodded, and he squeezed my shoulder before leaving.

"If you gotta go talk to her, I can wait," Liam said, which was nice of him, since he was practically oozing worry. I can't read people the way I can the imprints they leave, but I didn't need any talent to read him.

"It's okay." I'd waited thirty-three years—what was a few more minutes? Besides, I really liked Liam, and his presence here told me he had nowhere else to turn. I poured Liam a cup of tea before refocusing my attention on the worktable.

"Thanks," he muttered, clutching the cup as if it were a lifeline.

I stretched out my hands, my fingers tingling in anticipation. *Wait. Had Jake called the woman Suzy?*

In the letter from my birth mother, Suzy was the name of one of the owners of the café where she'd worked during her early pregnancy. I'd searched for the café, hoping the owners knew something about my biological family, but without luck. It had to be the same woman.

Concentrate, I told myself. I needed my wits about me to remember what I experienced. Imprints always repeated themselves in exactly the same way, so if I paid attention, I wouldn't have to reread something in order to tell Liam about it. That was a good thing because reading imprints—at least negative ones—was exhausting.

I dropped my eyes to the script, which proclaimed *For the Love of Juliet!* in large lettering. This seemed the most likely to have imprints, or it would if she'd cared about the part. No reason for more delay. I picked it up and the imprint began.

Excitement. I had gotten the part! Now all I needed to do was to impress the right people and I'd be on my way to Broadway. No more second-rate theater companies or staying in rundown motel rooms crammed with other actors. My chance at last! I was going someplace. My parents would finally understand my dream. And Liam would be proud. A wave of love and longing for my brother filled me.

"What is it?" Liam asked anxiously.

I shook my head, indicating that he should wait. Another imprint was coming on the heels of the other, a slightly older one, as I always experienced the most recent imprint first.

Anger. Resentment. Fear. All aimed at a sheet of paper tucked inside my script, the words blurry with my tears. It doesn't matter. I'm going to do my best, regardless. I deserved this chance. No way would I throw the audition because of a little threat.

The imprint faded, followed by others that were much older by at least four years. Apparently they recycled these plays, but the previous actors' emotions hadn't been forceful enough to give me an image. No matter. They wouldn't have anything to do with Rosemary's disappearance now.

I took my hands away before the imprints could replay. If imprints were really bad, I could get stuck in a loop and wouldn't be able to let go. This one had been mild by comparison, and Rosemary's love for Liam actually strengthened me.

Jake had reappeared in the room and was staring at me anxiously, ready, I knew, to hand me something with a positive imprint if it looked like I should need it. I found his concern both touching and annoying, which made me feel sad. I hadn't always resented him for knowing me so well. Or had I?

"Rosemary did get the part three days ago," I said, "and was really excited about it. She thought it was her big break."

Liam frowned. "Must be the connections then, because that place is kind of a dive. Not even as respectable-looking as the other theater place she was at."

That was odd, but I put it in the back of my mind to think about later. "There was an early imprint from last week that was strange," I continued. "I believe someone threatened her about auditioning."

"Threatened her?"

"Yes. Inside her script, I saw a sheet torn from a small notebook. She was upset about it, but unfortunately, I didn't see what it said or receive any indication of who had sent it. She was determined to go through with the audition despite the threat."

"Maybe the note is still here." He picked up the script and flipped through it without finding anything. "Guess that was too much to hope for."

"Maybe she didn't keep it. Or it's wherever she's staying."

"A threat could mean she's in trouble."

I hated to admit it, but he was right. "I'm sorry."

"What about the rest?"

I touched the square makeup bag. Nothing but a feeling of haste. Opening it, I felt the same urgency tinged with anticipation on the contents. I shook my head. Nothing from the gloves, as I'd expected, and the see-through mini purse with hair accessories radiated more hurry and a hint of frustration. Only the hairbrush was left.

Brushes were often good imprint-holders. Not because people cared about them so much but because they had all sorts of strong emotions while using them and staring into mirrors. Thoughts about their appearances, the people they were going out with, the people they were angry with. This brush was no different.

He'll hate this, but I don't care! I stared into the mirror as I dragged the brush through my long brown hair. Who does he think he is, anyway?

A noise and someone coming into the room. The briefest glimpse of a man's shadowed face. Turning to see who it was.

Sudden darkness.

Had she let the brush drop, cutting off the imprint? Or had something happened to her? I'd felt no pain, but the cutoff seemed too abrupt for her to have simply let the brush go. One thing for sure, whoever the "he" was, she'd felt so strongly about him that I'd been swept up immediately into the imprint. There'd been no separation between Rosemary and me. I always saw things as though I was experiencing them, but only with the strongest feelings did I temporarily forget who I was. It was always strange, even if it happened only for a few seconds.

More imprints followed on the brush—a dissatisfaction

with skin tone, frustration at a blemish, annoyance with another actress, anticipation of a performance. Nothing unusually important and already fading. I withdrew my hand.

"Well?" Eagerness filled Liam's voice.

I shook my head. "She was really angry at someone two days ago—Thursday afternoon—but the imprint cut off. I can't tell why. She could have dropped the brush."

"That was the day after she got the part." He frowned. "What should I do?"

"In light of the threat, I think you'd better go to the police."

"What if they think she just took off again?"

I felt for him. I mean *really* felt. Not the normal emotion I usually experienced for him but also the love Rosemary had left imprinted on the script. It had become my memory, and unless I wanted to consciously fight against it, I would keep feeling that way for him. I didn't bother fighting the emotion. They say once you help someone, you become responsible for them. Maybe that had something to do with my feelings now.

"Tell you what," I said. "You talk to the police—I'll give you the name of someone—and I'll go to the theater company this evening and see if I can find out more information." If anything violent had happened there, I'd probably be able to pick it up. "Tell me where they're located."

He set his half-finished tea on the worktable and pulled out his phone. "I have the address here. Do you have anything to write it on?"

"Text it to me." I gave him the number, feeling a bit guilty that already I was thinking not about his sister but of the woman I hoped was waiting out in the shop for me. Not that I didn't plan on helping him. I would—as soon as I talked to her.

"And if you have a picture of Rosemary, text that to me too,"

I added. "It'll come in handy when I ask people about her." Besides, I'd never actually met her in person, though I almost felt I knew her because of Liam, and it would be nice to see a picture up close.

Jake handed me my antique rings, and I automatically put them on, feeling the comforting buzz of positive emotions. Strange how this extra sense was normal to me now, like seeing or breathing. While it was often a curse, I wouldn't want to live without it.

I wrote down Shannon's name and number for Liam, promising to let him know if I found anything at the theater. He gave me a weak smile as I led him from the back room.

"Thanks," Liam said. "I didn't know what else to do."

"It'll be okay. We'll find her."

Thera eyed Liam as we emerged, but when she spoke it was to Jake. "You've got a lot of customers. I don't think Randa can deal with them all, and I've been too busy myself to get over there."

Jake looked through the double connecting doors that Winter and I had put in when Winter had owned the Herb Shoppe. "I'll go with you tonight," Jake said. "Okay?"

"Sure. If you don't have anything else to do." With his locs and chiseled physique, he looked tough, even though he was the most gentle man I'd known besides Winter, and having him back me up was always a plus.

He smiled and squeezed my arm. My stomach flopped a bit at the smile, which was why I was still confused about my conflicting feelings for him and Shannon. Any way I looked at it, I loved Jake.

Tearing my eyes away from his retreating figure, I looked

over my browsing customers, finally coming to rest on the stocky woman standing near my antique music boxes. Her shoulder-length blond hair was pulled back into a ponytail, the hair thick enough for the style to be attractive, though she had to be pushing sixty and by rights should have thinner hair. Her jeans and fitted T-shirt under her ski jacket were casual, but her confident bearing screamed self-assurance, as though she might be wearing a suit or designer outfit. She was paying more attention to us than the merchandise, so I figured she must be Suzy.

She met my gaze with a smile and came toward me. "Are you Autumn?" she asked, holding out her hand.

I nodded. "You're looking for Kendall?"

"Yes. I'm Suzy Olsen. Kendall lived with us for a bit in Hayesville before she came here. I was hoping to talk to the couple she was placed with during her pregnancy. I thought maybe they'd kept in touch with her after she left. I've always wondered what she ended up doing." Suzy stared at me with an unusual intentness that was unsettling.

"Summer and Winter . . . they're no longer here," I said, stumbling uncharacteristically over the words. "Summer died of breast cancer a long time ago, and Winter died last year in the bridge collapse. I'm their daughter."

Suzy's brow furrowed. "I'm so sorry to hear it. I didn't know them well at all, but the two times I did meet them, they seemed nice. Kendall wrote me a few times, and she spoke a lot about them. Good things. Excuse me if I seem to be staring, but you look a bit like Kendall. It's kind of strange. Like going back in time. But I don't understand how—"

"I'm Kendall's biological daughter. Winter and Summer adopted me."

Suzy's smile returned. "That explains a lot. I thought she'd decided on a couple from out of state, but it's great that you're here. Have you had any contact with your birth mother?"

There was nothing else to do but to tell her that Kendall had died from complications the night I'd been born. But I was glad not to have to explain it alone. The connection I always felt with my sister, the invisible line that seemed to link us and that I'd only ever felt with Winter and Summer, was becoming thick in my chest. I couldn't explain where in my chest or what caused it, but I envisioned this link as a cord between us, and feeling it this way meant she was nearby. Tawnia wasn't due to pick me up for dinner for a few hours, so Jake had probably called her.

I tried to be irritated that he'd been so presumptuous, but how could you fault a man like that? He was always looking out for me. The smothering had to come from my imagination.

Sure enough, Tawnia was approaching the door to my shop now, her daughter, Destiny Emma Winn, in her arms. I'd won the battle against a boring name for my niece, but in the three months since her birth, her parents mostly called her Emma, a name I didn't have anything against, but it seemed odd to give a child a first name and then not use it, so I called her Destiny. Tawnia didn't mind—a good thing since it was the baby's name.

Suzy followed my gaze. "I can wait if you need to help that customer."

"She's not a customer." I watched Suzy from the corner of my eye as Tawnia approached and saw her do the familiar double-take.

Since losing weight after her pregnancy, Tawnia and I looked more alike than ever. She had medium brown hair, a slim build, freckles on her narrow face and upturned nose, and her eyes were large and oval, set slightly too far apart for perfect beauty. She kept her hair long, and I opted for short, with red highlights on top, but our identical facial structure was unmistakable. Not to mention the color of our eyes.

"I don't understand," Suzy murmured.

"You wouldn't be the first." I greeted Tawnia with a smile and took Destiny from her arms. "Let's go to the back room to talk."

Destiny cuddled into me. Besides her mother, she loved me best, even before her dad, which wasn't too surprising since biologically I was practically her mother. Tawnia and I must feel similar to her. Of course it helped that I spent every moment I could with them.

Suzy kept looking between us. As we passed the counter, Thera gave me a wink, amusement and curiosity on her face.

"I'll be in back, if you need me," I said unnecessarily. We both ignored the fact that she already needed my help with the customers.

After Tawnia and Suzy had shed their coats in the back room, I invited Suzy to sit in the easy chair while I took the table and Tawnia chose the folding chair. I tucked my feet under me, Indian style, and laid the baby in the cradle formed by my legs before making the introductions, gratified at the surprised expressions on their faces. For Suzy's benefit, I also explained our separate adoptions and about Kendall's death shortly after our birth.

By the time I finished, tears stood out in Suzy's eyes. "That poor thing. She was never given a fair shake. First to be assaulted in her own house and get kicked out by her mother. Then to separate her babies . . . Oh, that poor, poor girl."

A tight feeling squeezed my chest, but I wouldn't let that get in the way of what I wanted to know. "What about her mother? Kendall left us a note that mentioned her mother was willing to take her back if she chose to place us for adoption. Her mother claimed to have stopped drinking. Do you know anything about that? Or where she lives?"

Suzy shook her head. "Not really. I mean, I saw her mother when she came in. I heard the fight—everyone in the café did, even though they took it outside—but Kendall didn't want to put her baby up for adoption. It was only later when she realized she couldn't do it on her own and that it wasn't fair for her baby that she changed her mind. She was only fifteen when it happened, you know."

Tawnia nodded. "We searched for your café," she told Suzy, "but we didn't know where Kendall was from, except that she had to get to Portland by bus or that sometimes you drove her. We'd hoped to find Kendall's mother, but the last name we had— Eaton—didn't go far. There were too many listings, and without a location, it was impossible. The adoption agency wouldn't give us an address. We were lucky to get the name from a former worker."

"Kendall told us her last name was Drexler. Not that it mattered; we paid her in cash."

Had Kendall purposely given the adoption people the wrong name, or were either of the names actually hers?

"So how did they allow a minor to give up a baby for adoption?" Tawnia asked. Between us, she was always the more detailed. "Wouldn't they have needed her mother's signature?"

"She became a ward of the state after her mom kicked her out," Suzy said with a shrug. "They weren't as rigorous about those things back then. Not like now." She paused. "My, this chair sure is comfortable."

I laughed. "Wait until you try to get out. So did you ever notice Kendall having any odd sort of . . . talent?" I could feel Tawnia's eyes on me and wondered if she feared I'd spill her secret. She didn't need to worry. I wouldn't tell Suzy mine, either, despite how good she'd been to our birth mother.

"I'm not sure what you mean," Suzy said. "She was a capable worker. She learned all the meals and drinks within a few days. She was friendly, though shy around men—especially those who tried to flirt. She spent a lot of time reading under the tree behind the café. But I knew her for only a few months. I regret to say there wasn't time to get very close."

Which meant if Kendall had an ability, she'd kept it secret.

"You were close enough," I said. "You gave her a place to work and saw that she was taken care of. That's more than her family did."

"What made you look her up now?" Tawnia asked. I'd been wondering the same thing.

Suzy shrugged. "My husband died a few years ago, and I sold the café. Too much trouble to run alone at my age. I've spent a lot of time visiting our children, and my daughter moved here last year. That's why I'm in town now, visiting my grandchildren. I drove by the other day and recognized the Herb Shoppe. I started wondering about Kendall. I really liked her. She was a good kid, and that's why I tried to help her. I knew Dr. Loveridge, and I figured Portland was far enough away from her mother that she could start fresh. I'm just sorry things didn't work out better for her."

There was nothing we could say to that. Kendall had been a victim, but she was also a hero to us.

"Are your eyes a different color?" Suzy broke the silence, looking from me to Tawnia.

Heterochromia was what she meant. Our right eyes are hazel, the lefts blue, a hereditary condition in our case, though we didn't know who gave it to us. Before meeting me, Tawnia had used a contact in her left eye to make both eyes hazel.

"We know Kendall didn't have eyes like ours, but what about her mother?" Tawnia asked.

Suzy shook her head. "Not that I know."

So far we hadn't learned anything. "Is there something you can tell us about Kendall that might help us find her mother?"

"I dropped Kendall off at her house once. They lived in Hayesville, on the other side of town from my café. I don't know the exact house, but I can pinpoint the area more or less, if you have a map. That is, if they haven't torn it all down. It was bad thirty years ago. I've been living in Salem the past few years since I sold the café, so I really don't know."

"I can show you a map," Tawnia said, rising. "Autumn has Internet access on her computer. If you'll come out here with me—?" I left them to it. Tawnia was the computer whiz, doing much of her design work from her computer. She'd gone part time since the baby and now mostly worked from home.

I looked down at Destiny, who'd fallen asleep in my lap, and thought about the young girl who'd given me life. She'd taken the harder, selfless path, and for us it had worked out. I was grateful.

I adjusted my position on the table, my hand coming against the script that Liam must have left. Rosemary's emotions flooded me again. I sighed. Whatever Tawnia and Suzy Olsen came up with would have to wait until tomorrow. Tonight I had a theater to visit and a missing woman to find.

I wondered if the play, *For the Love of Juliet!* was related to the original *Romeo and Juliet.* If so, I sure hoped Liam's sister didn't face as tragic a fate as the characters in Shakespeare's play.

Chapter 3

After closing my shop, Tawnia and I had dinner together at Smokey's, the organic restaurant across the street. Smokey's was a light, airy place with spotless tables and a long snack bar along the wall opposite the kitchen area. The restaurant always smelled heavenly. We often had lunch there during the week, but her husband, Bret, was out of town on business and she'd wanted company for dinner. I enjoyed eating with her because she was the one person I knew who delighted in food as much as I did, though I tended toward natural choices while she reveled in anything with ample amounts of white flour, sugar, and preservatives.

"So, when should we check out Hayesville?" Tawnia frowned over the copy of the map she'd printed. "It'll take about an hour to get there. We could go right now, if you're not doing anything tonight."

"Can't. Jake and I have plans." I didn't want to tell Tawnia about the theater or Liam's sister. If I did, she might insist on coming along, and I didn't know what I was up against. When I used my talent, things had a way of turning, well, ugly, and no way did I want my only sibling to be caught in the middle.

Tawnia wiggled her eyebrows suggestively. "Does that mean you two are back together?"

I sighed. "No." The fact is we hadn't exactly broken up so much as backed off.

"You're going to have to choose eventually."

She meant between Jake and Shannon, but I wasn't taking the bait. I experienced enough internal chaos about them without her adding to it.

She shrugged when I didn't answer. "There'll be time to look for Kendall's mother tomorrow morning. Better to do it in the daylight, anyway, especially if we're going door-to-door asking for information. We're going to look a little odd."

"Maybe you could try a drawing," I suggested. "Might save us time finding the right place."

Tawnia frowned as she always did when I mentioned her ability—not her ability to draw but the other talent that came with it. She didn't have much belief in her unusual gift.

"I've *been* drawing," she said. "Nothing weird, though. I only drew things like that when you needed help. It was probably just a heightened connection to you because of my pregnancy."

I suspected otherwise. Her ability to draw a scene that had happened across town or to people she'd never met was the reason I believed our gifts were hereditary. Our talents had evolved differently, but both were real. While I could read imprints left on inanimate objects, she drew scenes from the immediate past, and some of her drawings had helped me find the missing people I was searching for. In one notable case, her drawing had helped Shannon reach me in time to save my life.

I'd saved his since, though, so I didn't owe him anything. At least that's what I told myself.

"You aren't drawing anything because you don't *want* to," I said. "You never want to unless someone you know is missing or in danger."

Tawnia shrugged. "Think what you like, but I'm sure it's gone, whatever it was. Maybe it was giving birth to Emma, or maybe it just went. I don't know."

It wasn't like my sister to be so deeply in denial. Then again, she'd spent a lifetime trying to fit in, while I'd been taught to celebrate my differences.

She peeked under the table. "I see you're wearing the boots I got you."

"They don't hurt my back."

"Ha. The only reason you're wearing them is that it's freezing out there." She glanced through the window, where rain once again pounded the dark streets. It was a night when even single people would prefer to stay in and curl up with a good book.

I, however, had a theater to check out. I glanced at my watch. "I hate to cut this short, but I'd better get going." Jake and I hadn't actually set a time, but the sooner I got this over with, the better.

"Where are you going?"

So much for not telling her. I'd have to give her something. "To a theater. You know, the kind that puts on plays."

"Oh? What are they performing?"

"Actually, I don't know. I—uh . . ." I didn't even know if anyone would be at the building practicing, much less putting on a live play this evening.

"Well, I'm sure it'll be good. If Bret were home, I'd leave Emma with him and go with you." She smiled mischievously.

"Or maybe you'd rather I didn't." There she went with the eyebrows again.

I rolled my eyes. Sometimes married people had no idea how irritating they were. "Definitely, three's a crowd tonight."

Tawnia laughed and bent to pick up the car seat where Destiny lay snug and sleeping. "I took care of the tip," she said, "so don't worry about that."

We hugged at the door, and she plunged into the night, a useless umbrella over the car seat. The wind blew the rain in every direction, and though Destiny probably wouldn't feel it on her well-wrapped body, she'd likely awake and object to the rain hitting her face. If I were a vindictive person, I might wish she'd scream all the way home to pay Tawnia back for her prying.

Pulling my coat around me, I hurried to where I'd left my old Toyota hatchback, praying it would start. Tonight would definitely not be a good time for it to break down again. The wind pushed the rain inside my coat and chilled my body, and my teeth chattered at the onslaught. At this rate my jeans and the inside of my boots would be wet before I got to the car. I shoved my hands deep in my pocket for the keys, only to hit the weight of the Ruger still there. *Darn that Shannon. What was I going to do with the gun?*

Thankfully, the car started. I'd pulled out my phone to call Jake, but the passenger door opened, and he climbed inside. "Saw you leaving Smokies," he said. "I was catching up on some ordering." He thumbed toward his shop.

"Did you eat?"

"I had a late lunch. I'll grab something later. This isn't going to take long, right?"

"I hope not."

As I drove, we talked about Suzy and the possibility of finding Kendall's mother. Now that we had a real lead, I felt a sort of strange dread. Maybe we should leave well enough alone.

"Uh, Autumn, I'm pretty sure this isn't the right way."

I pulled my attention back to the road and looked at Jake, who was studying the address I'd pulled up on my phone. I didn't question him, because Tawnia and I had both long ago admitted that we were directionally impaired. "Which way, then?"

"How come you don't use the GPS on this fancy new phone of yours?"

"I'm not exactly sure how it works." The new phone had been one of the conditions of my consulting with the police department. They wanted—Shannon wanted—me to have the latest gizmos and probably to track me too, but I turned off the GPS locator first thing. No way did I want Shannon to pinpoint me at the push of a few buttons on his phone.

"Here we go. Push this application and put in the address here. Wait, first we have to turn on the GPS. Looks like it was off."

Following Jake's directions, I drove through the dark streets, which appeared even darker with the storm. "Are you sure it's here?" I asked. "This neighborhood is . . . well, there's nothing here. Just a bunch of old abandoned buildings and—"

"There." Jake pointed at a building awash with light, a beacon on the other wise deserted street. Near it I spied the sign, a sad-looking fluorescent affair about three feet long, that announced *Live Performances by the Portland Players Touring*

Theatre Company. There was another sign beneath, this one unlit, that might or might not contain relevant information.

"Do you think they actually perform plays here, not just practice them?" I asked. "Who'd come here to watch? No wonder they have to tour." I pulled into one of the parking places near the entrance and shut off the engine.

"It says live performances," Jake said. "But I wouldn't drive all the way out here."

Even the darkness couldn't hide the poor condition of the building. The area directly around the entrance had been painted recently—probably during the past summer—but even that was already beginning to peel again, as though no one had bothered to remove the old peeling paint beneath it before slathering more on top.

At least the rain had abated slightly, I noted as I climbed from the car. We walked onto the rickety porch and up to the double-door entrance, my eyes darting back and forth as I contemplated any potential danger as I'd been taught to do in my taekwondo training. Always alert and prepared. We sounded like Boy Scouts or something. With my earlier training as a teen and my recent intensive private and group lessons, I'd reached black-belt level in skill, though I had several tests yet to take before the rank was official. I felt confident with my training, especially as I'd come out on top during recent bouts with the black-belt students, but that was in the light of day, not in the dark at a place that looked straight from the set of a werewolf movie.

The front door was locked. What a letdown.

"It says it opens at seven for tonight's performance," Jake said, reading a printed paper taped to the door. "That's only a half hour from now. I mean, assuming this paper is current. It doesn't look too old."

"Let's check around back. With all this light, someone has to be here."

Jake nodded but more to appease me than because he wanted to go. He'd been dragged around enough in my adventures. If I were less selfish, I wouldn't have let him come.

As we retraced our steps, I was able to read the lower unlit sign: *The Comedy of Errors.* I wondered how long it had hung there.

Around the back of the theater, a dozen cars crowded into a tiny lot. A back door was propped slightly open with a brick, so I pushed at the door and went inside. I couldn't see much, as the room was poorly lit by a single, uncovered fluorescent tube on the ceiling, but at least it was significantly warmer inside. The room was filled with racks of clothing, tables full of props, and pieces of sets.

"Hello?" I called, glancing behind me at Jake, who fingered a set of swords on a narrow table.

He grinned. "Painted wood."

"Figures." I circumvented a rack of clothing, searching for a door leading somewhere else. On the other side of the rack, I ran into a short, rounded, balding man dressed in an ill-fitted dark suit. Beads of sweat stood out on his forehead.

"Oh," he said, peering up at me through the gloom. "Who are you? What are you doing here? The theater doesn't open for seating until seven. You'll have to wait around the front."

"I'm not here to see the play. I'm looking for one of your actors." I motioned behind me. "The door was open."

He gave an exasperated sigh and pushed past me. "I don't know how many times I've told them to stop propping the door open. Money to heat this place doesn't grow on trees." He hesitated when he saw Jake, who could be very intimidating with his locs, especially while holding a sword—even a fake one.

"Excuse me," said the little man. He stalked to the door, kicked at the brick holding it open, and pulled it shut.

"But Cheyenne isn't here, yet," said another voice behind me. The clothing rack that had cut off the path through the tables and pieces of sets rolled aside, startling me.

"Sorry," the newcomer said. He was also dressed in a suit but was taller than the other man by a few inches. He had a friendly smile, intelligent eyes, and what I could only describe as presence, despite his nondescript hair color and wiry build.

"I don't care if Cheyenne shows up at all," growled the short man, returning from closing the outside door. "If our actors can't be here by final call, they don't deserve to be in the play at all. One of the others will have to do her part. It's easy enough." He glared at me as if it were all my fault before adding, "How many times have I told you to have your friends come at a better time?"

The taller man shook his head, barely concealing his impatience. "I don't know these people, but for all we know, they may be with the press." To me, he added, "I'm Paxton Seaver, the director. This is Carl Walsh, our producer and stage manager."

"I'm Autumn Rain, and this is Jake Ryan."

Walsh's attitude changed abruptly. "Nice to meet you." He smiled so wide his teeth seemed to take up his entire face. A frightening thing to behold, and I wondered if he was wearing dentures. "I would be glad to answer a few questions for the press, but it'll have to be quick. We'll be seating people in a few minutes, and our play begins shortly after. We're performing

The Comedy of Errors. It's one of our most well-received plays when we're touring, and we like to do it frequently for our supporters when we're in town."

"We're not with the press," I said. "I'm investigating the disappearance of Rosemary Taylor."

Walsh's round eyes narrowed. "Well, when you find her, tell her she's out as Juliet. We're giving the role to Cheyenne, as we should have in the first place instead of trusting an unknown, no matter how talented she might be. People who don't show up for rehearsals even once are out, and she missed yesterday and today. These actors think they're all irreplaceable, but they aren't. We definitely made a mistake casting her."

"So you haven't seen her?"

Walsh shook his head. "Not since Thursday when we did a blocking of our next play as we always do at the first rehearsal."

"*For the Love of Juliet!*" I said, remembering the script Liam had brought me.

"Yes. It's a modern play that we don't typically put on, as it only uses four actors, but I've been wanting to do it for years." He straightened and took a breath that puffed up his chest. "It's a special favorite of an important family member." His confiding tone seemed to indicate that I should be aware of this person and should hold him or her in as high esteem as he did.

I glanced at Paxton Seaver for a clue as how to proceed. He smiled at me and shook his head, his expression of disgust vanishing as Walsh looked his way. "I haven't seen Rosemary, either," Seaver said, "and as Carl mentioned, now is not a good time to talk, since we are about to open."

I felt it prudent not to mention the lack of cars or patrons in the front. "I would appreciate if I could just look around on my own," I said. "I won't be long." Anxiety emanating from the prop room had worked its way into my voice. Imprints buzzed all around me, and I wished I could know before I touched them which might have something to do with Rosemary.

Walsh looked heavenward and shook his head. "I don't have time for this. Paxton, handle it. I must make sure the doors open on time and that Lucas and Millie have made up. I won't have their antagonism ruining the play." With that, he took another self-important breath and hurried down the path and through the door.

Seaver's nostrils flared, but he didn't say anything about Walsh's request, though I didn't think getting rid of unwanted guests typically fell under the duties of a director. "Perhaps you can come back tomorrow?"

For all his apparent friendliness, I had the distinct feeling he didn't want me here. I'd rather have dealt with rotund Walsh, who was at least transparent.

"I'm sure you know that the initial hours after a person disappears are the most important. Rosemary's been missing more than a day."

Seaver arched a brow. "Are you here in some sort of official capacity then?"

I could tell he didn't think so, what with my jeans and Jake's locs, and he would have been right, but I didn't want him to refuse to cooperate. "I do consulting for the police department," I said. "My investigation is not yet official, but Rosemary's brother is talking with a detective now. Depending on what I find, I may call them in."

Jake cast me a look that said he was fighting not to roll his eyes and laugh. With a return stare I dared him to do so.

Seaver frowned. "I think you'll find no one here knows anything. She was new to our company. None of us knew her well. In fact, Cheyenne knew her best, and she's not even here yet."

"That's okay," I said. "If I can't speak to the cast, I'd like to at least see where Rosemary might have stored any personal belongings or anyplace where she might have spent time."

He shrugged. "There's a women's dressing room next door. Look around, but please don't move anything or upset the cast. Actors are funny—the littlest thing can set them off, and we do have a performance tonight."

"All I want is to look around. You won't even know I'm here."

He gave me a flat grin. "That I sincerely doubt. As I said, actors are very aware of the unspoken. They'll assume something nefarious happened to Rosemary."

Nefarious? I bet before becoming the director, he'd been an actor himself.

"Come on," Seaver said. "I'll show you the room. Oh, wait, I need to prop the door open again for Cheyenne so she can get in. The door automatically locks, and our actors don't have keys."

"She'll be in the play anyway?" Jake asked, setting down the sword.

Seaver nodded. "Carl may be the producer, but I'm the director, and I have final say about who's in the play. Cheyenne's a great actress, and her part, though small, is crucial. Anyway, he'll barely notice." The derision in his voice was clear, and I wondered how he could stand to work with someone he obviously didn't like or respect. At any rate, it was a question that might or might not be related to Rosemary's disappearance. I filed it away in my mental bag of evidence.

"I only gave Cheyenne a small part in the first place because

I'd expected her to take the lead in the Juliet play," Seaver continued. "That was before Rosemary auditioned, of course. With Rosemary missing, it's fortunate I did it that way. Cheyenne will need all her attention for her Juliet character." Without waiting for a response, he brushed past us, heading for the outside door.

While we waited for him, I removed my antique rings, shoving them into my pocket before reaching out to let my hand run over a table of props. Imprints immediately jumped to life, but I let my hand stay on each item only long enough to determine that they had nothing to do with Rosemary. There were strong imprints on many of the props—jealousy, rage, love, excitement, expectation, hope. But, strangely, I couldn't tell if the events were real or lived only by the actor playing his role.

"Autumn?" Jake yanked my hand away from a glass that contained a particularly virulent imprint of someone planning to poison someone else. I knew it wasn't real since I'd experienced several retakes of the same scene, and yet it felt real.

It was the first indication I'd had that imprints could be faked. Or rather, that fake imprints could seem real if the actor was good enough at his job.

"I'm okay." I looked past Jake to where Paxton Seaver had returned and was watching us. "Ever thought about going on stage? Either of you?" he asked. "You have the right look, and presence. The chemistry between you is . . . good."

I wanted to laugh. Plays had been Tawnia's thing, not mine. She'd been involved in theater in college and had performed in community theater when she'd lived in Nevada, but pretending didn't sit well with my personality. "No, I haven't," I said.

"Me either." Jake's voice held mirth and a bit of mockery, but I doubted Seaver would be able to tell.

"If you'll come this way." Seaver indicated behind us.

He led us past the rack of costumes, through a door, and into a narrow hallway illuminated by an even dimmer light. Our feet clunked on the wood floor as I touched the wall to guide myself. I was relieved when Seaver tapped on a door on the right and opened it a crack. "Coming in!" he shouted, waiting mere seconds before pushing the door all the way open.

This room had ample light, which revealed half a dozen women sitting in front of mirrors or standing about in various stages of dress—petticoats, tights, and numerous layers seemed to be the theme. Only one woman had stepped behind a dressing screen for privacy, and even as we walked into the room, she reemerged to ask another woman to zip her up. Except for a few curious glances at me and a couple of admiring ones at Jake, no one paid us any attention. They were apparently accustomed to interruptions and lack of privacy.

The room seemed familiar, and I realized I'd seen it before in Rosemary's imprint on the brush, though only a slice of the room had been visible in her imprint, which probably meant she'd been sitting at one of the vanities close to the wall. Other actresses could have been present during the brush incident, and I wouldn't have seen them if she hadn't been thinking about them or looking in their direction.

Seaver gestured toward the back wall, where a built-in bookshelf had been labeled with names. "That's where they put their things, but everyone knows we aren't responsible if something left there goes missing. Rosemary might not have used it at all. Now, if you'll excuse me, I need to get dressed myself. I'm in the second scene."

"You're in the play *and* you direct it?" I asked, pulling my eyes from a woman with her red hair in an elaborate updo and so much eyeliner that her eyes dominated her face.

He shrugged. "We're a small company. Everyone does double duty." As he spoke, a blonde in a maid uniform walked over to the woman with the red hair and began to lace up a decorative bodice over her full dress.

"I won't be long," I told Seaver. He nodded and left the way we'd come in.

Jake and I walked to the back of the room, now garnering more looks from the actresses as we encroached upon their territory. A slender woman with black hair and a pale face arose from a stool where she was applying makeup to another woman. Her hair was barely an inch long and dipped into a sharp point in front of each ear, which emphasized her small nose and heart-shaped face. She looked like a delicate faerie.

"Can I help you?" she asked.

I nodded. "My name is Autumn, and I'm looking for wherever Rosemary might have put her things."

"The new girl?" She pointed at the bookshelf. "There, I guess, but it doesn't look like she left anything. I thought I saw something there yesterday, though, so she must have come in to get it."

"Think that means she's sacked?" asked the redhead.

"Probably." The faerie woman shrugged. "You know how Walsh and Seaver are about missing rehearsals."

"Yeah, but Seaver thought she was his ticket out of here," said the woman who had been behind the privacy screen, pausing in her attempt to form blond ringlets on either side of her face with a tiny curling iron.

"And what of it, Millie?" asked the faerie, bitterness oozing from her young voice. "We all want a ticket out of here. That's the only reason we stay with this lousy outfit. Otherwise, we'd kiss this stinking theater goodbye forever. Rosemary was just in the way, and I'll admit it—if none of you will—that I'm glad she's gone."

"Gosh, Erica, tell us how you really feel," said Millie.

"Just don't let Walsh hear you," added the redhead.

"Walsh," Erica snorted. "He's nothing but an overweight womanizer in a bad suit. Anyone who falls for him is dreaming. He'll never leave his wife. Or should I say her money."

Everyone suddenly became busy and wouldn't meet my eyes. I wondered what sort of relationship this woman had with the producer that she would dare to talk about him so condescendingly in front of everyone. Was she speaking from personal experience? She seemed rather young and pretty to succumb to his questionable charms. I'd give her maybe twenty-five or twenty-six. With only a few exceptions, they all looked about that age.

Jake shook his head slightly at me. *I know,* I thought, *something isn't right here.* What had Rosemary stumbled into? She wouldn't have been welcomed easily by this lot, so why had she accepted the role in the first place?

The faerie I now knew as Erica turned back to her makeup job. "Look around if you want," she said, dragging an eyeliner beneath her subject's left eye. "But I can tell you there's nothing to see. She wasn't around long."

"So none of you really knew Rosemary?" I asked.

She shook her head, eyeliner poised in the air. "She was someone Cheyenne knew—Cheyenne's one of our actresses. But some friend Rosemary turned out to be, taking the Juliet role right out from under her. We shouldn't even be doing that stupid play, as I keep telling Walsh. Only four actors. What are the rest of us supposed to do?"

"*The Comedy of Errors,*" retorted the redhead, "on the off night. Fat lot of good it will do us. It's old—no one important comes to see it anymore."

"At least we're doing what we love," Millie said, moving to stand next to Erica.

"Doing what we love?" spat the redhead. "Easy for you to say since you have a part in that stupid play—and a chance to be noticed."

Millie shrugged. "You know that's not my fault."

The redhead didn't deign to respond but turned back to her mirror. The other women in the room who hadn't spoken averted their gazes from her, as though not wanting to risk her wrath.

Okay, I thought, exchanging a wary glance with Jake.

"Did Rosemary have an assigned vanity?" Jake asked.

Erica shook her head. "We share them." She capped the eyeliner. "All done," she told the actress in front of her. "Sit down, Millie, and I'll do you." The women exchanged places.

Convinced that was the extent of the help we would receive, I began to do what I do best: touch things. One of the women had left a vanity, so I started there. I was aware of the heavy, subtle stares from the actresses as I intruded upon their space, though they averted their gazes if I glanced their way.

Imprints. A lot of them but old, faded, or irrelevant to my investigation. Resentment, excitement, and friendship were the reigning emotions, which, given the competitive and yet family-like nature of theater, seemed about right. There were no imprints regarding Rosemary. The redhead and some of the others might be resentful toward her, but there was no imprint that indicated foul play. Since she'd only recently won the part and had come only for the tryouts and one rehearsal, it was unlikely she had left many imprints in this room.

Still, I tried, trailing my fingers over everything until I could feel the animosity build in the room to a point that I became uncomfortable. Erica, now wearing a long raven wig that matched the color of her own faerie cut, had given up all pretense of doing anything and simply watched me. At least she didn't look away as the others did when I met her gaze.

Jake was looking around, too, inside the closets and cupboards that were built into the walls. When I finished the vanities, I started doing the same, but by then I'd lost hope of finding anything useful. Rosemary simply hadn't been here long enough. I'd need to find some other place to pick up her imprints.

"It's nearly curtain time," Erica said, bending to retrieve a dress that was spread over a chair. "What exactly are you looking for?"

"Something she might have left behind," I hedged. "There was a threatening note someone left her. Maybe it's here." It was probably a clue I wouldn't have divulged if I'd been a real detective.

"A threatening note?" Erica asked. "Poor thing. I had no idea." A few others nodded in agreement. The animosity fell a notch.

I opened another closet door. This closet had only top shelves and was home to a bucket, mop, broom, and a large round plastic garbage can lined with a black bag. Oddly, a high-heeled shoe stuck out from behind the garbage can.

It still had a foot inside. A foot that wasn't moving.

Chapter 4

I drew in a quick breath and reached for the can, my heart pounding furiously in my chest. *Oh, Rosemary,* I thought. *What am I going to tell Liam?*

Jake appeared at my side, helping me pull the plastic can from the closet. Tucked in the small corner space behind it sat a woman propped against the wall, her head tilted at an uncomfortable angle that told me she wasn't sleeping, though I couldn't see any blood or notable injury. She had long brown hair and was wearing some sort of costume. I didn't recognize her, but that did nothing for the anger I felt that someone could have hurt this poor woman and stuffed her in a closet. Behind a garbage can, no less. I felt no imprints from the garbage can, which was a good thing given the circumstances.

Because there was no one else around to do it, I knelt and put my fingers to her throat to confirm what I already knew. No pulse.

"She's dead," I announced.

I heard a scream behind me and turned in time to see the redheaded actress falling to the ground in a faint, her beautiful hair twisting in an unnatural angle. A wig.

"Vera!" shouted several of the actresses, rushing to the fainted woman's side.

I looked back at the woman I'd found in the closet

"Rosemary?" Jake asked me in a low voice.

The hair was similar, but I didn't think this was the face I'd seen in the mirror when reading the brush, though it was possible I hadn't been reading Rosemary's brush at all. Liam might have taken someone else's by mistake.

I turned to Erica, who had come to stand behind us, her pale face even whiter. "Is this . . . ?"

"Not Rosemary," she said in a weak voice. "That's Cheyenne."

Ah, the actress who'd missed this evening's final call. There was no stench, and I assumed she hadn't been here long, since they'd all been expecting her to show up any moment, and no one had mentioned her missing rehearsals.

"We need to call the police." I fished for the phone in my coat pocket.

"Wait," Erica said. "We'd better talk to Paxton first. We've got a play tonight."

"Who cares about the play?" Millie came toward us, tucking a blond ringlet behind her ear. "We're calling the police now, not after."

"You're right, of course." Erica shook her head. "Who cares what Walsh wants? Poor Cheyenne. I can't believe someone would do this to her." She ran a fingertip under one eye, as if blotting a tear. "I'll go tell everyone else."

Millie knelt next to me. "She looks so uncomfortable."

Her hand reached out, but I pushed it away. "Don't move her."

Millie blinked. "Oh, yeah." She stood and backed away to

stand with the other women who were either staring or helping the fainted redhead.

I stood and pushed Shannon's number on my cell phone without even considering calling anyone else. Jake watched me, his brown eyes occasionally going past me to the body.

"Hello," Shannon said. "What's up?"

I could hear rock music in the background. "I have a problem."

"Oh."

I had the faint sense that he was disappointed, but what did he think, that I was suddenly going to start calling to ask him out? I hadn't come that far in my acceptance of my feelings. Or his. Or become that careless of Jake's.

"Does this have something to do with that pup you gave my number to? Did you absolutely have to give him my cell number?"

"Sorry. I meant to give him the precinct. Actually, his case might be connected to the reason I'm calling. It's hard to tell, but it probably is. I think."

"Spit it out."

With a dead woman in the room, I was entitled to babble, but his words got me back on track. "I'm looking at a corpse right now." I wasn't actually, since my back was to the closet, but it was the same in principle. I'd actually touched the poor woman.

"Where are you?"

How nice of him not to ask for details, because I had nothing more to tell him. "I'm at the theater where Liam's sister had just started working before she disappeared, but it's not her." I gave him the address.

"Don't touch anything."

"I need to see if there are any imprints."

"Later. After the police finish. And don't let anyone else touch anything."

"Okay." I hung up, for once glad to comply. My stomach felt queasy, and I wondered if I was going to lose my dinner.

I looked at Jake, but his face was inscrutable as it often was where Shannon was concerned. Once the two men had openly baited and mocked each other, but after the last case where Shannon and Jake had fought members of a Japanese crime family side by side, they'd become friends, much to my consternation.

"He says not to let anyone touch anything," I said.

Jake stepped in front of the closet door and folded his arms, looking official and more than a little breathtaking.

"I knew we shouldn't do that play," Vera was saying. She was conscious again, and the other woman had helped her to a chair. Her red wig had been completely removed, and I saw through the hair net underneath that she was also a brunette, though her hair was slightly lighter than that of the victim's.

"Really Vera? Do we need to go there?" Millie said. "The play didn't kill her."

"No, but it's bad luck," Vera insisted with a sniff. "At least for us. You know what happened the last few times this company tried it. People ended up dead! Now it's happening again. Walsh has to cancel."

This was interesting. A play evoking such bad luck that people died? "What do you mean?" I asked.

Before Vera could reply, an older actress whose name I hadn't learned knelt in front of her and gently dabbed at Vera's tear-stained face with a tissue. This was the sense of family I'd experienced in some of the imprints earlier. When things got tough, love and loyalty overrode jealousy and competition.

"It's ridiculous," Millie said. "A play can't be bad luck."

Vera didn't take the bait but let her gaze fall on each of us in turn, as if aware that she now held center stage. "It's not ridiculous. I wasn't here then, but I've heard the stories. Every time the Portland Players tried to perform this play, something terrible happened. The first time two of the characters—the ones playing Juliet and Alex—missed final call on opening night. They were never found. That was like eight years ago. Two years later when they tried to do the play again, Juliet died of some mysterious illness. Then last time, four years ago, Juliet broke her leg during rehearsal, and the Ginger character was in a car accident and died. They've had to cancel the play every time."

"Chloe died because she had cancer," Millie said. "That was right before I started here. And car accidents and broken legs happen. I bet you those first two ran off together to work for another acting company. Good grief, Vera, it's just coincidence."

"Coincidence? Three times in eight years? And now a fourth time? I don't think that's coincidence. That play is cursed." Vera looked at me. "What else can it be?"

I would have thought it coincidence, if not for the fact that this time someone had obviously put Cheyenne in the closet. But whatever I might have responded was swallowed in Carl Walsh and Paxton Seaver's arrival. Seaver, the director, was wearing makeup and some kind of medieval outfit, complete with tights up to his knees. He was followed by Erica and one of the male members of the cast, also in costume and makeup. The new actor was broad and tall with dark, wavy hair, the epitome of what I'd always expected from an actor.

"Where is she?" Seaver demanded, his voice gruff. A line of anxiety creased his forehead.

I motioned toward the closet Jake was guarding. "Don't touch anything. The police are on their way."

Seaver and the male actor hurried to Jake, their gazes locking on what was inside the closet. With a muffle exclamation of disbelief, Seaver's hand grabbed at the door frame, as if he needed support.

The rotund Walsh clapped his hands together. "I know this is a tragedy, folks, but we have a play to put on tonight. We've got a full house out there. Curtain call is in fifteen minutes."

"We're still doing the play tonight?" Vera wailed.

"Of course we're doing the play," Walsh said. "We sold the tickets, and if we don't do this play now, we won't have money to pay you."

"Again," mumbled someone, but I couldn't identify who. Neither could Walsh, apparently, because he ignored the remark.

Seaver turned from the closet, his lips clenched together and eyes glittering with unshed tears.

"Are we sure she's dead?" asked the good-looking actor.

I almost smiled because his voice didn't match his looks but was at least two octaves too high for any man. If I'd been watching a play, I'd expect a character with his voice to be the comic relief.

"Oh, Lucas, of course we're sure." Millie shot him an evil look, which reminded me of something Walsh had said about Millie and a male actor being at odds with each other. Apparently they hadn't made up, though fighting with Lucas didn't seem to go with the rest of her positive character.

Maybe it's his fault, I thought.

"Well, she could be unconscious." Lucas shivered.

"Someone killed her and put her there," Vera said.

Lucas shook his head. "She could have had a heart attack."

"And then walked to the closet?" shot Millie. "And hid behind the garbage can?" Lucas obviously wasn't the brightest bulb on their marquee.

"She's dead," I said. "I checked for a pulse. And someone definitely hid her here."

"Does this mean I don't get to be Alex?" Lucas asked in his falsetto. "I mean, if we have no Juliet, we can't do the play."

Silence as everyone stared at him. He shrugged uncomfortably and said to me, "Who are you? Are you a new member of the cast?"

I sighed and shook my head.

Walsh clapped his hands together again. "Never mind. Everyone, back to your places. I'm opening the curtain in a bit, and you'd all better be ready."

With an accusatory glare at me, he marched to the door. "Come on, Lucas, before the others find out what's going on." By others I assumed he meant the rest of the male cast.

"The detectives will want to interview everyone," I said to no one in particular.

Seaver sighed. "They'll have their chance."

"After the play," retorted Walsh. "Now get going, ladies!"

I wondered how Shannon would react to that. Certainly this was a murder scene and no one would be allowed to leave, not even the customers I was sure were figments of Walsh's imagination. Well, that would be Shannon's responsibility and his call. I was sticking around only for the imprints.

"Hey," I whispered to Jake, "can you keep an eye on things

here while I look around? Now that everyone's going to be on stage or busy, I might find something more."

He nodded. "Be careful."

How did I know he was going to say that? I didn't bother to remind him that I was perfectly able to take care of myself now. I'd been training for months. Besides, the killer had to be long gone or at least wouldn't attempt anything more now that everyone was aware of the murder and the police were on their way.

The backstage of the theater was alive with movement. Actors scurried past me carrying props and costumes, and two were working on a wooden set. One cluster of actors practiced lines, Lucas among them, and I was surprised to learn he could lower his voice so well. It sounded a bit fake, sure, but then all acting did to me.

I didn't see Walsh and Seaver as I nosed about, my hands once again trailing over everything from props to walls and spare costume pieces someone had dropped on the floor. It was exhausting to experience the lives of a group of people who as a matter of course blurred the lines of reality and make-believe. Some scenes I knew were faked because of the language, but others made me shiver with the realism.

I knocked on each door that I entered but besides a small office and the men's dressing room, now deserted with the preplay frenzy, there wasn't much to see. Nothing I touched pointed to Rosemary's disappearance or poor Cheyenne's death. I even went onto the darkened stage and touched the props there. Nothing.

Peeking through the curtain, I saw that the seats in the small stadium theater were indeed full of patrons. Whatever opinion I had of Carl Walsh, he had apparently come through in dredging up an audience. Of course, none of the attendees knew there was a dead woman in the women's dressing room. Shaking my head, I headed back to the prop room to see if I'd overlooked something there.

"That must have been terrible," came a voice from around a bend in the hallway. "I wish I could have been there for you."

"It was horrible! She was just sitting there, stuffed in a corner. I didn't really like Cheyenne, but to end like that—behind a garbage can in a closet. It isn't right. And now there's a killer on the loose. I'm so scared!"

"It'll be okay. I won't let anything happen to you. I promise." Abrupt silence that probably meant kissing.

I kept walking, wanting to know who these actors were, though I already suspected the identity of one. They pulled apart as I rounded the corner.

"Hi, Vera," I said. She had replaced her red wig and fixed her makeup—all but the lipstick that was now shared by the male actor next to her. Or maybe it was his lipstick. One never knew with actors.

"Oh, it's only you," Vera said, her voice slightly hostile.

"Who is this?" her friend asked. He had blond hair and was a little on the short side for a man, but he was broad and strong looking and had a certain appeal in the way he smiled.

"She's looking for Rosemary," Vera said, pushing her lips into a pout. "She's the one who found Cheyenne."

"I'm Autumn Rain," I said.

He smiled again and held out his hand. "Beautiful name." Trust an actor to say that. People usually thought my name was odd. "I'm Trenton Cauley. Nice to meet you."

"You too." He shook hands well, not like a limp fish, and I found myself liking him more than I liked the dramatic Vera.

"Well, I'd better let you two go," I said. "I know your play is starting."

"Oh, no! She's right. See you later, love." Vera grabbed the sides of her dress and fled down the hall, apparently all her fear of murderers having vanished. I tried not to roll my eyes.

Trenton Cauley gave me an obviously admiring look, which in my book made him a player, a ladies' man, and I wasn't interested in more drama.

I nodded and moved down the hall toward the prop room. The large space was as dim as ever but now it held a sense of foreboding I hadn't experienced earlier. Murders do that to you—not that I knew much about murders. Most of the cases I consulted on involved missing people I eventually found alive.

This time I ran my hands close to the props, not touching them unless I felt a prominent tingling that signaled a stronger, more recent imprint. Anything connected with a murder or kidnapping would be strong. Usually, I'd avoid clothes altogether, as they weren't good receptacles for imprints, too often being washed, discarded, or taken for granted, but costumes were different, so I made sure to check all the clothes racks.

Then I felt her—Rosemary. She was trying on a dress in front of a mirror, her contentment palpable.

I finally get to be Juliet. So what if it's a modern play and I have to fall in love with a muse instead of a real man. It's a good part, and I just know it's going to mean my big break when Mr. Walsh's aunt from New York sees it. It's my turn at last!

The recent imprint faded to earlier emotions that were irrelevant, and nothing else on that clothes rack shed more information.

So Rosemary had come to the Portland Players with an agenda, a hope that it would be her big break. Liam and the script had already hinted at such, but now I had solid confirmation. No way would Rosemary have left of her own free will.

A noise pierced my consciousness. "Hello?" I called. "Is anyone there?" I paused to listen and heard nothing. The noise had probably come from the hallway. Of course if someone was in the room with me and was trying to hide, I wouldn't be able to find him in this decades-old collection without more light and several helpers. It would be too easy to duck behind a rack or slide under a table.

Goose bumps rose on my skin. Nothing like the dark to evoke images of crouching attackers or more bodies hidden in closets. Instinctively, my hand went to the gun in my pocket, but that brought up the whole question of whether I could actually use it to shoot someone.

Shaking my head, I bent to the table near the rack of clothes. Something seemed out of place here, but what? There were dishes, a box of costume jewelry, a slew of hats, and a hammer—a hammer that radiated strong imprints I would have to read.

The moment I reached for it, I heard a rushing sound. Something heavy hit me, spinning me against the rack of clothes that shot away with the impact. Thankfully the rack and clothes were heavy enough not to go far, and I didn't hit my face on the concrete floor when I fell. Or at least not too hard. My body protested the jarring, even as I forced it to move, trying to shove away from my attacker, fear arching through me. The dark-clad figure reached for something on the table.

Jumping to my feet, I sidestepped another rush. My attacker stopped short of running into the rack and whirled to face me, hammer in hand. The figure was wearing all black, including a ski mask and a thigh-length coat that hid his build. The hand with the hammer jabbed in my direction, but I blocked it and threw a punch that landed with a satisfying crack. The figure curled momentarily in pain, dropping the hammer.

I took two steps forward and kicked it away. Now we were on equal footing, and with my training, I might have the advantage. I still had my gun too, though I worried it might end up being used against me at this close range.

The attacker launched at me again. Not exactly an intelligent martial arts move for the untrained, so he either knew nothing or was sure of himself. I turned before the impact, grabbing his arm and using his forward movement to roll him over my back where he slammed onto the floor. His grunt of surprise filled the quiet. My shoulder ached where his boot had caught me on the way over, but I reached for his mask. He jerked away, rolled from me, jumped to his feet, and ran to the outside door.

I sprinted after him, reaching the door as he rounded the side of the theater. By the time I got to the front, he was nowhere in sight. Only the full parking lot and cars lining the street both ways for a quarter of a mile greeted my arrival. Puddles of water reflected the tiny slice of moonlight peeking through the overhead clouds. He could be hiding anywhere.

At least it wasn't raining, though my breath came in soft white clouds. My shoulder throbbed, and my face felt slick. When I touched my right cheek, my hand came away wet with blood. I'd hit the floor harder than I'd thought, or perhaps I'd been scraped by something sharp on the clothes rack.

I searched the darkness, though I had no idea what I would do with the attacker if I found him. A car so far down the street that I couldn't identify the make roared to life and sped out of sight.

I kicked at the ground in frustration. He'd gotten away, leaving only the hammer behind as evidence, but since he'd been wearing gloves, it wasn't likely he'd left an imprint.

As I debated what to do, two police cars and two unmarked vehicles drew up in front of the theater, blocking the street. Two officers emerged from each car, and Walsh hurried from the front of the theater, where he must have been watching for them. I knew Shannon would be among the officers and detectives and that he'd want to talk to me, but an idea wouldn't leave me alone and I had to take care of it first. When the assailant had grabbed the hammer, had he been trying to hide evidence or simply searching for something to stop me from doing whatever he thought I was doing?

There was only one way to find out.

A coroner's van pulled up as I turned to go around the theater and back inside the prop room. The hammer lay where I'd kicked it. I knelt beside it and touched my finger to the handle.

I gasped at the mental image.

Hate and rage filled me, so great there was no way to contain it. I felt the hammer in my hand, saw it rise. In front of me was the back of a woman's head, her identity obscured by her long brown hair. I brought the hammer down hard, and she crumpled at the impact. The hammer fell to the ground.

I snatched back my hand as the images disappeared, my body shaking all over at the terrifying scene. The hammer had definitely been used as a weapon, but for the life of me, I couldn't identify either who had received or who had delivered that terrible blow.

Chapter 5

$\mathcal{I}$ hadn't fainted, and I'd been able to remove my hand from the hammer without help from either Jake or Shannon. That meant I was learning something or that the imprint, though horrendous, had been too short to hold me in a repeating loop. I suspected the latter, but for whatever reason, I was grateful Shannon wouldn't find me mopping the floor with my face—again.

Now to find something to wipe my cheek before Shannon and his crew showed up looking for me.

I was too late. Already I could hear Walsh coming in the back door, complaining about the brick holding the door open, how it was impossible to stop the show, and his concern about inconveniencing his customers.

I stood and grabbed the nearest thing I could find for my cheek—a winter scarf that was so full of dust, I'd have to wash my wound thoroughly later to be sure it didn't become infected.

"Autumn?" Shannon peered through the dimness. "That you?"

He came toward me, sturdily built and compact, each movement unwasted and undeniably graceful.

"Hi, Detective Martin." Better to keep it formal in front of Walsh and the other three police officers.

"I thought I told you to stay with the body." He took several steps closer.

I shrugged. "Jake's got it. No one will have touched anything."

"I can personally vouch for all my actors," Walsh said. "None of the people in my company has anything to do with this dreadful act. We vet our actors very carefully."

Which likely meant he hired any halfway decent actor willing to accept substandard pay, but Shannon would discover the truth about the company's financials without my interference.

"I'm sure you do," Shannon said dryly, his eyes not leaving mine. "What happened to your face?"

"I, uh, was looking around in here and had a little run-in with a guy in a black mask," I told him. "I chased him outside, but he took off in a car just before you arrived."

Shannon's expression darkened. "You get the license plate or a make?"

"Too far away. Too dark."

Everyone was interested now, especially Walsh, who looked ready to accuse me of lying.

"I did, however, find something of interest," I added. Something I didn't want to talk about in front of Walsh. "If I could talk to you privately."

Shannon finally dragged his gaze from my face and waved the other officers to go on without him. "You know the drill. I'll be along in a minute." He smiled at Walsh. "If you'd be so kind as to show them the way."

Walsh's jaw jutted from his round face, but he didn't

object. I wondered if he was as compelled by Shannon's eyes as everyone else always seemed to be. Okay, maybe not everyone. Maybe just me.

"Let's have it," Shannon said when they were gone. "What happened?"

I told him everything, from the moment I arrived at the theater to reading the imprint on the hammer.

"Don't you have your gun?"

"I didn't need to shoot him." The weight of the small pistol weighed more heavily than ever in my coat pocket.

"He tried to hit you with a hammer."

"Rather ineptly."

His hand went to my chin, turning my face so he could examine it. "Then what's this?"

His touch burned my skin, but I couldn't tell if that was a good or a bad thing. "That was me falling."

His hand dropped. "Okay, so where's this hammer?"

I pointed to where I had kicked it earlier, nearly under the table. "You won't find any of my attacker's prints, though. He was wearing gloves, those thin, socklike ones."

"You sure it was a he?"

"Actually, no. He wasn't really big, so I suppose it could have been a she. At any rate, I didn't receive any other imprints when I touched the hammer. Just one of someone attacking a woman with long brown hair."

"Our vic?"

"I'm not sure. She does have long hair, though, and it's the right color. Like Tawnia's, only longer. It could be anyone. I couldn't identify the person wielding the hammer, either. All he concentrated on as he struck was the hair."

"He or she."

"Right. As for the murdered woman I found tonight, I didn't see any blood."

"You might not if she was killed somewhere else and then shoved into that closet. In fact, that's likely. Who attacks someone in a closet? The murderer might have thought to hide the body until there was time to dispose of it without being caught."

Body. How sad to be reduced to such a word. Not woman or man. No names, just "body" or "vic" or "it."

"We'll know more once we have the cause and time of death." Shannon took a glove from his pocket. He and his coworkers seemed to carry around disposable gloves the way most people carried chewing gum. The glove was followed by a plastic bag to hold the hammer. He marked on the outside with a pen.

It said a lot about his increasing trust in me that he didn't spend fifteen minutes trying to talk me out of what I'd seen, and that warmed my heart much the way his hand had warmed my chin. Time was when he'd have threatened to lock me up for trying to sway the investigation with my ulterior motives, whatever they might be.

"Where's Paige?" I asked, realizing I hadn't seen his partner.

"It's her day off. Mine, too, before you ask."

I knew that meant he'd come in because I was involved, not because he was the most successful detective on the force, though that could very well be the case. "Well, I'm glad you're here."

He smiled and suddenly the space between us was too small. I swallowed hard and looked away.

Jake is here, I reminded myself. *He's my boyfriend.* Except that he wasn't, not really, not anymore, though he wanted to be, and I wanted him to be. Maybe.

"Anything else you want to see here?" Shannon asked, his voice thick with amusement—or perhaps something more.

There were many items I should probably touch, but I was feeling reluctant. "Not unless I have to. The imprints here are strange. It's hard to tell which are real and which took place on the stage."

"What about the hammer?"

"That was real." But I was already beginning to doubt myself.

If I touched it again maybe I could verify . . . No. I knew what I'd seen. That was real rage, and the woman must have been seriously hurt. The strength behind the blow had been real.

Without further discussion, I led Shannon to the women's dressing room, where his men had already finished with pictures and were well into dusting for prints in the closet and on the garbage can.

Jake was standing back from the others, his hands in his coat pockets. He blinked at my face, taking two steps toward me. "What happened?"

"A guy knocked me over in the prop room. I scraped myself on the floor. Don't worry. I'm okay." That explanation would have to hold him for now.

His jaw worked, but he nodded without further comment. Then his gaze met Shannon's and his head dipped. "Shannon."

"Jake. Thanks for guarding the body."

"No problem, but next time I'll go with Autumn."

"Next time?" Shannon arched a brow. "Let's hope there's no next time. Not for this." He chuckled, and Jake grinned.

It still unsettled me to see them act so civilly when once they'd been at each other's throats. Fact was that with my indecision, they both had more reason now to dislike each other, but apparently saving each other's lives this past summer had created a permanent bond between them. It made things horribly awkward for me.

We were joined by an incredibly young medical examiner, who knelt near the body. Shannon didn't feel a need to insert himself into the activity around the corpse but seemed content to wait for the initial conclusions. Meanwhile, his sharp eyes took in the two actresses still present—Erica, who looked out-of-time with her long black wig twisting along her face in gentle ringlets, and a woman with blond hair I'd overlooked before.

"You will try to be discreet with this investigation, won't you?" Walsh came to stand before Shannon, twisting his hands. "I don't want my customers disturbed. In fact, I'd rather they didn't find out."

Shannon shrugged. "Depending on time of death, we may have to detain them all."

"Not necessary. Some of my ladies were in here at least an hour before any of our guests arrived, so it must have happened before then. Our guests have nothing to do with this. This murder had to have been accomplished this afternoon when we left rehearsal for an early dinner." His nostrils flared in distress. "If this gets out, it's going to ruin us. Simply ruin us!"

I stifled an urge to roll my eyes. "Think of it this way," I said. "You'll probably be more packed than ever once people hear a real live murder happened here. Do you have any murder mysteries in your repertoire? Maybe you could start a murder dinner theater."

Walsh glared at me. "Why are you still here?"

"Where else would I be? I'm a witness now. Besides, I still don't have any clue where Rosemary might be."

"Believe me—I want you to find her. With Cheyenne gone, I don't have anyone else to play Juliet."

"Look," Shannon asked, "did any of your actors not show up tonight—or leave early? Someone was prowling around a short time ago in your prop room."

"Everyone showed up on time—except for Cheyenne." Walsh's brow furrowed. "And everyone is still here and accounted for. I gave one of your officers a full list, including my director and the janitor."

Shannon nodded. "So earlier on our way in you said Cheyenne was here for your afternoon rehearsal. Did she leave with everyone else?"

"I don't know. I didn't see when everyone left. I told them they could go and then went to my office to get my keys. But I already told this to your officers. Now, if you'll excuse me, I must get back to my duties. Can't have any actors missing their cues. Erica, come with me. You're on soon."

Erica reluctantly followed him, her eyes lingering on Shannon. "I gave a statement to one of your detectives, but I'll be back, if you want to talk to me yourself." Gone was the woman with the attitude I'd met before. This woman was from another time—warm, compliant, soft.

Must be the costume, I decided.

"Thanks, ma'am," Shannon said.

Erica frowned and left the room, the ma'am title apparently not falling well on her shoulders. I stifled a laugh, though she was a beautiful woman, with or without the wig, and if she decided to pursue Shannon, there was absolutely nothing

I could do about it. He might even appreciate the attention in light of all the trouble I gave him.

After a moment's hesitation, the unnamed blond actress also hurried from the room.

The medical examiner arose from the body, shaking his shaggy dark head. "I believe the cause of death is poisoning. There's no other apparent trauma, and with her skin still so pink and that bitter almond smell, it's almost a given for cyanide."

"I didn't notice any smell," I said.

The doctor pushed up his glasses and gave me a flat stare. "The ability to smell cyanide is genetic. I am particularly sensitive, and I know what to look for."

"Autumn, this is Paul Carter. Paul, I think you've heard of Autumn Rain."

Paul nodded. "Nice to finally meet you," he said without real feeling, though his gaze was intent.

I could think of a whole lot of things I'd rather be doing. "You too," I said, feeling a bit dissected with the way he was staring at me. Probably the scientific part of him wondering what made me tick.

"So no wound on the back of her head?" Shannon said.

Paul's gaze shifted back to Shannon. "Not a thing. She's been dead at least three hours, which puts the time of death around five. We'll know more after the autopsy."

"When you're ready, move her out." Shannon turned to his other men. "None of the theater personnel can leave until you get a full statement and contact info from everyone. I want prints, alibis, and whatever else you think is necessary."

"So the patrons can leave?" asked an officer.

"Yes, but we'll need to make sure they're really patrons.

Inform the suits outside to keep an eye out for anyone who seems suspicious." Shannon looked at me. "The guy in the black mask, was his car here when you arrived?"

"I don't think so. There were no cars out front or parked along the street at all. Only those in the back." I frowned. "But that means he was likely not responsible for the murder."

"Maybe he came back, thinking to move the body while everyone was busy with the play."

"But if he killed her when no one was here, he should have taken care of it then when no one was around. It doesn't make sense to return or to hang around until the body is discovered." My mind was racing. "Maybe he's not connected to the murder at all. Maybe he has something to do with Rosemary's disappearance instead."

"Could be." Shannon looked skeptical.

"I don't see how he could be involved with Rosemary," Jake said. "She was barely here a few days."

"Are you actually agreeing with each other?" Oops. I'd said that aloud.

"The poison may have been administered somewhere besides this room," Paul, the medical examiner, said into the silence that followed, as though there had been no interruption in his report. "We haven't found anything related in the closet or garbage bin. But given the signs, death was quick, so the poisoning likely took place in this theater."

I sighed. "Cyanide basically doesn't allow the body to use oxygen, right?" You learn the oddest things as the child of hippie parents who owned an herb shop. "Are you saying she smothered to death while her killer watched? And then he moved her here?"

"Her heart probably gave out before she suffocated." Paul

gave me an apologetic smile, which made me like him a tiny bit more. I guess you had to develop a cold outer shell when you worked that kind of job. I knew Shannon had. "She probably went into a coma and then was moved here so time could finish the job."

"We need to tear this place apart looking for any signs of poison," Shannon said. "We'll also have to check the homes of the entire acting company. Look for any possible cyanide connection."

Poison. What a terrible way to go. "Wait," I said, remembering something from earlier. "Could the cyanide have been administered in a glass of lemonade?"

Shannon, Paul, and Jake's eyes were all on me now. Paul nodded. "The addition of the acid in the juice would help it work even faster."

"There was a glass," I said, "in the prop room that had an imprint. I saw freshly poured lemonade and someone stirring in a white powder. I thought it came from a play." I hadn't paid a lot of attention to the imprint, but I remembered the fear beating in the actor's heart and impending triumph as he or she mixed the liquid. Of course, the imprint had ceased after being set down, so I hadn't witnessed the result, and since similar earlier imprints had repeated afterward, as though the events had taken place during a rehearsal, I'd assumed it was fake, though the more recent imprint had felt vivid. Perhaps the murderer had simply acted out his plan several times before finally committing the deed. Then again, it could be completely unrelated.

"Show me," Shannon said.

We hurried down the hall, accompanied by Jake, but when we reached the prop room and the table where I'd seen the glass, it wasn't there.

"I remember the glass," Jake said. "Autumn looked, well, involved while reading it." Which meant I'd freaked him out, something I'd done a lot of this past year.

"The guy in black," I said. "He must have taken it."

"Maybe." Shannon looked thoughtful. "Or someone else already here could have taken it when you found the body. That means it may still be here. I'll get everyone looking."

"What about Rosemary?" I asked.

"She doesn't yet seem to be connected to the murder."

"She received a threatening note, and there was something else weird in one of her imprints." I explained about the hairbrush and how the scene had shut off so abruptly.

Shannon studied me in silence for a minute. "What does Rosemary look like?"

"Narrow face, wide forehead. Green eyes. Long brown hair." Lightheadedness assaulted me as I thought about my description, though neither of the men could possibly see my reaction in the dim light.

I took a deep breath before adding, "Her hair was long enough that she could have been the woman I saw hit with the hammer."

If so, given how hard she'd been hit in that imprint, we might not be looking for Rosemary but her body.

Chapter 6

Everyone looked for the drinking glass. That is, the officers and detectives searched while Jake and I waited. At least they'd taken away the body and most of the theatergoers had cleared out. The police had even begun allowing the actors to leave. I hadn't been permitted to touch anything on the body, but they had allowed me to test the closet for imprints. There was nothing. Cheyenne had definitely been unconscious when she was carried there.

Jake yawned. "This could take all night."

"You're right. We should go home. They can contact me later if they find the glass."

"That's the best idea I've heard all night."

I was convinced my attacker had taken the glass, but even if he hadn't, I didn't know what more I could see if I read it again. Maybe looking at the person's hand as he or she held the glass would tell me if it was a man or a woman. Otherwise, the police would have more success with their forensics.

"There is one thing," I said. "I'd like to talk to Erica. I still don't have any clue about where to keep searching for Rosemary, and with the murder on their hands, finding her isn't going to be a priority for the police. Didn't Erica say something about Cheyenne knowing Rosemary and that was how she came to be here?"

"Something like that." Jake stifled another yawn. "There's Erica now. While you talk to her, I'll go tell Shannon we're leaving."

"Good idea. I'll meet you out front."

I cornered Erica by the door to the women's dressing room. She'd removed her wig, but the heavy makeup she still wore contrasted sharply with her casual jeans.

"Leaving?" she asked, running a hand through her pixie cut.

"Yeah. But I wanted to ask you a question first."

"Shoot. Though maybe I shouldn't answer. You brought a lot of trouble down on us tonight."

"Better now than when the trail was cold. Or when the body started stinking."

Erica grimaced. "Thanks for that vivid picture. What do you want to know?"

"You said Rosemary was someone Cheyenne knew. How close were they?"

"I heard them talking about Rosemary sleeping on her couch. Maybe she let her stay a few nights. I really don't know. Rosemary showed up for tryouts, but Cheyenne wasn't happy when she got the Juliet role."

"So who's going to do it now?"

She snorted. "Not me."

"I thought you didn't believe in a role being cursed."

"No use tempting fate. Why don't you do it? You could investigate us all better that way. You might find out what happened to Rosemary."

"What's so important about that play?"

Erica rolled her eyes. "Walsh has a connection on Broadway, an aunt, and every year she and her friends come to visit and to watch one of his plays. Several times in the past they've offered actors jobs, and it makes their career. Except they haven't chosen anyone in the past five years, and Walsh is getting desperate. The chance of being chosen is the only reason most of us still work here."

"I see." Rosemary's choice of this dive was making more sense now.

Erica laughed at my expression. "What, you didn't think we stayed for the great working conditions and the excellent directing, did you? Our actors are good, though, far better than this company merits. But if there isn't a real chance of actors being chosen to star in New York, no one is going to work for Walsh, and his business goes under."

"So why that particular play?"

"He heard it's one of his aunt's favorites."

"Did anyone else try out for the part beside Rosemary and Cheyenne?"

She shrugged. "You'll have to ask Paxton. He and Carl held the auditions. Some of the others watched, but I wasn't there that day. I suggested doing another play, one that used more of us, but no one listens to me."

"With so few roles, you'd think everyone would fight over the parts."

"Well, on the whole, we're a superstitious bunch, and they really haven't had a lot of luck with this play. If they want a Juliet now, I bet she'll have to come from the outside."

"Could you tell me where Cheyenne lived? Maybe her neighbors know something about Rosemary."

"Maybe. Or Cheyenne's roommates. Six of them rent a house together." Erica gave me general directions to Cheyenne's as she walked me to Walsh's office to write down the exact address. I was glad for the explanation.

Thankfully, the annoying Walsh wasn't in the office, though a uniformed policeman on his hands and knees was searching under the desk. "I'll need these drawers opened," the detective said, pointing to the desk. "Two are locked."

"Walsh usually leaves his keys here." Erica retrieved a set of keys from a cup on the desk and tossed them to the detective, who nodded his thanks. Then she opened a notebook and began copying Cheyenne's information from it onto a sticky note. I'd expected her to bring up an employee file on a computer, but apparently Walsh didn't have one.

Cast pictures and posters of their past performances filled the office walls. They seemed to be organized by the year, and as I went back in time, I could identify many of the actresses I'd met today. After a few years, only a couple familiar faces cropped up, and after six, there was no one I knew. I went back further, just to make sure.

Wait. Was that a younger Erica? The woman had long black hair and her face was rounder, but the nose and eyes could be the same. I stepped closer for a better look, squinting my eyes. It was hard to tell in a picture.

Erica came to stand beside me, the sticky note in her hand. "Is that you?" I asked, pointing.

She laughed and shook her head. "I wish. I was in college then, studying hard. I didn't join the cast until two years later. Here." She pointed to a poster where she was lying on the ground and an actor was trying to pull her to her feet. "That was me six years ago."

It looked like her—the heart-shaped face, short hair, small nose, and large eyes. She'd been younger and those brown eyes held a glint of mischievousness that was missing now, but it was her.

"That was my first real role—out of college, that is."

"Didn't the company try to do the Juliet play that year?" I might have remembered wrong what Vera, the actress with the red wig, had recounted about the play's history.

She nodded and pointed to a woman in a picture next to the poster. "That was Chloe, the actress who died—of cancer, they say. I didn't know her well."

My eyes shifted back to the picture from two years earlier. "So which of these actors were the ones who went missing on the opening night of the play the first time they tried it?"

She shook her head. "I really don't know. Walsh or Seaver might. Anyway, here is Cheyenne's address."

"Thanks." I tucked the sticky note into my pocket.

Erica was still looking at the old picture, a blank expression on her face. I wondered if she was thinking about the girl who resembled her, who perhaps Walsh and Seaver had been trying to replace when they'd hired Erica. Or was she thinking of the couple who'd gone missing?

I turned to leave, but her voice stopped me. "Hey. You seem to know that cute detective—is he seeing anyone?"

The officer going through the desk stopped searching and stared at us, as if awaiting the answer himself.

Her interest probably explained why she was being so helpful. I swallowed hard. "Not that I'm aware of."

"Good to know." Turning, she preceded me from the room, her hips moving in an exaggerated swing.

In the hall, I walked resolutely toward the front of the

theater. Unfortunately, the only way I knew to go was through the stage, where I found the director, Paxton Seaver, in an armchair watching officers comb the seating area.

He looked up when I appeared. "What are they looking for?" he asked.

"The murder weapon." Though the glass wasn't actually a weapon.

"And what would that be?"

"I can't say."

"Can't or won't?"

I shrugged. "Same thing. Ask Detective Martin."

"I don't know if Carl is right about us losing business by Cheyenne's death, but we need to find a new Juliet."

"Before Walsh's aunt visits?"

He gave me a tiny grin. "You get around, don't you?"

"I hear things. Some I just guess. Right now I'm guessing that you and Cheyenne were more than friends." His reaction at seeing her body in the dressing room had been unmistakable.

His eyes dropped to his hands, and several heartbeats passed before he looked up again. "She was furious when I gave Rosemary the role of Juliet, but Rosemary was exactly right for the part—sarcastic, witty, and the chemistry with both male actors was great. Cheyenne is more the good fairy type, you know. The sweet character, the one knights fight over and the evil villain tries to conquer, only to have her hero sweep in and save her at the last minute. She didn't understand. We fought. Now she's gone, and I'll never be able to tell her I'm sorry."

I wondered if his not choosing Cheyenne had more to do with keeping her in the company than with Rosemary's talent. "What did Walsh think?"

"He was thrilled to find Rosemary. That only made Cheyenne more upset. She confronted him several times. With both of them gone, he's not sure what to do now."

"The play is that important?"

"To Walsh it is."

That went with what Erica said and also brought up an angle I hadn't considered before. If Walsh had the most to lose by Rosemary's disappearance and Cheyenne's death, someone might be trying to destroy him.

"I'm sorry," I said.

"You would be perfect for the role." Seaver stood and took my hands. "Come back on Monday, okay? We're having new tryouts. I'll walk you through it. Think of it as saving the theater."

"I don't know a thing about acting."

"Yes, you do. Every day you act. We all do." His comment unsettled me, but I couldn't pinpoint why.

"With any luck, I'll find Rosemary for you." I pulled my hands from his and sauntered to the steps leading down from the stage. Feeling Seaver's eyes digging into my back, I hurried up the aisle, through the lobby, and to the front door where Jake was pacing.

"There you are," he said. "I was wondering if you'd had another run-in with a man in a mask."

I laughed. "I think he had enough the first time."

"So, you up for a late snack?"

"I can't."

"What? You turning down food?" Jake brought a hand to his heart and staggered. "Never thought I'd see the day. Though I guess I can't blame you after what happened tonight. Kind of feeling a bit sick myself."

"It's not that." I could always eat. "It's Tawnia. She has plans to find where our birth mother's mother lived. To see if we can contact her. She's picking me up bright and early tomorrow."

He gave me a half grin. "How do you feel about that?"

"I do want to know, but now that we have a real lead . . ." I shrugged. "It's just been so long. I want to know about my roots, especially since Winter and Summer are gone and they don't have any extended family to speak of, and I'd like to learn more about Kendall. But at the same time, I wonder if I should leave well enough alone."

He snorted. "Like that will ever happen."

I punched his arm with a little more force than I'd intended.

"Ow." He took my hand. "Kidding. Of course you have to follow the lead, or you'll always wonder. I'll take a rain check for the food, but let me know how it goes tomorrow."

"I will."

I dropped Jake off in front of our stores where he'd left his car. "Call me if your car breaks down on the way home," he said.

Normally he would have kissed me, and for a moment I wanted him to. I wanted to feel normal, to not have to think of Cheyenne dying or about Rosemary out there somewhere, possibly fatally wounded. I didn't want to think about a certain detective.

He hesitated, as if he could sense my uncertainty, or as if he too wanted something more. Then he smiled and gave me a wave and sauntered to his car.

I watched him go, torn between calling him back and going home to make myself a nice cup of lemon tea to drink in bed. Rain began falling again, and he hurried to his car, making my decision for me. I pulled back into traffic and began driving for a while without noticing where I was going.

I was heading home. At least that's what I thought, but ten minutes later as I looked around me, I realized my subconscious had other plans. Fortunately, my subconscious was better at directions than I was and when I stopped to examine the map on my phone, I wasn't far off the mark.

The section of town I was looking for was filled with small, older houses. Bungalows, really, some in a sad state of disrepair. Flowers in pots lined the porch of one bungalow, and though the contents were long dead, the colorful pots, illuminated by the streetlight, gave character to the house, which I suspected by the light of day might look rather garish.

According to Erica, Cheyenne had lived here with her roommates.

Shannon was going to kill me, especially if I let hints about Cheyenne's death mess up his investigation. But I wasn't here for Cheyenne. I simply wanted to know if any of her room-mates had information about Rosemary. If she'd been the one hit by the hammer, she could be lying somewhere hurt, if she wasn't already dead, and if she was out in this cold rain, her prospects would be worse. I couldn't go home and curl up in my comfortable bed unless I at least tried the only lead I had.

It was late, but these women were presumably single, like me, and that meant ten-thirty was early. They might not even be home yet from their dates or wherever they spent their Saturday nights.

Flipping up my hood and pulling my coat tighter around me, I went up the uneven walk, my flat boots splashing in shallow puddles of rainwater. The smell of rain on the pavement filled my mind with images of clean. I wished it were warm so I could pull off these confining boots and feel the wet pavement against my feet.

On the covered porch sat several wood chairs, one of which was broken. There was also a pair of soaked boots, which I hoped signaled that at least one roommate was home. Ignoring the bell, I knocked on the door in the off chance someone was sleeping; a knock was easier on the nervous system than a doorbell.

My phone buzzed with a text, and I glanced at it. *Found glass in dishwasher at the theater. No fingerprints. Saving it for you.*

Great. I guess it wouldn't hurt me to read the glass again. Simply washing didn't remove imprints from most objects, perhaps because they were embedded deep within the atoms that weren't overly disturbed by a little hot water. Often I'd had to pass up great antiques for my store because of negative imprints I knew I couldn't remove or stand to be around. I wouldn't sell such things anyway, though no one would know the difference, at least not consciously. Clothing and other things made of fabric were the exception, as they lost a bit of themselves at every washing, making even strong imprints fade rather quickly—if anyone had cared enough about them to imprint something in the first place, which didn't happen often.

Though I never saw anything more on subsequent readings, I hadn't been paying close attention the first time I'd read the glass because I believed the imprints had come from play-acting scenes, not real life. They still very well could have.

I didn't answer Shannon's text. He'd catch up to me eventually.

Shannon was like that. Always turning up when I least wanted to see him. Must be his profession.

I heard a brief creaking, and the door opened abruptly with no footsteps to warn me. A woman stood framed by the light. She was tall and model thin, with long golden blond hair and a figure I suspected hadn't come naturally. Eyebrows plucked to perfection, makeup artfully applied, and a sleeveless red dress that screamed "Look at me!" In her hand she carried spiked heels.

"Oh," she said in a low, husky voice. Obviously she'd been expecting someone else. "May I help you?"

"Sorry to disturb you so late. I'm an acquaintance of Cheyenne's. Is this her apartment?"

"Yes, but she's not here. She had a performance tonight." The woman peered around me into the rain, as though looking for someone. "She performs practically every night or is rehearsing. She's an actress, you know." She squinted at me and did a double take at my hurt cheek, which I ignored.

"I just came from the theater."

"You did? Then why would you come here to see Cheyenne?"

"The play's over, so I came to ask her about my friend Rosemary. Someone mentioned that she knew Cheyenne. Said maybe Rosemary had slept here a time or two."

"Yep. She did. She was looking for a place to stay, and right about that time one of our roommates up and got married, so Rosemary took over her contract."

I couldn't believe my luck. "Rosemary lives here now?"

She shrugged. "Yeah. Haven't seen her in a few days, but I don't keep the same schedule as Rosemary and Cheyenne. I leave for work while they're still sleeping, and I'm home after they're gone. Then I'm either asleep by the time they come home or still out if it's the weekend."

Not much help there. "Look," I said. "Here's the thing. No

one has seen Rosemary since at least Thursday. She didn't show up for Friday rehearsal. Everyone's worried."

The woman's brow furrowed. "That's strange. Anyway, Cheyenne might be able to tell you more. She's the one who knew her."

What to say to that?

A familiar white Mustang drove up to the curb.

"Look, my date's here," she said. "I'm sorry, but I can't talk to you anymore, and I can't let you wait here alone for Cheyenne. You'll have to come back later. You understand."

Of course, I understood. I could be some wacko with a secret agenda and a gun in her pocket. "It's not your date," I said. "It's the police."

She blinked at me. "Are they looking for you?"

"Do I look like I'm running?" What was it about me that she assumed I was a criminal? I was even wearing shoes, for crying out loud.

"No need to be rude."

"I'm sorry. I just need to see Rosemary's room. She's missing, and she could be hurt."

The woman was no longer paying attention to me. Shannon and an Asian detective who had also been at the theater reached the porch, badges in hand. "I'm Detective Martin with the Portland police," Shannon said. "This is Detective Huang. What has she told you?" He shot me a blistering stare.

"Only that Rosemary is missing," I said before the room-mate could answer. "This is her apartment, by the way, and I'd like to see her room."

Shannon relaxed. "If you don't mind," he said to the woman, "we'd like to take a look around."

She frowned. "I don't understand. What's going on?"

"I'm sorry to have to tell you," Shannon said. "Cheyenne's been murdered."

The woman gasped and put her hand to her lips. "Oh, no! How? Why? Who would hurt her?" She clung to the doorknob for support.

"That's what we're trying to find out. The sooner we take a look, the closer we'll be to figuring out what happened."

"Don't forget Rosemary," I added. "She's still missing."

Though I'd already said it several times, this information finally seemed to register as a concern for the woman. "Missing? Do you think we're in danger, that they're after all of us?"

"Until we know more, we really can't say." An impatient note had crept into Shannon's voice. "We won't even know for sure what killed Cheyenne until they finish the autopsy."

The woman turned a shade paler but still made no move to let us in.

"Look," Shannon added, "I know this is a surprise, but this is a murder investigation."

"Oh, of course. I'm sorry. Come in." She opened the door wider, looking past us to the street outside. Her date was apparently late. "There's no one else home at the moment." She gulped as though remembering that Cheyenne would never be coming home. "What should I do?"

"Just tell us which room was hers."

"And Rosemary's," I said, removing my winter gloves and stuffing them into my coat pockets.

"Cheyenne shares with Courtney over there." She waved a french-manicured hand toward a narrow hallway. "First door on your right. Rosemary's in the end room with Bonnie."

I headed immediately to Rosemary's room, but Shannon reached out to stop me. "I'll go first." He glanced at the other detective. "Huang, you start in our victim's room."

Well, at least he hadn't ordered me to come back after his investigation was over. Of course, that didn't mean he was happy with me.

"I can't believe you came here," he said when we were alone in Rosemary's room. His eyes flashed a bit dangerously, which instead of making me want to back off gave me a little rush of excitement.

"I'm helping a friend."

"There's a murderer loose."

I narrowed my eyes. "Exactly. Rosemary might be in danger—if she isn't already dead."

Ignoring me, he scanned the room. "Nothing seems out of place." He pulled on disposable gloves and opened a few of the drawers in the dresser. "Clothes are still here."

"Closet looks divided in two," I added. "Half for each roommate. No big gaps."

"If she really is missing, you're right that it's probably connected to the murder. I'll need fingerprints before you disturb anything. I have more detectives coming."

"I can't read imprints unless I touch things."

"I need to help process the other room. You'll have to wait."

"Can't he do it alone?"

"He's not that experienced yet."

Huang had been around for as long as I'd been consulting with the police, so what did that say about me?

I rolled my eyes. "You've got to be kidding."

He wasn't.

The roommate's boyfriend, or whoever she was waiting for,

hadn't shown, so I sat with the now-sullen woman in the small living room, waiting for the detectives. I learned her name was Mallory and that she worked as a paralegal at a law firm. I was a bit surprised that she wasn't a model or a wannabe actress, and I felt a little chastened at my chauvinistic attitude. Just because a woman looked like a model didn't mean she had aspirations to be one. Some beautiful women had as much brains as beauty.

When Mallory arose to check the street once more, I went with her, more out of sheer boredom than anything else. As we emerged onto the porch, a shadow at the corner of the house caught my eye.

"Did you see that?" I asked.

"See what?"

"I thought I saw someone go around your house."

She scanned the street. "There are no new cars out here. Maybe it was just the moon breaking through the clouds."

"I don't think so." I leapt from the porch, my leather boots squeaking and making me long to remove them. My steps led around to the side of the house where the narrow space between houses made me feel almost claustrophobic. Had I really seen anything? Or was it just a shadow?

My gut told me I'd seen something, and investigating Rosemary's disappearance made it my job to find out what. Adrenaline kicked in, overriding the frustration I'd been feeling with my enforced wait. After the attack in the prop room, I was itching for a fight.

The rain was still coming down, though less convincingly. The dead grass beneath my feet felt soggy and unsteady. Rounding the back of the house, I spied a figure dressed in black, standing on a stepladder and doing something to a window.

It was Rosemary's room.

"Stop!" I shouted, running toward him. This time he wasn't getting away.

The masked face swiveled in my direction, holding oddly still for what seemed like several long seconds. Then he launched himself at me from several rungs up the ladder. My breath fled in one gush as we fell to the ground.

e struggled on the wet grass, dampness seeping through my jeans. He aimed a punch, but I moved my head to the side and used his momentum to push him off. I followed up with a kick—a difficult move from a prone position—and was rewarded with a fist to my right ribs.

Ow.

So he wanted to get serious, did he?

I didn't know much about wrestling, though we did some in our taekwondo classes just to cover the basics. It was all about position and leverage. He grabbed my right arm, and I relaxed enough to set him off guard before I took hold of him with my other hand and rolled him over me to the other side. We tumbled like that several times, around and around on the sparse, waterlogged lawn, neither getting in a good punch. He wasn't trained, I could tell that much, or at least not well trained, but he wasn't giving up easily either. He was strong enough that I would have to wear him down. At least he didn't seem to have a knife or gun on him.

With a deft twist, he broke free and was up and running

before I realized what he was doing. I dived after him, barely catching the bottom of his boot. For a moment, I feared I'd be left with only the boot, but he fell, splat, onto the soggy ground. I gave a low chuckle.

He kicked at me and started to his feet again. I jumped up and landed a blow to his abdomen, halting his progress. A shove and a bit of maneuvering, and he was face down into the grass—mud now—where we'd been struggling.

I jumped on top of him and twisted his arm around his back before he could roll away, forcing it up toward his shoulder blades. He howled.

"Sorry," I said quite insincerely, spitting out mud that had somehow worked its way into my mouth. My uncovered hands felt like ice cubes. Was this really the same guy from the prop room at the theater? Though he was dressed similarly, I couldn't say for sure.

"Are you finished?" asked a bored voice.

I turned to see Shannon and Detective Huang standing behind us, the gleam of cuffs in Shannon's hands. Even Mallory had braved the rain, though she now wore boots and held an umbrella; she must have been the one to give Shannon warning. I'd have to thank her later.

"About time you got here," I muttered.

A partial grin touched Shannon's mouth. "You don't enjoy mud wrestling?"

From what I could see of myself in the lights coming from the surrounding houses, I was a mess. I was also freezing. "It's fun. You should try it sometime."

"Who's your friend?"

"He was trying to get into Rosemary's room. He might be the same guy who attacked me at the theater."

Detective Huang picked up something from the grass, showing it to Shannon. "Looks like he did plan to get in."

Shannon squatted and snapped the cuffs on the arm I was holding before forcing the other arm in as well. "Glass-cutting equipment," Shannon said to my captive. "You aren't very smart, are you?" He motioned for me to get up and pulled the man to his feet. I tugged off his mask.

I expected to see someone from the theater, though that didn't make much sense once I thought about it. All of them would have had access to the prop room and the entire theater without resorting to a mask. This man I had never seen before. He was short for a man and slender, but his face was perfect, and his brown hair was cut in the long shag that seemed to be so popular among the twenty-something crowd.

"I don't know what you're talking about." The man glared first at Shannon and then at me. "Either of you."

"Why don't you tell us what you're doing here?" Shannon asked.

"Yeah, why don't you?" Mallory's husky voice was tinged with anger. "You were supposed to pick me up half an hour ago."

I blinked in surprise. "This is your boyfriend?"

"Just a date. His name is Grady Mullins. I met him when he helped Rosemary move in. I thought they were dating, but when he called me this morning and begged me to cancel plans with my girlfriends so we could go out, he told me they were just friends."

"I can explain," Grady said. "I left something with Rosemary, and I need it, but she's not answering her phone. No one seems to know where she is. When I saw you had company, I thought I'd just get it from her room first, so I wouldn't have to make a big deal out of it."

I snorted. "Cutting open the window isn't a big deal? Tell us another one."

"I bet whatever it is, going out with me was just an excuse." Mallory gave him a deadly look. "What, did you think I'd invite you in for a drink, and you could search Rosemary's room at will?"

Grady didn't deny it.

With a small cry, Mallory turned and stalked around the side of the house, her boots making squishing sounds in the grass.

His loss, I thought. I couldn't understand what the golden-haired beauty saw in Grady Mullins anyway besides his pretty face. She was already half a head taller, and the heels she'd had in hand when she answered the door would definitely make the night awkward. Besides the physical difference, his character obviously wasn't much to appreciate.

"When was the last time you saw Rosemary?" I asked Grady.

"Wednesday before lunch. She came to tell me she'd gotten the part of Juliet." He grimaced as though the words tasted bitter.

"Came where?" Shannon asked.

"To the theater—her old theater where she's been working for the past two years. She came to let us know we'd have to cast someone else for the part she was supposed to play."

"Oh, you're an actor." That explained a lot.

Shannon's lips quirked at my words, but he didn't comment.

Grady drew himself up to his very unimpressive height. "Yes, I am." He darted a look in the direction where Mallory had disappeared. "I'm Rosemary's boyfriend, too. We've been dating a year now."

"Then why don't you know where she is?" I asked.

His gaze dropped to the ground. "We had a little disagreement."

"What about?" I asked.

"Nothing important."

"What are you here to get?" Shannon pressed. "You were just about to tell us, right?"

Grady shook his head. "I know my rights. I don't have to say anything."

"Unfortunately, the law also says that breaking and entering, or attempting to do so, is against the law. We'll question you further at the station."

"What about her?" Grady pointed at me. "She attacked me!"

"Oh, and I thought it was you who jumped off that ladder and flattened me into the mud." I rolled my eyes.

"I want to press charges," Grady insisted.

"Shut up." Shannon shoved him roughly forward. "You're lucky she didn't shoot you."

Oh, that's right. I had a gun.

Grady blinked. "Fine. Take me in. But I'm not saying a word."

"Your decision, but while you're sitting in the car waiting, you can think about telling us what you were doing at the theater and what you had to do with the murder there."

Grady's jaw dropped. "I don't know what you're talking about."

"Oh?" I said sweetly. "Then why aren't you asking who's dead? I mean, if you care so much about Rosemary." I wished we had more light so I could see his expression better, but it was enough to have him stunned into a short silence.

"Well, it wasn't Rosemary, was it?" he asked finally.

No one answered. Shannon motioned for his companion to take Grady. "Oh, and don't put him in my car. I just had it cleaned. Wait till the others get here, and put him in the back of a squad car." He turned to me, grinning, his face as unguarded as I'd ever seen it, though maybe it was the lack of proper lighting.

"Paige is going to hate that she missed all this," he said lightly.

"There's always next time."

He lifted a finger to my chin and wiped off some mud. I shivered inside, a thing I knew couldn't be blamed solely on the cold. "You want to go home?" he asked.

I shook my head. "I need to look at Rosemary's room. If she was hit by that hammer, she might not last much longer." Provided she wasn't already dead, of course.

He took another step, his eyes glittering even in the darkness. A warmth shuddered through me. The tension between us was so taut that I could almost see it like a line tying us together, bringing us closer. Moments ticked by. I could see the rugged planes of his face, maybe even the premature crinkling of the skin around his eyes that told how much he was in the sun. Droplets of rain clung to his sandy hair, making the ends curl even more than usual. If one of us didn't come to our senses soon, we might do something we'd regret.

He shook his head, and a few drops of water sprayed me. "I'd better get back to work." His voice was so low and soft, I barely heard him. I wanted to reach out to stop him from leaving, but that would be totally stupid, wouldn't it? Besides, he *was* working. So not the right time, even if I had things clear in my mind.

Some women might think that having two guys in my life wasn't all bad, but for me it meant limbo because I wasn't a player. I didn't want to hurt either of them, though maybe I was fooling myself about that possibility where Shannon was concerned. Any way I looked at it, he was tough.

I walked with Shannon around to the front of the house, neither of us speaking. The strain between us was heavy, and I almost longed for the days when that awkwardness came from wanting to rip the other's head off instead of the tension we felt now. On the porch, I removed my coat and boots, which would at least prevent me from ruining the carpet. My pants, hair, and face were still caked with mud.

"The guys will finish soon," Shannon said. "Why don't you clean up in the bathroom?"

I passed a pouting Mallory sitting on the couch, noticing that the other detectives had arrived and were heading with their crime kits to the back room.

The bathroom was small, and towels hung on every available space—the towel bars, the shower curtain rod, the edge of the sink, and the side of the tub. Cosmetics and makeup crammed the sink counter, top of the toilet tank, and the mirrored medicine cabinet, which had been left open. Thin lines of mold had grown around the plastic baseboard, though the shower and tub combo was scrubbed clean.

I looked worse than I'd expected. The two-inch-long scrape on my right cheek was already turning purple, even beneath the layer of mud. My hair was plastered to my head with mud in the back, and bits of mud were scattered throughout the rest. Good thing I didn't have long hair. Picking up one of the towels, I used it to turn on the water. Faucets weren't usually good carriers of imprints, except in domestic violence cases, but I didn't want to risk any ugly memories until I was halfway decent. If someone had to pick me up off the floor, I'd rather be a bit less repulsive.

Muddy water filled the sink as I washed my hands and then more gingerly my face. My wound stung, but I wanted to get out as much mud as possible since I wouldn't be able to put comfrey salve on it until later. When that was clean, I set about pulling as much mud as I could from my hair. The lukewarm water felt hot on my cold hands, but at least the feeling in them was coming back. Only a good washing could salvage my jeans, and I didn't bother to do anything with them except scrape off the biggest splotches of mud on the knees.

I took my time, knowing the police would need even longer to process Rosemary's room. I had a big bruise on my left arm, and the aches in my legs and torso told me I probably had quite a few more I couldn't see.

After I finished cleaning up, I forced myself to touch everything in the bathroom—sink, faucets, toiletries. If the police searched for prints here, they'd find a lot of mine, though knowing Shannon, he'd already seen everything in here that he wanted to see. I found no useful imprints, and I was glad no one was around to notice the shimmer of tears in my eyes that signaled my relief that Rosemary hadn't been hurt here.

When I emerged, Shannon was nearby holding a plastic bag with a glass I recognized from the theater.

"It tests positive for poison residue, even though it went through a dishwasher cycle. Perhaps because the theater's dishwasher is as ancient as the building itself. It's up in the air whether or not we'll find anything else useful, but the outside has no prints, so you can do your thing."

My thing. The only thing I really wanted to do was drop into bed and sleep for a week. But I had a murderer and a missing woman to find.

He opened the plastic bag, and I reached in to touch the glass. No use taking it out. This time I was prepared for the imprints.

I'll teach her a lesson she'll never forget. In the thirty seconds it will take for her to pass out, she'll finally know who is in control. Glee and a sense of power spread through me. Delicious. Euphoric. I couldn't wait.

The part of me who was Autumn felt horrified.

I dumped a spoonful of white powder into the glass of pale yellow liquid and stirred thoroughly with the long spoon. I set the glass on the silver tray waiting on the counter. Next to it was another glass that looked exactly the same. No poison for that one.

I couldn't see the poison container, but a glimpse of hands revealed light skin, which let out a few of the actors and actresses. The image cut off, and a new imprint started.

I stirred a powder into the glass, only this time it came from a pink sugar packet. This will solve my problem, I thought. But there was no real emotion as I placed the glass on the silver tray that was sitting on a table. Beyond the table I could see the stage curtain.

Another similar scene played out, and I was beginning to feel I'd watched enough. The difference between the first scene, which was the most recent, and the next two scenes was obvious to me now. The first was real; the others, playacting.

Wait. Another imprint came from at least eight years earlier.

Here I was again, mixing something into the glass, this time a liquid. I caught sight of a small brown bottle. I'd teach them both a lesson. They wouldn't take this chance from me. A thrill inside gave me strength. This was true power. Their lives in my hands. I set the glass on the silver tray on top of a dusty crate next to another identical glass. No stage or curtains in sight.

"Autumn?"

I kept touching the glass, but nothing more came. When the imprints began repeating, I pulled my hand from the bag, feeling that I was about to be violently sick.

"The murderer is white," I said. "And the poison was a white powder put into a glass of lemonade. Mixed in the kitchen at the theater, I believe. That's about it."

"Male or female?"

"Not a person with big hands. I'd say a strong woman or a slender man. Hard to say. But it wasn't the first murder."

Shannon stared at me. "What?"

"Eight years ago someone mixed a liquid from a small brown bottle in this same glass with the intent of killing two people. I couldn't tell where it happened, but it wasn't any place in the theater that I recognized."

I waited for him to question me further, which would shed welcome doubt on my own impressions, but all he said was, "The same person for both murders?"

"I don't know for sure, but I'd say yes. The feelings were much the same. The method too. They were different from the other scenes where the glass was used as a prop to mix pretend poison. Sugar packets. Pink."

I was shaking inside, and I felt weak clear to my toes. Almost, I longed for the crazy power and anticipation I'd felt during the first and last imprints, but I knew the negativity and the feelings that were so opposite mine were what was making me feel fragile. I took a deep breath and hurried on.

"You should also know that tonight I heard something about two actors going missing on an opening night. That was eight years ago as well."

Shannon was making notes, seemingly unconcerned by what he once might have considered the power of suggestion. One moment I heard two actors were missing, and the next I read an imprint in which someone was planning to poison two people around the same time. Even I was skeptical, or would be if I hadn't experienced it for myself.

"We'll check into the disappearance eight years ago," Shannon said. "See if it really happened." He paused, and his voice grew softer. "You okay?"

"Sure. It's just getting late. Look, are your guys almost finished?"

"They are with Cheyenne's room. Would you like to look at that first?"

I wanted to say yes, but I didn't feel I had the strength for two more rooms. I bit back my pride. "Not today. I can't really help her anyway. It's Rosemary I'm worried about now."

"The cases are probably connected."

He was right, but Jake would have taken the hint when I said I didn't want to look at the room. He would have protected me from further exposure regardless of the effect on the case— or cases. He wouldn't have felt compelled to be so honest about the need for my input. For a brief moment I hated Shannon.

"Okay," I said.

I turned and went into the bedroom, not bothering to see if Shannon followed. The room wasn't messy, but it had that not-quite-together look that told me it had been thoroughly searched.

The fingerprint dust around key points was still apparent, though someone had made a halfhearted attempt to clean it up.

Once again I started touching things, and it was apparent from the beginning that I was not on Cheyenne's side of the room. From the imprints on the knickknacks, writing utensils, books, and alarm clock, this woman was a first-grade teacher who loved the children she taught and who dedicated hours of preparation to her lessons. She was also an avid lover of historical romance novels and had a crush on Mike, a fifth-grade teacher at her school, who was also single. She owned a pearl necklace her parents had given her when she graduated from high school; it filled me with such love that I felt stronger and more than a little envious of the good memories.

If my birth mother had lived, she had been close enough to my adoptive parents that I might have seen her, if not regularly, then at least sometimes, and once Summer died, she might have had a guiding hand in my life.

I pushed the thoughts away and hurried through the rest. A little self-consciously I opened drawers, hoping to find nothing that would ruin my image of the teacher or connect her with the murder. It was with a sigh of relief that I moved to the other side of the room.

Two more different women couldn't have existed. While the teacher was calm, shy, careful, steady, and loving, Cheyenne's imprint showed impracticality and loud confidence accentuated by bursts of insecurity, jealousy, rage, kindness, and despair. She was a study in contrasts.

I picked up the pen on her night table, and a vague imprint from last night filled my head: *I stared down at the pen in my hand, resignation filling me. I will do it.*

But I didn't know what "it" was and the imprint was too brief and unfocused to give me a hint.

"Nothing," I said to Shannon. "But did you find something she wrote on? The pen indicates she was planning something last night."

"We found a journal, but the last entry only talks about how excited she is to have the part of Juliet since Rosemary didn't show up to rehearsal. We'll have someone go through it for more."

"I'm done here. Sorry I couldn't help more. Her roommate seems nice, though. A teacher. A good one."

One of the detectives who had arrived with the reinforcements looked at me, disbelief evident on his face. Not someone I'd worked with before and apparently he was doubtful of my ability.

Join the club, I thought. Even I didn't believe it if I thought about it too much.

Finally, I was in Rosemary's room, which showed the same minor displacement as the previous room, along with the fingerprint residue. I started on one side, but when the first imprint on a glass dog knickknack showed me the hands of an old woman presenting this beloved gift to her white-haired granddaughter on her eighth birthday, I set it down, not waiting for the earlier imprints that would surely be on it, and went to the other side of the room. Even if Rosemary had been blond as a child, which I didn't believe, Liam had once told me he didn't know anything about his grandparents. The odds were this imprint belonged to the other roommate. I wondered now if Liam's grandparents had died or if they were estranged from their family, just as Rosemary was now.

So much time wasted, I thought. I felt angry that anyone would throw family away for which I'd give anything.

We had good years. It was Winter's voice in my mind. Just what I knew he'd say if he could speak to me. Always a glass-half-full kind of guy. He was right.

Again the police detective I didn't know watched me with narrowed eyes. The man had dark hair and was bulky, though his bulk looked like muscles rather than fat. One look at him might scare even the most hardened criminal. I wished Shannon would tell him to leave, or call his partner, Paige, who knew and believed in me.

Shannon saw my stare. "Warren, would you mind?" Warren nodded and reluctantly left the room.

"Thanks," I said. "He was making me nervous."

"He makes everyone nervous. He's new."

"I figured by the way he stared. Most of your other guys have seen me around enough by now to limit their staring to when I'm not looking."

He laughed. "By the way, your prints were the only ones they found on the hammer, but there was some blood residue. They're doing DNA. They'll compare it with Rosemary's and everyone else in the case."

That was good news. "So, did you find any reason for the boyfriend trying to break in?"

"Maybe." Shannon withdrew something from inside his jacket—another plastic bag. "A note." He passed the bag to me.

"Don't take the part," I read through the plastic. "You'll be sorry."

"You don't look surprised."

"There was an imprint on something her brother brought me that said she'd received a threatening note. But I thought it'd be a little more detailed. You think the note is from the boyfriend?"

He nodded. "Probably. We'll see if his prints are on it."

"I might be able to tell you right now."

He hesitated. "Okay, but be careful. It'd be a shame if you smeared the only print."

I hadn't expected that he'd let me taint the evidence this way. Guess I was no longer the last resort. Smiling inside, I reached in the bag and, bending my finger, placed a knuckle in the middle of the writing.

Anger came in a rush, filled every part of me until I didn't know what to do with the emotion. How dare she take the part! New York has always been our thing, but now she's only thinking about herself.

Then another, more poignant emotion. Maybe Rosemary wasn't just leaving the company. Maybe she wanted to leave me.

Well, she'll be sorry.

The imprint vanished as fast as it had appeared. Nothing more followed, and I grabbed back my hand as it began to repeat. Feeling dizzy, I sat abruptly on the bed and took a deep breath. Shannon took a step toward me and then stopped himself. He gave me a moment.

"I'm pretty sure it was him," I said. "It felt like him. When she decided to leave her old theater company and take a part in the Portland Players, he saw it as her abandoning him too."

"You think he did something to her?"

I shrugged. "He was angry enough. But there was no solid plan or anything in his mind, just the anger."

"Sometimes that's all that drives them. We'll have to look into him very carefully. Hopefully, he left a fingerprint or two on the note as well."

"It's likely, seeing as he was so anxious to get it back. Is that all they bagged from here?"

"That was it. They took a few fingerprints and got her toothbrush for DNA."

My dizziness had passed, so I arose, noting that I'd left a smear of mud on Rosemary's bedspread. With resignation, I held my hands over the objects on her desk and the nearby shelf, touching only those that radiated a slight buzz.

Rosemary's imprints showed her to be a kind, strong, determined person who'd had little encouragement in her short twenty-one years of life. It was amazing she'd come as far as she had. Despite the lack of support, she was loving, fun, and full of life, instead of bitter and obsessed. She was the kind of person who did nice things for others just to see them smile. Rosemary was definitely a person I'd like to get to know, if I ever had the chance.

Most of her imprints had to do with her work, her hopes, and her dreams. She had a tendency to buy objects that represented her acting roles, and she would often hold them as she practiced her lines. Besides these, I found the music box Liam had tried to steal from my shop, and on it the strong loyalty and love they shared was clear. She had kept a few letters from him inside the box, but the imprints on them weren't strong.

I'd finished almost everything before I touched the rock. It was an ordinary small stone, with a childish happy face painted on it, and *I love you* in awkward writing on the back. As I held the rock, the urge to throw it was strong and very recent. Last Thursday recent, the day Rosemary had disappeared.

He's always demeaned my dreams. Why did I think this would be any different?

"*Sorry,*" *my father said, standing with clenched fists in the middle of the women's dressing room at the theater. "If you come back and show some sense, maybe we can work something out. But what you do now is an embarrassment to us." His expression was frightening.*

I'd made a terrible mistake. I shouldn't have asked him to come. He'd never, ever bend. I had to get out of here.

I started for the door, only to be yanked painfully back by my hair. "Don't you dare leave while I'm talking to you! Show some respect for once in your life—or I'll make you show it!"

The imprint faded, and another one from years earlier took its place.

The same rock sat on my opened hand, looking large because my hand was so small. "Here, Daddy," I said. "Look."

"Oh, what is it?"

"A princess. She's the one in the play we saw at school today. I'm going to be her when I grow up. I mean in the play. It was magic."

"No, sweetie. That's only a fake life, not a real job. You're old enough now to understand that you need to do something of value. You're good at English and science. You should think about pursuing one of those. In our family, we don't do acting. That's low class. Look, I have to go back to work. Make sure you have your homework finished before I get home."

Sadness as he left both me and the rock. "But I made it for you, Daddy," I said softly. Except he wouldn't want it. He didn't believe in princesses—or magic.

I set the rock down, filled with a child's keen disappointment. That she'd kept it all these years said something, but I wasn't sure what. "We might have another suspect," I said.

"Someone she argued with on Thursday afternoon at the theater. He was angry, maybe even violent."

"Who?"

I sighed. "Her father."

Chapter 8

I wanted nothing but to go home. I didn't feel like explaining the imprint in detail or discussing the case with Shannon. I didn't want him to find anything else for me to touch. I turned and left the room.

"Autumn!" Shannon hurried after me, but I didn't stop. On the porch I found that someone had put my muddy coat in a huge plastic sack. I wasn't about to put on my boots, so I shoved them inside with the coat. I shouldn't freeze too badly driving home.

I felt something warm go around my shoulders, and I turned to see Shannon, who was now coatless. "You can return it later," he said. "I have a regulation one in the car I'll use."

It smelled like him, turning my stomach upside down. Or was it inside out? "Thanks," I said.

"You going to be okay?" His eyes burned into mine. I hated the way he did that.

"I'm tired. But I'll be fine." I felt somewhat of a failure, though. I mean, what use was a gift like mine if I couldn't find a friend's sister who might be lying unconscious somewhere bleeding? I'd wanted solid evidence about someone she went to see, or someone who confronted her—not to witness a fight with her father.

"We have the boyfriend. I'll interview him. He might know where she is."

I managed a smile. "You're getting pretty good at that."

"At what?"

"Reading my mind."

"I don't have to read your mind. Your face tells me everything."

I hope it wasn't telling him I wanted to curl up in his warm arms and feel safe. But I knew what he meant. Living with hippie parents where almost anything was okay, I'd never learned to be great at fabrication. I'd never needed the skill. On the other hand, Tawnia, raised in an environment with strict, overzealous parents who'd banned or limited almost every activity, had developed a talent of duplicity. Not that I was condoning my upbringing by any means. It had come with more dangers than I cared to admit, and for the most part, I'd simply been lucky. Tawnia had survived as well. She loved her parents and claimed she owed her career to them. Still, she was aiming for a happier medium with Destiny.

"Good night," I said, aware of other eyes upon us. I couldn't tell if the detectives and officers were wondering what I'd found, or if they were curious because they suspected Shannon had a thing for me.

As tough as they were, my feet froze on the wet sidewalk, but it was better than the muddy alternative. My soul sang with joy at feeling the connection of the earth through the cement. Even so, I hurried to my car, praying once again that it would start. Thankfully, the car roared to life, reminding me that I should get the muffler checked before someone at the precinct gave me a ticket for noise pollution.

Shannon was still watching me from the porch as he talked with several colleagues. I could tell, though there was no way to really know he watched me for sure.

I had it bad.

What about Jake?

I pushed the thought away. What I needed was rest, and then I'd be able to figure out what to do next in my search for Rosemary. There had to be something I was missing.

I drove home without thinking, letting myself into the lobby and my ground floor apartment. The place greeted me with its familiar array of antiques I couldn't bear to part with. I thrived on both the clutter and the positive feelings left from the former owners. Normally I'd get something to eat and cuddle under the afghan Summer had made before she died, but I was too tired even for food, and the mud was a deterrent because I couldn't wash the afghan and risk obliterating the imprints. I didn't have many from my mother.

Heading for the bathroom, I shed Shannon's coat and my clothes and stepped into the shower, letting the hot water push the cold from my veins and the numbness from my toes. The remaining mud slithered down the drain. I stepped into my robe to dry off, coated my cheek with comfrey ointment, and fell into bed.

After the rotten evening, you'd think I'd have terrible dreams or at least dream about the case. I didn't. My sleep was disturbed only by the fact that it was so deep and undisturbed, almost like passing out. I awoke only once in the middle of the night, feeling a craving so deep for protein that I almost climbed from bed, but sleep claimed me once again before I could make the decision to get up.

Time passed in sweet oblivion.

"Autumn! Autumn! How come you didn't answer the door?" My sister's voice came to me through a fog. "Did you forget I was coming? Good thing I brought your extra key, or I'd have had to drive all the way back home."

I managed to pry one eye open. "You could always get one from the neighbors."

I went through more spare keys than anyone I knew. Though I'd finally begun locking my apartment, I shared my parents' philosophy: If a person needed something bad enough to steal it from me, maybe he needed it more than I did. Tawnia told me that was ridiculous, that there were plenty of people who would steal me blind for no reason at all.

"What's with the trail of clothes?" She set Destiny down, still in her car seat. "And all that mud?"

I shut my eye and moaned as last night came rushing back. No wonder my body felt bruised all over.

"You look terrible," Tawnia added. "Worse than terrible. Your face is all bruised and cut. And why aren't you dressed? Is that a robe?"

I tried opening the other eye, but it wouldn't open and neither would the first. "I'm just tired."

She was silent a long, disapproving moment. "You were reading imprints, weren't you?"

"Yes." My sluggish brain found the word.

"Well, you have to be careful. Now where's that picture I drew for you? The new one."

The second because I'd ruined the first by jumping into the Willamette to save what I thought was a child trapped in a trunk. The new one was in my pants pocket from Friday, as I'd forgotten to transfer it to the clothes I wore yesterday, but I couldn't make my lips move again. I wanted her to leave me alone and let me sleep.

With an exasperated sigh, Tawnia began searching. She was thorough, so I knew she'd find it. I drifted off to sleep, thinking of a huge steak lying next to a side of organic baby potatoes slathered with a ton of real butter.

The next minute Tawnia put something on my palm and sandwiched it between both of my hands, holding them together for good measure.

Love filled me. My sister's love.

I saw the drawing forming beneath my hand, and with each stroke of my colored pencils, I thought about my sister and how much I loved her. How grateful I was to have finally found her.

At last my drawing was finished. I glanced over to compare my version to the original photograph, the first we'd ever taken together. It was perfect.

"I love you, Autumn," I said aloud. "Whenever you need a good imprint, you can touch this and feel that love."

I did feel Tawnia's love. It wrapped around me, filling up the gaps left by the horrors of the night before. Blotting out the unnatural glee felt by the person who'd murdered not one but possibly three people with poison. Dimming the thrill of immoral power brought by slamming a hammer into an unsuspecting person who had done me wrong. Soothing the jealousy of whoever had written the threatening note and the unhappiness Rosemary felt in regard to her father. All of it was pushed to the back of my mind, still memories but containable and logically recognizable as not mine, though I'd lived the experiences.

I believed the imprint on Tawnia's small drawing was so powerful because of her own unusual gift. For months, I'd used the drawing for its soothing properties, and the imprint never seemed to fade.

Strength rushed through me as my mind cleared. "Thanks," I said.

"You need food." She squeezed my hand. "You got this?"

"Yeah."

"I'll be back in a minute. Emma and I will make you something to eat." Tawnia picked up the car seat and left the room.

I lay there and let the imprint warm me. Tears came to my eyes, knowing that while Tawnia and I had spent our growing up years apart, we would never voluntarily be separated again. Come husbands and children and jobs, we would be there for each other.

I was sitting up when she returned, carrying a plate loaded with food. I grinned. Only my sister, who shared my appetite, could know how much that appealed to me now.

"You're looking better already. Hurry and eat. I'm dying to hear about the mud."

The way she said it was strange. "You drew it, didn't you?" I asked.

"Eat." She waved at me to shut up. "I'm going to get Emma from the kitchen."

"Destiny, you mean."

She laughed. "Eat."

I did. There were at least half a dozen eggs and bacon loaded with wonderful fat, all naturally produced on a farm and something even my sister knew how to cook. Three pieces of whole wheat toast layered with organic raspberry jam. The hash browns were a little undercooked, but that was better than her normal burned ones. The glass of whole milk from a grass-fed cow topped everything off nicely.

"I would have made you buttermilk biscuits since you like them so much," Tawnia said, setting Destiny, sleeping in her car seat, beside my bed, "but you know how they turned out the last time."

Yeah, like pioneer hardtack, of which I wasn't particularly fond, but I wouldn't say it aloud. "Thanks." I sighed and set my empty plate aside.

"More?" she asked.

"Maybe after I get dressed."

"Okay, but we should hurry if we're still going to Hayesville this morning. I'd like to get back before one."

"What did you draw?" I asked.

"What's with the mud?" she countered. "And that's not your coat I hung up."

"It's Shannon's."

"So he was there while you were in the mud?"

There was nothing else to do but tell her. I wouldn't be able to keep it from her anyway, and if I tried, she'd just go to Shannon and Jake herself. I told her about Liam coming to see me, what had happened at the theater, and how I'd ended up in the mud.

She scowled at me when I was finished. "I can't believe you let me think you were on a date with Jake. And both of them should know better than to let you read so many imprints. What would have happened if I hadn't come over today, huh?"

"I would have slept it off and then gotten up and eaten something." I felt a chill as I said it because I didn't know if it was true. What if I hadn't been able to wake up?

"You know the drill. You eat before you sleep. Lots of protein."

"Okay," I said. "Anyway, I didn't want to drag you and Destiny into it."

"Well, I am in it." She reached for her large bag, which was next to the car seat. She carried everything a person could ever want in that bag. If I was half as prepared as she was, I would never get myself into such trouble.

She pulled out a drawing pad. "I was trying to think about Kendall last night. You know, where she might have lived, where her mother might be now, and this is what I drew." She slapped it down on the bed, open to the first picture.

"Cheyenne," I said. Not just Cheyenne but Cheyenne in the closet as I'd found her. The second drawing was of two people on the ground, one atop the other. Their faces were unrecognizable, but I knew it was me and Rosemary's boyfriend, Grady Mullins, as we struggled in the mud. My coat was the same, as were the boots. It was a wonder Tawnia hadn't come breaking down my door last night.

The third picture brought me up short, a coldness seeping over me. A figure of a woman lying on a floor, her face partially obscured by long dark hair. Even in the drawing she was too still. Something matted in her hair. Since the drawing was in pencil, I couldn't be sure it was blood.

"Do you think it's Liam's sister?" she asked.

"Possibly. Or whoever else was hit by the hammer."

"It could have been you."

"No, Rosemary's boyfriend was too inept. It must have been him in the theater prop room. I think he was trying to retrieve his threatening note."

Tawnia's face wrinkled. "Why would he go there to find it before he checked out her apartment? That doesn't make sense."

She was right. Rosemary had been at that theater only a day or two. There was no reason for Grady to believe she'd take the threatening note there. So maybe it hadn't been him in the prop room. I'd have to think about it. The poisoner had to be connected with the theater, and whoever it was must have put the glass in the dishwasher there after giving it to Cheyenne. But if that was the case, what did the black-dressed figure want?

"Let's talk about it on the way," Tawnia said, throwing me a blue shirt and my multicolored, sleeveless broomstick dress. "You'll have to do something with your hair, too. It dried funny."

Ten minutes later, dressed and with my short hair newly wet, I found her in the kitchen brushing the dried mud from my boots.

"Sorry about that," I said. "I hadn't planned on rolling around in the mud. Guess I should have sprayed them off last night."

"Not if you didn't have time to stuff them so they wouldn't shrink. A lot of water isn't good for leather. Look, this is taking it off just fine. You can wear them now. Later we'll try a little leather soap and a thorough oiling. They'll be as good as new."

I bowed to her greater knowledge of footwear and made myself a bagel sandwich to take along, tucking it into my bag. Already I was feeling much better.

"I put dinner in the Crock-Pot at my place for after we get back," Tawnia said. It was the one dish she did well.

"Good." I picked up Destiny, who had awakened and was staring at me with her big eyes.

"Don't forget your gloves," Tawnia said. "You've read enough imprints for now."

"I'm more worried about a coat. Mine needs washing."

"I already stuck it in the machine. I'm glad it wasn't wool. You'll have to wear Shannon's, if you don't have another one."

"I'll find something." I wasn't going to wear Shannon's coat again. No way. It was too, I don't know, possessive. Too reminiscent of a childish crush. I felt warm and safe and loved in that coat— feelings too dangerous to perpetuate.

Finding something else wouldn't be easy. Unlike with antiques, I didn't hang onto a lot of clothing. If I didn't love it enough to wear it often, out it went. Still, there should be something I could scrounge up.

Tawnia turned to me, hands on her hips. "You should kiss him."

"What?"

"Shannon. Try it and see what happens. Then you'll know how he makes you feel. So just pucker up and smooch already."

Tawnia was a great believer in kissing to reveal truth, but I'd thought I'd felt it already with Jake. My attraction to Shannon pretty much obliterated that idea. Though I was a great believer in fate and the universe sending back to you what you sent out, I didn't subscribe to the one true love ideology. True love involved decisions and commitment, and I wasn't sure I was ready for either.

"Not making a decision is actually making one," my sister added quietly.

"He would have given his coat to anyone," I retorted.

"Yeah, but not this." She retrieved something from the cupboard, holding it between two fingers as if it stank. "I found it in your coat pocket. I know how you feel about guns, and this has Shannon written all over it."

"I took a course." I set Destiny back in her seat and took the gun from Tawnia. Removing the Ruger from its protective pouch, I popped out the magazine and checked the barrel to be sure it was still empty before replacing it. Not that Tawnia would have racked it, but I didn't want to chance it going off without my knowing about it.

The gun had no external safety because Shannon believe those could be a detriment if you had to use the gun in a pinch and forgot to take it off. The safety could also be knocked off accidentally and the gun shot before you realized it. Definitely not a good thing around children who are curious about buttons. Better to develop the habit of racking and then firing. Unless I knew I would be entering a questionable situation, of course.

"I see."

"Don't worry," I said. "It's going in a safe. Shannon promised to make the department spring for one. I'll make absolutely sure Destiny will never have access. It's only for when I'm investigating."

"I'm glad you're taking your safety seriously, Autumn," Tawnia surprised me by saying. "Though I don't suppose you'd ever really shoot someone."

I was silent for a long moment and then said quietly, "I would if they threatened you or Destiny."

She hugged me tightly. "I love you, you know?"

"I do know." I hugged her back. "We should go."

I found a coat in the back of the closet, one that had belonged to Winter. It was ragged and old but reliable, a lot like he'd been. There weren't any positive imprints on it, but it comforted me to wear something of his.

"Gloves?" Tawnia asked.

I shook my head. I couldn't find the gloves that had been in my coat pocket last night before my tussle with Rosemary's boyfriend. Probably they were somewhere on her back lawn.

At the last minute, remembering my promise to Shannon, I slipped the Ruger into my pocket.

Chapter 9

*I*t was one of those rare winter days in western Oregon when it actually stopped raining. There was no way either of us would trust my car for the long trip, so I relaxed as Tawnia drove south on the freeway, enjoying the prospect of doing nothing for the fifty-seven minutes it would take to get to Hayesville. Destiny was asleep in her car seat, a bemused expression on her tiny face.

Except now that I was feeling well, my mind wouldn't stop going over the previous day's events. The way I saw it, I had more suspects than leads in both the murder and Rosemary's disappearance. Of course, I was more concerned with Rosemary at the moment, though I couldn't deny that the cases seemed linked. Mentally I arranged my suspects in order of most likely.

Grady Mullins, who claimed to be Rosemary's boyfriend. If he'd sent the note, he might have gone even further to force her to do what he wanted. Next was Mr. Taylor, Rosemary's father, who'd never approved of his child's dreams and who in Rosemary's imprint was guilty of using excessive force.

There were also people from the theater who had access to both women. Paxton Seaver, the director who claimed to love

Cheyenne, could have had reason to get rid of Rosemary, despite his admiration of her acting skills. He might have regretted his decision to cast her. Or a lover's spat with Cheyenne could have ended in murder. I didn't know if he'd been with the company long enough to have attempted the first murders eight years earlier, but it was possible.

Carl Walsh, the producer and stage manager with the New York connections, also had access to both women. Though he seemed to have the most to lose with Cheyenne and Rosemary out of the picture, there could be undercurrents I wasn't aware of yet and probably wouldn't be unless I could touch his belongings. I assumed he used the office, but I hadn't found anything unusual there. Maybe the police had found something in his locked desk drawers. I'd have to ask Shannon. Or better yet, his partner, Paige Duncan.

Next came Erica with the black pixie haircut. The lovely, bitter actress seemed to hold no love for Rosemary and also appeared disdainful of pretty much everything and everyone else as well. Her comments about Walsh had seemed out of place for an employee, and that bugged me. That and her fascination with Shannon.

Then there was Millie, who, unlike the other actresses, had a part in the four-person play. She might feel the role didn't give her the attention she deserved, and Rosemary's absence created the possibility of her moving to the more important role. She had problems with at least one fellow actor that concerned Walsh, so maybe she was hiding bitterness behind her positive attitude.

Lucas, the handsome, self-absorbed, high-voiced, dumb-as-a-log actor, could also be hiding something. He might not be as dumb as he looked. Maybe he'd gotten rid of Rosemary because he'd wanted Cheyenne to have the part. Or maybe he'd killed Cheyenne when Rosemary went missing because he didn't think she was as good and would ruin his chances of going to Broadway. These actors were serious about their jobs. But serious enough to kill? Maybe he thought if he got rid of Cheyenne, Rosemary would return in time to save the show.

Last on my list was the actress Vera, who claimed the Juliet play was cursed, but underneath her fake red hair, she might be using the play's history to clear a spot for herself. After all, she also had brown hair similar to both Cheyenne and Rosemary. Or maybe her ladies' man boyfriend, Trenton, had strayed, and she was seeking revenge.

The murderer could also be one of the other actors from the theater. With the insight I'd received from the imprint on the glass, I suspected the killer would prefer to be close to the action to learn if he or she was in danger of discovery. He might even be enjoying giving misleading information as he played the role of his life. Or her life.

None of my scenarios explained who had attacked me in the prop room.

"Autumn, what are you doing?" Tawnia glanced over at me. "Who are those people?"

I looked down to see that I'd written the list of names and brief notes beside each one on a fresh page in Tawnia's drawing pad. "They're suspects," I said. "But the most likely don't seem to have motives involving both Rosemary and Cheyenne. The cases might be connected, but the acts are so different—one obviously premeditated and the other committed in a moment of passion."

"Yeah, but both could be murder."

"Then why haven't we found Rosemary's body? I'm hoping

that means she's still alive. If she was the one hit with the hammer, the assailant might not have actually wanted to kill her, just get her out of the way for a while."

"Do you think she's the one in my drawing?"

I turned to that page to examine it more thoroughly, mentally comparing the figure to the picture of Rosemary that Liam had sent to my phone. "It's hard to tell with all that hair, but I think so. Maybe if I showed it to Liam or her roommates, they could identify her or something she's wearing. Too bad there's nothing in the picture background to tell us where she might be."

Tawnia fell silent, her top teeth worrying her bottom lip. I knew she was concerned with the reappearance of her so-called gift, and I wasn't sure what to say to her. At least we were taking a step toward understanding why we might be this way. I didn't exactly think something was wrong with us, something that needed to be fixed, but it would be nice to know if these abilities were in our family history, like our directional impairedness and heterochromia.

"Bagel sandwich?" I asked, offering mine to her. When in doubt, offer food.

"Thanks." With swift movements, she snatched the sandwich, unwrapped the top, and took a bite.

"Hey, I didn't think you would actually accept it." I reached, trying to get it back.

She held it away from me. "Relax. I have a full cooler in the back seat. All your favorites. You can thank me after you eat."

A short time later, with an even fuller stomach, I dozed. When my sister eventually awakened me, I felt completely restored to my usual self.

"I plugged in the address on the GPS," Tawnia said. "We're

almost there." Nervousness laced her voice, which was unusual for my confident sister.

My eyes wandered over the houses we were passing. "Suzy wasn't joking when she said it was a dive. I mean, these houses are falling apart. At least some of them are."

"I know. There's nothing wrong with being poor, but I can't help imagining what Kendall must have gone through. I read her letter again last night, and she didn't seem to care about being poor. She just wanted love." She paused and then added, her eyes mournful, "If I ever find him, I'm going to kill him."

I knew she was talking about the man who'd taken advantage of a fifteen-year-old girl in the middle of the night on her birthday. My first inclination was to feel the same way, but I knew Winter and Summer would urge caution. "We've all done things we aren't proud of," Winter had been fond of saying, "and you can't judge someone until you've walked in their shoes."

I wasn't exactly prepared to forgive my birth father, if I ever caught up to him, but I would hear him out. Regardless, the information he had about my heritage was the important thing. I certainly didn't plan on having any kind of a relationship with him.

We fell silent as we came upon a group of dwellings that were obviously new. "They've destroyed the old houses," Tawnia said. "If they've rebuilt all of the houses in this section, we're not going to find anything."

"We can still talk to the neighbors. Situations can change. Maybe someone built a new house on their old property." But we both breathed a sigh of relief when the next turn took us back to the older houses. These were not in complete disrepair, and some of the yards were well-tended. Still, there were not many signs of life, though that wasn't unusual on a cold Sunday morning. Many folks were probably taking advantage of the weekend and sleeping in.

Tawnia pulled to the curb. "This is the road. Suzy thought it was the second or third house. We might have to try them all."

"I still think that while you were drawing, you could have at least drawn the house where Kendall had lived," I said with a smirk. "It would have been more helpful."

"Too bad. Get out and start walking."

She slid from the car herself, retrieved Destiny's stroller from the trunk, and ensconced the child in enough blankets to warm half a dozen babies. When Tawnia wasn't looking, I slipped my finger down Destiny's back to make sure she wasn't sweating. But a few minutes walking proved Tawnia right. Without the rain, I'd thought it would be warmer, but the day was crisp and cold. A strong wind blowing in from the north had me wishing I were in the stroller with the baby.

No one answered at the first door. At the second, we raised a grouchy, bearded man still in his pajamas. No, he didn't know any of the people we asked about. At the third house, a child answered, and her young mother was also no help. So on it went. All the way down one side of the street and up the other. We went to the next block and began again.

On the fourth house there, a pretty blonde answered the door, still in her pajamas and her hair mussed with sleep. She had a toddler on her hip and a smile for us. We explained our quest, already knowing she was too young to have any knowledge of Kendall and her mother.

"I really couldn't say. This is my grandmother's house. She's letting me stay here. But she lives close by, and you could ask her. She's lived around here all her life, and she knows everyone, old or new. If you'll wait a minute, I'll write down her address." She returned shortly with a sheet torn from a notebook. "Her name is Mariel, and she lives three streets over in the new houses."

The new houses. It figured. Already we were backtracking. "Thanks," we told her.

"We aren't getting very far," Tawnia lamented.

"Well, we knew it could take a while."

We decided to finish the street before trying the woman's grandmother's. Both of us moved with a gritty determination. We had at least another hour before we had agreed to drive back to Portland.

With no other leads, we climbed into the car, waited ten minutes for Destiny to nurse, and then drove to the address. I liked the two-story house immediately and not only because of the happy yellow siding and the red door. The walkway was lined with flowerbeds, and even though it was winter, I could identify several dormant herbs. More flowerbeds sat against the house, and I bent to see what else was planted underneath winter's gray shroud.

"You coming?" Tawnia asked, leaving Destiny and the stroller at the base of the stairs to the narrow porch.

A brown nut of a woman with white hair pulled into a ponytail opened the door, wearing surprisingly hip jeans and a T-shirt. "Good morning," she trilled. "How may I help you?"

Tawnia grinned. "Are you Mariel?"

"That's me."

Tawnia launched into our explanation—which was a good thing. Though I'd joined her on the steps, I was still thinking about the herbs.

"Oh," Mariel said, her smile widening. "You must be talking about Laina Drexler. You say you're Kendall's daughters?" She shook her head. "I always wondered what happened to Kendall. She was a beautiful child. Good girl too. Used to watch my baby for me. Always knew I could trust her to do a good job. Not like some of the neighborhood kids who'd set the kids in front of the TV while they robbed you blind. And she and Laina needed the money." Here her smile faltered, and I knew there was much, much more to the story. My interest in her herbs was completely forgotten.

"Do you have some time to talk to us about them?" I asked.

"Or do you know where we might find Laina now?" Tawnia added.

Mariel opened her door wide. "Come on inside. It's too cold to talk out here, especially with that baby."

I went inside while Tawnia scooped Destiny from her stroller.

Welcome heat washed over me as I went into the room Mariel indicated.

"Beautiful baby," Mariel cooed, briefly touching Destiny's chin. "Have a seat, if you'd like."

I sank into a plush, new-looking floral couch that appeared to have come from another era. I was wearing my antique rings, but I was careful not to touch anything. I was finished with imprints for a while.

Mariel didn't sit but stood in front of us, her head slightly cocked. "Now that I know you're Kendall's girls, I can see the resemblance. Even after all these years. How's she doing anyway?"

"About that," I said. It was always hard, this part. Talking about Kendall's short life and our separation.

When I finished, Mariel sank to the love seat opposite us. "I'm so sorry to hear that. I was glad when she left home, even though I was Laina's best friend. Maybe her only friend. Laina didn't give that girl a fair shake."

"Did you know Kendall was expecting when she left?"

"There were rumors, but nobody knew anything for sure. I always thought it was strange because Kendall was a shy little thing. Stayed to herself a lot. She wasn't the type to go out with boys, you know. Laina did eventually tell me in confidence that Kendall was expecting and that she wanted her to give up the baby. Apparently Kendall didn't want to. Laina had done the same thing herself as a teen, you know, and she'd never been able to pull herself up. But I still don't see Kendall as that type of girl. I mean, she'd seen all the boyfriends her mother had, one after the next. She didn't want to be that way."

"She was raped," I said. "By her mother's boyfriend."

Mariel's face paled. "The poor child."

"I take it you had no idea," Tawnia said.

"No idea at all. I mean I knew Laina and Kendall had some sort of falling-out but not the specifics. Laina was drunk a lot in those days. I remember a time when she was talking all jealous-like about her current guy leaving because of Kendall. It was crazy, ridiculous, of course, and I thought at the time it must have been the drink talking. Or the drugs. She did them in those days as well."

Mariel sighed and shook her head. "Anyway, a few months after Kendall left, Laina finally went to one of those programs and got help. There was no more crazy talk after that."

"Did Laina ever mention Kendall when she was sober?"

"Just to say that she'd disappeared from the place across town where she was working. The only thing the owner would say was that she was living with a nice family. She wouldn't tell Laina where. Laina tried to go through the state, but somewhere along the line she'd lost custody, so that didn't get her far. I'd always hoped they'd make up."

"They might have if Kendall had lived," Tawnia said. "In the letter she left us, she said her mom offered to have her come home if she gave up the baby for adoption. Kendall wasn't happy about that at the time, but she later realized it would be best for the baby—for us—so they might have made up if they'd had more time."

Mariel shook her head. "Sometimes life just ain't fair." We nodded in agreement.

"So," Tawnia asked, "do you know who the boyfriend was?" Her voice was deceptively casual, but I recognized the emotion behind it. My stomach clenched as I waited for the answer.

Mariel shook her head. "There were so many of them, you know? Again, that was because of the drink. She always picked the wrong guys. After she cleaned up, she lived here for about three or four more years, and we became really good friends. She worked as a clerk at the gas station. Then she got married and moved away. I was glad for her. She was only a few years older than you two by then, I expect. She had Kendall when she was only sixteen."

She let us digest this for a minute before adding, "I learned about plants from Laina. She had a green thumb. Everything she touched blossomed—after she cleaned up, I mean. Her yard looked beautiful. Too bad she wasn't as good in the kitchen. But she got a husband anyway. An electrician, if I remember correctly. Or maybe he was a mechanic. I forget. But he did something responsible."

I also had a green thumb, and I'd raised herbs since my childhood. I'd thought that was because my adoptive parents owned an herb shop, but maybe there was more to it than that.

Tawnia didn't share my green thumb, though. Or my ability to cook.

"So, is Laina still alive?" I asked.

Mariel clicked her tongue. "I expect so. She'd be about my age now—sixty-five or sixty-six. But we lost touch. Last I heard, she'd moved to Salem."

"That's not too far from here, is it?" Tawnia asked.

"About fifteen minutes."

Tawnia bounced Destiny on her lap, trying to keep her from fussing. "I don't suppose you remember her new last name."

"Let's see." Mariel squinted and looked up at the ceiling. "It was something really different, but I can't remember exactly what. Walker? No, that wasn't it. Hmm."

Tawnia leaned forward. "Maybe you have an old letter from her?"

"We weren't much for writing. We usually talked on the phone. Anyway, I don't save letters. It's only clutter. But I think it was Wallace—no, Walkins. Or maybe Walkling. Yeah, it was either Walkins or Walkling. I'm sure of it."

"Thanks," Tawnia said. "That'll narrow our search."

"I have a few friends, too, that I can call and ask. They might remember the name. A lot of us were there at the wedding, though none of them still live around here. At least none that I can think of."

Tawnia handed her a card and rose to her feet. "If you learn anything, I'd appreciate a call. But you've already been a great help. Thank you so much."

"Look," Mariel said as she accompanied us to the door. "What Laina did back when Kendall was a kid wasn't right, but she suffered a lot afterward. What I'm saying is to not be too hard on her. She was young and poor and all alone. She did the best she could. It wasn't good enough for Kendall, but what can you do? By the time Laina was old enough to really handle motherhood, the alcohol already had her in its clutches."

I nodded. "Don't worry. We're not out to hurt her. We only want to find out about our history. You know, medical, ancestry. That sort of thing." About our strange talents, our eyes.

"We don't expect anything from her," Tawnia added.

Mariel smiled. "Oh, but she'll be happy to see you. Really happy. I know it."

Tawnia and I bade Mariel farewell and walked back to the car in silence. We'd found what we'd hoped to find and learned a little more about our young birth mother.

"It's so sad," Tawnia said, sliding into her seat and bringing Destiny to her breast. "One thing leads to another. If Laina had waited to have a child. If Kendall had been at a friend's the night of her birthday. Or anything. It could have all been different."

A lot of things could be different. No powder in a glass of lemonade could have meant a life saved. A hammer put in its proper place might have prevented a crime of passion.

"But it wasn't different," I said. "Only the future can be different."

"I hope that Laina's . . . I hope that she's . . ." Tawnia didn't finish.

"I know," I said. "I hope so too."

There was no option of going to Salem right then. Even if Laina was still living there, we both agreed that it would be best to let her know in advance who we were and why we were coming. Besides, the phone book might not lead us to her directly. We might need Tawnia's Internet skills to pinpoint her whereabouts.

"You okay going directly to church?" Tawnia asked me after she buckled Destiny into her car seat.

"Isn't that why you made me wear this dress?" The boots didn't go all that well with it, especially once I took my coat off, but people there were accustomed to seeing me without footwear. Besides, I think they kind of enjoyed having their own resident eccentric.

Now that I knew I could do nothing further about my past, I was back to thinking about Rosemary. The next step was going to see her parents to determine if they knew anything. I'd take Tawnia's drawing along to see if they thought it was Rosemary.

Tawnia said nothing as I tore the drawing and my suspect list from her sketch pad. "If you do another and it shows anything else, let me know," I told her.

She nodded. "You'll be careful?"

"I'm just going to talk to her parents tonight. I should show this to Shannon, though."

"Ah." Her grin was back.

"Don't start. There is nothing between us."

"We both know you're lying."

"Okay, then. What about Jake?"

She sighed. "I know. He'd be hard for me to give up."

"You're no help."

"Do you need help?"

I rolled my eyes and kept my mouth shut.

After the church service we went to Tawnia's to eat her Crock-Pot dinner of pork, carrots, celery, and potatoes. It was every bit as good as I'd hoped. When I'd downed two huge helpings, I was ready for a nice nap, but the vision of Rosemary lying on the ground somewhere compelled me to continue my sleuthing.

"When's Bret coming home from his trip?" I asked as my sister drove me back to my place.

"Tuesday, I hope. I don't like staying alone."

I would have volunteered to stay with her, but her house was simply too far away from my shop for convenience. "You're always welcome to stay with me," I offered.

She shook her head. "Not enough room with all those antiques."

I'd expected that reply. While the shelves and corners in my apartment were crowded with, well, just about everything, Tawnia's house was sparse and completely orderly, a legacy from her adoptive parents. To me, my apartment was comfortable and homey while Tawnia's decor was a little too high class and a bit stuffy. But I still loved her more than anyone else in the world.

I leaned over the backseat to say goodbye to Destiny. "You're bringing her by the store tomorrow, aren't you?"

"Yeah, but I only have to be at work for an hour. I wouldn't even go if it weren't for the mandatory meeting. I get more done at home. Fewer interruptions."

I knew it galled her a little not to be over the creative department at the advertising firm anymore and to have been reduced to a simple team member, but that was a small price for having Destiny. "See you then."

"Call me if there are any developments," she threw after me.

"I will. And you call me if you find Laina."

"Oh, I'll find her. I feel it."

Was that her gift speaking? I decided not to ask.

I hurried into my building as fast as I dared. My legs already felt icy in the cold air, and darkness, with its accompanying thermometer drop, was well on its way. I'd change into something warmer the minute I got inside my apartment.

I unlocked the door and froze as I heard movements in the kitchen. "Who's there?" I called. Maybe I should rethink giving out so many keys.

Except maybe it wasn't someone I knew. Chills crawled up my spine. I eased off my coat, letting it drop to the floor, and brought my hands to the ready.

Chapter 10

"Hi." Jake's body filled the kitchen door frame, his skin appearing more bronze because of the light behind him.

I breathed a sigh of relief and lowered my hands. "Man, you scared me."

He chuckled. "Sorry. I came to see how it went in Hayesville. I was just about to leave you a note."

I'd expected him to ask about Rosemary and the murder, but then I remembered he hadn't been around for the rest of the excitement last night. For all he knew, I'd come straight home.

"Oh, that. Yeah. We found a lady who knew our biological grandmother back then. She gave us her name, and Tawnia's going to search for her. She moved to Salem almost thirty years ago." I shrugged and bent down to pull off the boots, sighing with relief to have my feet free.

"You eat yet?"

"Tawnia made Crock-Pot."

He arched a brow. "Edible?"

"Actually, yes."

We stood looking at each other a little awkwardly. "I just came home to change," I said. "I'm going to see Rosemary's parents."

"Why?"

I hesitated. "She had a confrontation with her father. It's probably nothing—they found a guy trying to break into Rosemary's apartment last night, and he's the prime suspect."

"But they still haven't found her."

"No." Shannon would have called, but I didn't tell him that. Though the men were on good terms, I didn't need to rub my connection to Shannon in Jake's face.

I handed him Tawnia's drawing of the unconscious woman. "That's why I want to see what the fight was about and if her parents have any idea where she might be. If this is Rosemary, I'm not sure she has much time left—if she's still alive at all."

He studied the drawing. "Tawnia did this?"

"Yeah."

"I'll go with you, if you like."

I really wanted him to, but from what I'd gleaned from Liam about his parents, I felt I was likely to get more from them alone than with Jake. He could be intimidating with those locs.

"I'd better go alone. Or with Liam."

"You're positive it's not dangerous?"

"They're Liam's parents, upstanding people in the community. I'm sure it'll be okay. Even if they have no clue as to her whereabouts, I might find imprints Rosemary left that can tell us something." I added this last reluctantly, hoping he wouldn't make a big deal out of it.

He must have heard the tension in my voice because all he said was, "You want to hang out when you get back?"

"Sure."

At that he took a tentative step forward, his hands going to my shoulders. "I've really missed you, Autumn."

"I've missed you too." It was the truth. Jake had once been everything I wanted, but I'd changed since my gift emerged. I wasn't as fragile as I'd been at Winter's death, and I didn't need Jake as much as I had. He was a little too dependable and, well, always there. It didn't make sense, not even to me.

Maybe it was all an excuse. Maybe I was simply afraid of where we were heading. It would be so easy to fall into his arms, to let his lips work their magic, to find a future with him as Tawnia had with Bret.

Not as long as Shannon was in my blood.

I hugged Jake, which I knew was actually a way of holding him at arm's length while pretending everything was normal. I didn't fool either of us.

"What time will you be back?"

"I can text you when I leave their house."

"Okay. See you then." He started for the door.

I went toward my room, turning around only once when I heard the door softly shut. I frowned and whispered, though he was no longer there, "I'm sorry, Jake."

Pushing my feelings aside, I hurried to change into my heavy army pants and black sweatshirt. I called Liam as I went to the kitchen for a quick cup of herbal tea. He didn't pick up, so I texted him to call me as soon as he could.

The kitchen light was still on, and right away I saw the new herbs on my small table. A dozen different seedlings, all ready for replanting in my nicer pots.

Jake. That man knew what I liked.

As I waited for the water to boil and for Liam to call back,

I placed the herbs on the rack in front of my kitchen window with the rest of my collection. I'd had a run of bad luck with the new fluorescent lighting I had rigged for winter, and several of my best plants had died. These would fill in the gaps. Smiling, I pulled some leaves from one of my thriving mint plants, tearing them several times to put into my hot water.

Liam called as I finished. "Hi," I said. "I need to visit your parents. Can you give me the address?"

"I'm here now for Sunday dinner. But why do you want to see them?"

"Because a lot has happened since I last talked to you. Rosemary's roommate who works at the same theater was found dead yesterday. Poisoned. Your sister's disappearance might be connected."

Except for a deep breath, he was silent as he digested the news. "I knew something was up. Do you think she's okay?"

"I don't know. I really don't know." I wanted to tell him about the hammer, but that wasn't the kind of information you shared over the phone. "Text me the address," I said gently. "I need to talk to them now."

"Is it okay if I'm here?"

"Sure."

His text came through as I poured the tea, leaves and all, into my mug. Clapping on the lid and adding a small straw, I hurried from the kitchen, stopping only to pull on my boots and Winter's coat. I was glad to have the hot mug in my hands as I braved the night chill.

My car started on the second try, which wasn't half bad. I used the tea to warm my insides until the heater started spewing something that resembled tepid air about ten minutes later. It took twenty more minutes until I found the address, which was in an upscale section of town, one I didn't often have reason to visit. The house, however, was ordinary, smaller than all its neighbors.

My phone rang before I turned off my engine, so I left it on as I answered. Tepid air was better than frigid. "Yes?"

"Hi," Shannon said. "Thought you'd like to know that the boyfriend did write the note and so far he remains our best suspect for Rosemary's disappearance. As for the murder, we've checked out all the theater personnel, and so far we've found nothing unusual. Our detectives are visiting each of them now to see if they turn up any more clues, but we have no reason yet to get search warrants for their homes. If it wasn't for the imprint you read about the two other possible murders, I might want to pin the murder on Rosemary's boyfriend as well. He knew the victim. Maybe he didn't want her to take Rosemary's place in the play."

"After making it so Rosemary couldn't do it? Doesn't seem likely. And even if he was around eight years ago, he would have been really young."

"Twenty, in fact, and I've seen murderers a decade younger. But in this case I happen to agree with you about it being unlikely. My gut tells me we've got the wrong guy."

"For the murder?"

"For both. He's a hot-headed kid, and he's definitely not telling us everything, but even if he hurt Rosemary, I don't think he knows where she is now." A grim determination in his voice told me he'd probably be up half the night further interrogating the guy.

"If he doesn't know where she is, then he probably didn't do it. No one has reason to hide her if he didn't do something wrong."

"I've seen stranger things."

Yeah, like someone who reads imprints. There was a time when he'd have said it aloud, and I would have said something snotty back to him. I kind of missed those days. It had been simpler.

"So many of these perps lie even when they don't have to," Shannon continued. "The only thing it accomplishes is to slow down the investigation. I have to make sure that's not what's happening here. Oh, and one more thing. I went out to talk to Rosemary's parents this morning. I stopped by to see if you wanted to come along, but you weren't home."

He had? That was a first. It was still usually his partner who called me in on their cases. "Ever hear of a phone?"

"I called. There was no answer."

I had left my phone in Tawnia's car during our morning excursion and hadn't checked messages. I wasn't good about checking them ever, I was the first to admit. "Sorry, I was with Tawnia. We were talking with a lady."

"What a relief. I thought you might be getting mugged again."

"Very funny."

"So, did your appointment have to do with Rosemary?"

I hesitated. I didn't know if I wanted to tell him. Then again, this was a man I was considering starting a relationship with. Maybe.

"We found a lady who knew our birth mother's mother. We're trying to discover more about our relatives."

He was quiet a moment, and I was relieved he didn't rattle off some snarky comment. "How'd it go?" he asked finally.

"We're close to finding her, I think. Whether or not it's a wise idea, I don't know." I glanced at the house aglow with lights, feeling uncomfortable with the whole subject. "What about you? How'd it go with Rosemary's parents?"

"I found nothing new. I don't like the Taylors, though. They're hiding something. Maybe not about Rosemary, but they're hiding something, all the same."

"If I find out anything, I'll let you know."

"You going to see them?"

"I'm here now. In fact, I'd better go in or they might think I'm staking out their house."

"Okay. Well, let me know."

By his lack of protest and how quickly he hung up, I figured he didn't consider the couple dangerous despite his suspicion of them. I was glad. After last night, I'd had enough adventure. Though now that I thought about it, I supposed the room in Tawnia's drawing of the unconscious woman could be inside this very house.

Wonderful, I told myself. I didn't even need someone else to spook me. I could do it all by myself.

I realized I'd forgotten to tell Shannon about Tawnia's drawing. Anyway, it hadn't helped at all, so it wouldn't likely break the case, even if her parents or brother could positively identify her.

Turning off the engine, I climbed from the Toyota and slammed the door. As I trudged up the walk, a strange reluctance settled over me. Dread. The feeling of hidden eyes watching me. I fought the urge to run back to my car and drive home.

Pausing, I carefully surveyed the area. There was no sign of anyone, though the many mature trees and bushes provided plenty of places for someone to watch unseen. Had the person responsible for Rosemary's disappearance or Cheyenne's death followed me here? But why? Surely, he—or she—wouldn't think that I was a danger to him, not now that the police and all their resources were on the case. Unless he knew about my talent and thought I'd discovered something.

The attacker at the theater might not have been Rosemary's boyfriend. That, of course, meant he could be in the shadows watching me.

Ridiculous, I thought. Whoever attacked me in the theater had been there for something completely unrelated to me.

Nevertheless, I let my eyes roam back and forth as I continued up the walk. I thought about removing the gun from my pocket and holding it as a deterrent but pushed the thought away. Anyone watching might feel that much more threatened. If I were attacked, my hands and feet were the only weapons I'd need.

Unless the stalker had a gun.

Before ringing the bell, I purposely removed my rings and touched the doorknob just to see what might be there. Nothing but the faintest impression of relief. Relief to be home. Though it wasn't strong, I could tell it was fairly recent—within the last week. Nothing unusual about that. It had to be from Liam, though, or some other relative, because there was an equally impressive garage attached to the house. Likely the elder Taylors used that means to enter the house.

I raised my hand to the bell, but the door opened before I reached it, and Liam poked his nose out from around the side of the door. "Oh, you're here. I've been watching for you."

I hoped that explained the odd watched feeling I'd experienced.

"Look, about my parents," he rushed on. "They, uh, well—could you not mention that I went to see you about Rosemary? They don't know I kept in contact with her. They wouldn't be very happy to find out, and I need their support if I'm going to finish college. Okay? Can you do that?" He stared at me anxiously.

"But the police have already been here."

"Well, when I talked to that guy whose number you gave me, he said they'd have to talk to my parents, and I told him the same thing I'm telling you. He was cool about it. Not like the movies at all. You know, when they spring your secret just to get a reaction. I was there the whole time, and he barely noticed me."

I was surprised Shannon had been so accommodating. Yes, Liam had a certain something that had made me like him—even in the beginning when he'd stolen the music box and made rude comments about my not wearing shoes. Maybe that was because at the same time he'd been blushing furiously, obviously, as he confessed later, smitten with me. I'd found him endearing and kind of sweet, like a kid brother or a young neighbor child you couldn't get rid of. Shannon must also have liked the boy after having met him because, Shannon simply wasn't that nice. Or maybe it was only me he'd never been nice to. No, I'd seen criminals shaking under that intent gaze. The only answer had to be that Shannon hadn't found anything to gain by telling the Taylors about their son's concern with Rosemary.

"Well?" Liam pressed. He looked about ready to faint.

"Okay. I'm just a friend she missed lunch with. That good enough?"

"Yeah, but make sure they know you own a business. That you're not an actress."

At least that was the truth.

"Okay, I'm going in the back door. Give me a few seconds and then ring the bell."

Before I could protest or warn him about the person I'd felt watching me earlier, he took off around the house.

I waited five seconds and rang the bell. It was a presumptuous bell, with a grand tolling that went on for thirty seconds. You'd think their house was three times its size with that sort of annunciation every time a visitor arrived.

"I'll get it, Mom," I heard a voice say. Liam opened the door. "Hello?"

Oh, brother. "Hi, I'd like to talk to your parents," I said. "If they're home."

"Mom, Dad," Liam called. "It's for you."

A few seconds later a woman wearing a gold-and-black pantsuit appeared in the entryway behind Liam. Her stylish blond hair reached just below her chin. A man in dress pants and button shirt followed, the gray streaks in his brown hair looking more distinguished than mature. There wasn't much of Liam in him that I could see, except for his height.

"Don't yell, dear," the woman said to Liam, her eyes coming to rest on me with an apologetic smile. "May I help you? You haven't been in an accident, I hope?" This I guessed was in regard to the bruises and cut on my face.

"No, nothing like that. I'm Autumn Rain, an old friend of your daughter's, and I was hoping I could chat with you a few moments. I own an antiques shop here in town, or I would have come sooner." Let them derive from that whatever they wanted.

"Oh, a friend of Rosemary's." Mrs. Taylor glanced at her husband. "Isn't that nice, dear?" He smiled, which I took as a good omen and not only because the smile bore some resemblance to Liam's. Apparently Mrs. Taylor took it that way, too. "Come in," she invited.

As I followed the Taylors to a sitting room, I glanced at Liam, who hovered nearby, twisting his hands. The behavior seemed so unlike the confident boy I knew, and for the first time I really understood why he'd stolen the music box from my store. He didn't feel his parents were people he could go to where Rosemary was concerned.

Why? It didn't make sense. Many children disappointed their parents—maybe all children did at one point or another— but that didn't mean you ignored or stopped loving them, did it? I knew what Winter and Summer would think about that. No matter what I did or thought or tried, I knew they would love me, and maybe that made me more reckless, more cautious, or more naive. I don't know, but in any case, I made it to adulthood relatively unscathed.

"What a nice picture." I touched the top of a family portrait from the table near the chair where Mrs. Taylor indicated for me to sit. Love seeped through me. Three years ago when they'd taken this photo, Mrs. Taylor had been full of joy because of her family.

More pictures of them dotted the walls, but none were more recent. Not only had the Taylors not removed Rosemary's photographs, but they hadn't taken a new picture without her. I could feel nothing of Mr. Taylor on the frame, so I could safely assume that pictures were his wife's realm.

Mrs. Taylor's eyes ran over my black sweatshirt and army pants. At least Winter's black coat, though old, was more stylish than mine. Belatedly, I realized I should have stayed in my dress for this interview.

"So, how do you know Rosemary?" Mrs. Taylor asked.

My throat felt suddenly dry. The only thing to do was to plunge into my own questions and press on until they kicked me out. "It's been so long, I don't even remember, but she's been missed since she left town, I can tell you that. The strange thing is that she missed lunch on Friday, and Rosemary would never not show up like that. I was worried, so I went over to the theater, the new one she started at, and they didn't know anything. The frightening thing is that while I was there, the girl who replaced Rosemary was found poisoned. She's dead."

"Poisoned?" Mrs. Taylor's face lost all color. She turned to her husband. "The detective who talked to us didn't say anything about a murder."

Mr. Taylor didn't speak for a moment, and I couldn't read the impassive expression on his face. "I'm sure that's because the cases are not connected, dear. The detective mentioned a young man Rosemary has been dating, and he is, I understand, the primary suspect in her disappearance. But as I told the detective, I'm sure Rosemary will turn up."

He turned his head to include me. "You have to understand that these types of people simply don't respond or act the way we do. They aren't responsible. Rosemary probably found a better opportunity and neglected to inform her employer that she changed her mind. She's done stuff like that all her life. It's a fickleness we were unable to correct."

I glanced at Liam, expecting him to say something, but he was slouched on a chair, staring at his hands. Mrs. Taylor wouldn't meet my gaze, either. I was beginning to understand how it was. They all deferred to him, even when they didn't agree. Whether out of habit or because of fear, I couldn't say.

"The role Rosemary was doing had a possibility of taking her to Broadway," I said as though Mr. Taylor hadn't spoken. "The director believes she is very talented, better for the part than any of the company's other actresses. This was Rosemary's big break, and it was very important to her. She wouldn't have missed it. I'm really worried."

Mrs. Taylor's forehead creased with more anxiety. "Broadway?"

"Apparently, the producer has contacts there. As you can imagine, he was very upset about her disappearance. All her clothes and belongings are still at her apartment, except for her phone. No one has found that yet."

"She'll show up." Mr. Taylor looked at me with ice in his eyes. "Meanwhile you should let the police handle things."

I hated the dismissal in his eyes. "Actually, I consult for the police, and I'm interested in the case because of my connection with Rosemary. My visit isn't official, but they know I'm here."

"Oh?" He arched a brow. "And what do you do for them?"

"I make observations."

"I see." That meant nothing useful in his opinion. Probably right up there with acting.

"But you sell antiques," Mrs. Taylor said brightly. "In that cute little store in the shopping district."

I hadn't told her where I worked. My eyes went briefly to Liam, who was now staring at his mother. *She knows,* I thought. *She knows Liam was working for me.*

"Yes," I said. "Next to the Herb Shoppe. My parents used to own that store as well. I grew up working there."

"Antiques are wonderful things," Mrs. Taylor went on. "I've been meaning to buy a few antiques myself. Haven't we, dear?" She smiled at her husband, who nodded absently.

"I can help you with that anytime," I said. Not that I thought she'd follow through. If she did know about my connection with Liam, she wasn't bringing it up around Mr. Taylor, and he apparently wasn't paying close enough attention to the conversation to understand the subtleties. Perhaps because of a guilty conscience?

"Look, can I offer you some coffee?" she asked. "It's so cold out there. I'm sure you could use some warming up before you leave."

Was that a hint? "I'll take herbal tea, if you have any," I said. "Maybe lemon or chamomile?"

"I have an apple-cinnamon tea I simply adore. Will that be okay?"

"Sure."

Mrs. Taylor arose and swept from the room.

"Could I use your bathroom?" I asked no one in particular. I'd had too much tea on my drive, and besides, I needed to touch more objects. A bathroom on the main floor wouldn't reveal as much as the master bathroom, but it might hold some clues.

"Show her where it is," Mr. Taylor told his son.

Liam walked me to the hallway and pointed out the room. I went slowly down the hall, touching pictures and items on the half-oval table against the wall. Nothing. Liam made a strained sound in his throat, and when I glanced at him, he cast me an imploring look.

Sorry, Liam, I thought.

It was time to get serious. I was mostly convinced that Mrs. Taylor didn't know anything about Rosemary's disappearance, but I felt her husband was hiding something. After I found out all I could, I'd have to confront him about the imprint on Rosemary's princess rock.

I pulled open the single drawer in the table against the wall and ran my hands near the contents. A small picture radiated such strong imprints that my hand seemed to move closer of its own volition. A young girl stared out at me, standing next to two people I assumed were her parents. The blond hair told me it wasn't Rosemary, but the costumes on the adults and the obviously fake backdrop had me confused. Why would Mrs. Taylor keep a picture of actors in a hallway table?

My finger touched the frame and images washed over me, coming from only months before.

Longing. I wanted to see my parents. It wasn't enough anymore to listen to my husband's excuses. Who cared what they did? It wasn't as if they were beggars in the street. They hadn't even met my children. For all they knew, I was dead. But I kept track of them. It was easy enough on the Internet, and they never had to know I read everything I could about their performances. Barry never had to know.

Random, less focused imprints came on the heels of that one— similar longings that spanned years. These were followed by another clear imprint of anger and resentment, followed by a rash vow: *I'll cut my parents from my life to please my husband. It's the only way.*

The earliest imprint was more than thirty years earlier and belonged, like all the others, to the young girl in the photograph, Mrs. Taylor. *Pride, excitement, laughter, love. My parents are so cool. I'm so lucky.*

I pulled my finger away as the images began to repeat.

Liam had taken several steps toward me. "What?" he asked.

It was a lot to process. "You told me once you didn't know your grandparents. Is that right?"

"They died before I was born. Apparently, my grandmother lived with us a few years when Rosemary was a baby."

"Your dad's parents?" He nodded.

"What about your mother's parents?"

He shrugged. "I have no idea. I think they died when my mom was in college."

"No," I said, handing him the photograph. "They were very much alive two months ago."

His eyes were riveted on the picture, no doubt taking in the costumes and the theater backdrop. Then, with a quick peek behind him, he slipped the tiny photo, frame and all, into the pocket of his jeans.

I studied him for several seconds before walking the few remaining steps to the bathroom. I let the water run in the basin while I opened cupboards and slid my hands over everything. The few objects that tingled with imprints weren't helpful or relevant. Well, at least I'd found the photograph. I'd text Liam for a copy. It might be a long shot, but maybe her grandparents had something to do with Rosemary's disappearance. The theater world couldn't be all that big, could it? I'd have to ask Paige to run a few searches through her contacts at the station and see if we could find them.

I returned to the sitting room as Mrs. Taylor arrived with a tray. I accepted the tea without sweetener since all she had was plain white sugar. The tray also held a delicate array of cookies, which Liam inhaled with gusto, though it couldn't have been long since he'd eaten dinner.

"When was the last time you saw Rosemary?" I asked between sips.

Mrs. Taylor looked startled. "Two years ago before she left town. She hasn't been back since."

"But the company she was with is based here. She was home last year for a while."

Mrs. Taylor's eyes again refused to meet mine. Her voice was soft as she said, "I know."

Something had kept Rosemary away, and I was betting it wasn't her mother. Well, I'd always known it would come to this. I turned to Mr. Taylor. "I understand you went to see Rosemary at the theater on Thursday."

Mr. Taylor's gaze sharpened, but he didn't respond.

Still my turn, apparently. "I also know you had a disagreement and that you grabbed her hair."

Everyone had gone completely still, though whether it was from surprise that he'd seen his daughter or because I'd suddenly turned into a viper, I couldn't say.

"How could you possibly know that?" Mr. Taylor demanded.

"You didn't think Rosemary would tell anyone?"

"Who knows what Rosemary will tell people. She's an actress. Everything she lives is a fantasy."

"But you did see her there? Can you tell me what you talked about?" I tried to remove the accusation from my voice. "It could help my investigation."

"Your investigation?" he sneered.

"At the moment, the police are a bit more concerned with the murder than with your missing daughter." I pulled Tawnia's drawing from my coat pocket without unfolding it.

"But I believe Rosemary is hurt, perhaps severely, and if we don't find her, it might be too late."

A gasp from Mrs. Taylor, but nothing from Liam or Mr. Taylor. I hadn't expected Mr. Taylor to show emotion, but Liam should have been upset with this information.

Unless he was hiding something from me.

"Well?" I pressed. "Did she say anything about problems she was having? Any confrontation with anyone?"

"No." Mr. Taylor's voice was clipped. "I offered to help get her back into college. She refused. End of story."

"Did she tell you about her new part?"

"Maybe. The details didn't interest me."

"Is there anything else you remember?"

"No. Nothing." His jaw clenched tight. "Our visit had nothing to do with wherever she is now."

Clearly I wasn't getting any more from him.

"Does anything in this drawing seem familiar?" I passed the picture to Mrs. Taylor, who paled as she glanced at it before giving it to her husband.

Mr. Taylor's nostrils flared. "Is this supposed to be Rosemary?"

"I was hoping you could tell me."

"Where'd you get this?"

"I can't tell you that. I can only tell you it's evidence."

Mr. Taylor shook his head and gave a grunt of disapproval as he thrust the drawing back at his wife.

She studied it. "I don't know," she said. "It could be Rosemary. The hair is longer, though, than when I last saw her."

"Can you identify her clothing?"

She shook her head. "I haven't seen her in so long." She stared straight at me as she spoke, and I had the feeling she was avoiding her husband's eyes.

Liam had come to stand at his mother's elbow, but he also shook his head. "Well, maybe her roommates can tell me more." I reached for the photo. Too bad the roommate closest to her would never talk again.

"Your coming here has been a waste of time." Mr. Taylor stood, dismissal in his face and every rigid line of his body.

"Maybe." I took a last sip of the warm cinnamon and apple tea and stood as well, but because I hated to let such a disagreeable man win, I added, "I have one more question. Did Rosemary know that Mrs. Taylor's parents are actors?"

Mr. Taylor's face flushed red, and he cast his wife a glare, but she lifted her hands helplessly. Liam stared at his father, one hand shoved in his pocket, perhaps fingering the small photograph.

"Who told you that?" Mr. Taylor demanded.

"No one," I said. "I'm a good observer." Without another word, I showed myself out of the house, feeling their eyes tracking me to the door.

I hurried to my car, hoping that whoever I'd felt watching me outside earlier had long gone. Or that it had been Liam, though why I'd have felt dread from him, I couldn't say.

I checked the backseat before I got into the car and locked all the doors before turning on the engine.

I hoped no one followed me home.

Chapter 11

*L*iam came to see me the next day as I was finishing my whole wheat turkey sandwich from Smokey's. I'd been expecting him because I'd texted him and told him that if he didn't come to see me, I would tell the police he was withholding information. When he arrived, he looked like a college student who'd pulled an all-nighter for a final. Monday afternoons were customarily dead, so we had the shop to ourselves.

"Hey, are your eyes different colors or is it just the light?" he said a bit weakly.

"You look terrible, Bean Pole."

"I've been researching on the Internet all night. I found them."

"Your grandparents?"

"They own a little theater in Washington. Have for all their lives. They write plays and cast them and also act. It's just a little place, apparently, and they close down every now and then because of a lack of funds, but some of their plays have been picked up elsewhere. They seem to be well known, and people have a lot of good things to say about them." He sat down on the stool behind the counter. "How could my parents keep this a secret for my whole life?"

"I get the feeling your father doesn't approve of acting in general, and your mother, well, according to the imprints on the photograph, she had a falling out with them. For what it's worth, she regrets all that now, and she's kept track of them for years. From a distance, apparently. They may not even know you exist."

Liam raked his hands through his hair. "It's so . . . so hypocritical. My father gave Rosemary such a terrible time about what she wanted to do, but it was in her blood, you know? Something she *had* to do. She lives for it. And she's really good. Whenever I watch her, I really feel the part, you know?"

Though acting wouldn't be my first choice for any child of mine, Winter had always taught me to let life be the dream-killer instead of mocking or being too realistic in regards to others' dreams. Support them, help them, encourage them, show them options, and if for some reason they didn't make it, you stepped in to help pick up the pieces, keeping your relationship intact. If you did what Rosemary's father did, you lost every chance of a relationship with the child. Perhaps that was why Winter had helped me start my antiques shop instead of insisting I take over his herb store.

"Maybe he was trying to protect her from disappointment," I said. I didn't believe it, but I wanted to soothe the pain on Liam's face.

"It's her life. If she doesn't at least try, she'll always regret and wonder. Besides, she could always do something else with her talent, like my grandparents. She doesn't have to end up in New York." He grimaced. "Do you think my mother gave up her dreams because of my father? I don't even know if she ever had any."

"You'd have to ask her."

He put his elbows on the counter and let his head drop to his hands in apparent misery.

"Why don't you tell me what you've been hiding from me?" I prompted. "You knew your father went to see Rosemary, didn't you?"

His head rose slowly. "She told me she was calling him. Then after their meeting, she was just gone. No more texting, and she didn't show up for our lunch. Nothing. And my dad was stalking around the house when I went over to snoop around. You know, to see if my parents knew where Rosemary was."

"Do you think your father did something to Rosemary?"

His reddened eyes filled with tears. "I don't know."

"Has he hurt any of you before?"

"Not physically. But you saw how it was last night. He's always had a temper, and all my life I've been afraid he's going to explode if I don't do what I'm supposed to. What if that's what happened with my sister? What if he finally exploded?" He let his head drop again and groaned.

"You should have told me on Friday what you suspected. I told your parents last night that I thought Rosemary was hurt. What I didn't tell them was that in an imprint I saw someone hit a girl with brown hair like Rosemary's in the back of the head with a hammer. Hit her hard. That drawing I showed you last night looked like the girl I saw."

He grimaced. "It's Rosemary. I'm sure she was wearing that same blouse in a picture she sent me. Do you think my father might have done something to her?"

"I don't know, but I'm going to have to tell the police."

"Will they take him into custody?"

"Not unless they find proof, but they may have enough for a search warrant on any properties your parents own. I'd like to see the picture of Rosemary with the blouse, and I'd also like to see the info you have on your grandparents. If Rosemary learned about them, they might know something."

"Could she be with them?" he asked, sounding like a lost child.

"If that was the case, don't you think she would have contacted you by now?"

He shoved himself to his feet, looking worse than ever. "I'll send everything to your phone during my next class. I can't miss it." He sniffed hard. "You will find her, won't you, Autumn? Please?"

"I'll try."

I watched him leave, feeling helpless. Time was ticking away for Rosemary, and I was no closer to finding her. If her father had some role in her disappearance, how did that fit in with the murder? Were they not connected after all?

I was concentrating so hard on my thoughts that I didn't notice Jake come through the connecting doors until he put an arm around me. "Was that Bean Pole who just left?"

"Yeah."

When he saw my expression, he removed his arm and leaned against the counter to get a better look at my face. "What's wrong?"

"He thinks his father did something to Rosemary. And he might be right."

"So that's why you were so quiet last night." He'd come over to watch a DVD, and I'd been grateful for his presence, but I knew I hadn't been good company. Even so, it was fun being with him, though we'd lost the ease between us. In a strange way, the added tension was exciting in and of itself. I had to be careful I didn't do something I would regret—one way or the other. I loved Jake and didn't want to lead him on.

I sighed.

The bells over my door tinkled as a woman came into the shop—Liam's mother, her blue eyes looking bright in her thin face. Just when I thought things were winding down, or at least heading for a breather, they grew more complicated.

Jake, thinking she was a customer, thumbed toward his store.

"I'd better get back. We can talk later. Holler if you need me." I nodded, and Mrs. Taylor and I both watched him leave. He cut an impressive figure. Watching him made me wish I had taken more steps toward him last night.

Maybe.

"Hello," I said to Mrs. Taylor, walking around the counter to greet her. "How are you?"

"I know how you helped Liam, and I want you to know I'm grateful. You helped give him direction in those months before he graduated from high school. He'd been different since Rosemary left, and you made a difference."

"He's a good kid, and he was a good help to me."

"I'm sorry about how my husband treated you yesterday."

"Did you ask him about going to see Rosemary?"

She nodded. "He says she called him and asked him to meet her. He was upset when he arrived and found it was a theater."

"What did he expect? She is an actress."

"I don't know. Maybe he hoped that she wanted to come back. Return to college." She sighed and let her watery eyes drop to the floor, blinking twice at my bare feet. "Barry doesn't understand what it's like. The drive. I never had it, but my parents did. They lived for the theater. They would never leave it."

"You had a falling out?"

She nodded. "I wanted a part in one of their plays. I was often in them, but I wasn't very good, so it was just the little parts. The acting gene skipped me, I guess. The first year I was in college, I badly wanted this certain part, but they gave it to someone else. To someone a lot better, I realize now. At the time, all I saw was that she was a girl I hated, someone who'd given me trouble in high school. It was right about then that I met Barry. He was so smooth and romantic and so different. He hated the theater, and I was glad. Glad to have another world to live in that didn't revolve around my parents or make-believe. Needless to say, they didn't get along with Barry, and since I'd pretty much cut myself off from them, I didn't care. I haven't seen them since my wedding, which they nearly destroyed by coming in costume, by the way. Barry was mortified, and his parents, who paid for everything, were even more so."

"In all these years you never got together with them?"

She tucked a strand of blond hair behind her ear, her eyes flitting to the door as though at any minute expecting her husband to appear. "I talked to my mother once on the phone, after Rosemary was born, but Barry was worried they'd influence her. Like I said, he doesn't understand that sometimes these things are in the blood."

In the blood. Like my eyes and my odd gift. Someone had given both to me and to my twin. I wondered if Tawnia had found out anything about our biological grandmother.

"I thought I was doing the right thing at the time, but now, because of Rosemary, I think I was wrong." Her eyes met mine, pleading with me. "Do you really think she's hurt?"

"I'm afraid so. Liam says it's not like her to stay out of contact so long."

"They were always close." Tears started down her cheeks. "I failed her. I've really failed her."

"Mrs. Taylor, when your husband went to see Rosemary, they argued. She turned away, and he grabbed her by the hair. Rosemary was frightened."

"How do you know this? Did she tell you?"

"Not directly. There was a sort of witness." This wasn't the time to explain about imprints. "What matters is that Rosemary went missing right after talking to your husband. He might have been the last person to see her. Do you think he's capable of violence?"

Mrs. Taylor's tears were falling faster now, and her voice was a whisper when she said, "I don't know. I really don't know."

"Is there anywhere he might keep her if he didn't want her to leave?" *Or if he was trying to hide a body,* I amended silently.

"Just the house. We do have a cabin, but it's an hour's drive. We don't go there much."

"Would he have had time on Thursday evening to go there?" She shrugged. "I don't know. He always works late."

She wasn't much help, but if she allowed the police to search the cabin, it would save time getting a search warrant— provided a judge would even let us have one. "Will you let the police search the place?"

She nodded. "I just want my daughter back."

"I'll talk to the police. You can expect someone to contact you today, hopefully right away. Do you have a number where I can reach you?"

As I took down the number, Mrs. Taylor gazed around the shop, though it was apparent she wasn't seeing anything. "Thanks for your help. I . . . if you talk to my parents, will you tell them I'm sorry?" She turned toward the door without waiting for a response.

How sad to have purposely walked away from your own parents. I felt a moment of panic, of remembering when I was on the bridge before it collapsed, Winter in the car at my side. I would give anything for him not to have gone with me that day, but one thing I'd learned is there is no going back where death is concerned. Not ever.

"Mrs. Taylor," I said to her retreating back.

"Yes."

"Both your parents are alive. It's not too late."

She nodded, but I could see it made no difference. Not now. She was too far under her husband's spell. Maybe if I found Rosemary alive that would change things. Rosemary would insist on knowing her grandparents, and her mother would have the support she needed to break free.

I'd have to go back to the theater. Somehow everything connected there. I'd get Liam to send me a picture of Mr. Taylor and ask if anyone had seen him. Someone had to remember his visit, maybe even overheard something. If not, I'd touch everything there, searching for the one imprint I needed to find Rosemary.

I dialed Shannon's number, but this time his partner, Paige, picked up. "Hey," I said. "Where've you been?"

"Missing all the excitement, apparently. But I had a lovely weekend." Her voice lowered. "I met someone new. Someone I think might be important." We had reached the point in our relationship where she confided such things, and I listened. I was glad for her.

"So help me if he turns out to be an attorney . . ."

"No, I had enough with the last one. This one's a doctor."

"That's good in your line of business."

She laughed. "He's hot too."

"I hope he holds up to Shannon's background check."

"Are you kidding? That'll be nothing compared to the grilling my dad and brother will put him through. Even my grandfather will pull strings." I'd forgotten for a moment that hers was a family of police officers and detectives. "That's exactly why none of them are going to know for as long as possible. No spilling to Shannon."

"My lips are sealed. So what about the case? Any news?"

"Shannon's just finishing up another interview with the theater producer, Carl Walsh, which is why I have his phone. He's trying to get the inside scoop on everyone connected with the theater. By the way, eight years ago two of their actors did go missing on the night of an opening performance, and no one had a clue until they didn't show up. The rumor was that they ran away together, but we can't find any trace of them. No taxes filed, and none of their relatives have heard from them. Nothing. So either they ran away to another country, changed their identities, or they're dead."

I knew which I thought was most likely. Though I'd seen only one glass prepared with poison eight years ago, the killer had planned two.

"So far, only Walsh, the director, and two of the male actors were connected to the theater eight years ago," Paige continued, "and both those actors were basically part-time child actors.

There are five actors who have been with the company six years, but most have been there less than four. Obviously, not a company that holds employees for long."

"Maybe there's a connection with a relative of one of the current actors."

"I'm working that angle now. So far, I've come up with nothing. It's hard to know where to begin. There are close to thirty actors in the company."

"Walsh has the most to lose by actors going missing or dying. After all, he's the producer and the manager. Think of the revenue losses he had that night eight years ago if he didn't have understudies."

"They didn't, which was unusual in and of itself, so I'm told. I'll be honest. I don't like the man, but I don't see a motive."

I had to agree with her on both accounts. "I may have found out something about Rosemary, but I don't know how it ties in with the murder." Unless Rosemary's father had a connection to the theater company I didn't know about.

Then again, with Barry Taylor's hatred of the profession, maybe there was a connection. He could have had an altercation with one of the actors, was trying to cover up an affair, or any number of other variations. If we could find a connection, we might have a clearer picture of the man.

"Well, spill it," Paige said, shaking me from my thoughts.

"It's Rosemary's father." I outlined my conversations with Liam and Mrs. Taylor, as well as my own thoughts about Mr. Taylor. "I know it's a long stretch, but at least it's a lead."

"I'll send someone to check out the cabin and the surrounding area. But most cabins have a lake nearby. If he is guilty and he dumped her there, we may have to wait until spring to find a body. It's been pretty cold the last few days. If the lake is small enough, it could have frozen over."

Body. "I'm still hoping she's alive." I wanted that for the family. I liked Mr. Taylor less than I liked Carl Walsh, and I wouldn't mind finding him guilty, but Liam and his mother had suffered enough.

"If they find anything at the cabin, I'll have them save it for you to read."

"Thanks."

Paige was one of the few officers who had embraced and used my talent from the beginning. With her encouragement, I'd learned to use it better and help put bad people behind bars. Her belief in the face of Shannon's initial skepticism was probably what had made me stick with helping the police in the first place. My willingness had absolutely nothing to do with the fact that Shannon's eyes turned my insides to liquid even back when I used to annoy the heck out of him on purpose.

Hmm.

"Let me know," I said.

"What are you going to do? I know you won't just be sitting around."

"Hey, I'm at work. I gotta make a living somehow. Consulting for you guys doesn't pay enough."

She laughed. "Okay, that's what I'll tell Shannon. He always asks." Amusement was thick in her voice. "When are you going to put him out of his misery?"

"I don't know what you're talking about. Look, I'm hanging up now. But I want to meet this doctor of yours—and touch some of his things."

"Maybe. I don't know that I want to know."

"Yes, you do. It's better to know. Remember the attorney?" But I knew what she meant. I purposely stayed away from Jake and Shannon's belongings, even though, at least for Shannon, I really wanted to know more. I hadn't even been to his house, which was probably for the best. I knew how he'd feel about me reading his things. Or I knew how he once felt about it. Maybe he'd changed his mind.

"Hey, they're coming out now. Walsh looks like he's in a hurry. He's saying something about auditions. Looks upset. I'll talk to Shannon about Rosemary, and if he needs information, he'll call."

"Thanks." I'd barely hung up when the cord of connection I felt with my sister began to thicken. I wondered if it was this way with all twins or only those with our strange talents. Of course, I'd felt it with my adoptive parents as well, and she'd only ever felt it with me.

I went around the counter and was halfway across the room when the bells above my door signaled its opening. As usual, Destiny was in Tawnia's arms, which I quickly rectified by grabbing her. "Hey, baby, how're you doing? Did Momma bring you for me to watch while she goes to work?"

"The meeting was postponed until Wednesday," Tawnia said. "But we have news, so I thought we'd come in anyway and share."

"It's about Laina, isn't it?"

"Yes. Laina Drexler Walkling, our biological grandmother."

Chapter 12

Before Tawnia would tell me anything, she insisted on my updating her about the case. I would rather have kept her out of it altogether, and she must have suspected my feelings. Reluctantly, I filled her in, including my plan to return to the theater and show Mr. Taylor's picture around.

"Your face looks worse than yesterday," she informed me when I'd finished. "You sure you haven't done anything else to it? No more strange figures attacking you in the night?" She was only half kidding. Maybe that was the reason she'd insisted on the update.

"I'm fine. Bruises always look worse before they get better." She didn't need to know that my arm and ribs still ached from the tussle outside Rosemary's.

"Why don't we go to the theater right now?" she said. "I can tell you about Laina as we drive, and I can help you once we get there."

I looked pointedly down at Destiny. "What if it's not safe?"

"It's broad daylight, and there's two of us. Plus, all the actors. Nothing's going to happen. Whoever killed that woman is long gone by now or at least lying low. They have no reason to do anything to us. Besides, it was a poisoning, not a shooting or something of that nature, and we aren't going there to eat or drink. If we see anyone mixing lemonade, we'll run for the hills." She laughed.

"Someone was hit with a hammer," I reminded her.

"Only when she was alone. We won't be. You still have that gun, right?"

"Yeah." I stifled a sigh.

It wasn't so much taking Tawnia that worried me because she was probably right about the danger level, but taking Destiny to the theater seemed like something we shouldn't do. However, Tawnia wouldn't leave her with anyone but me or Bret—and sometimes her neighbor Sophie—not that I blamed her. Destiny was an angel while we were holding her, but she'd reached the age where she would usually cry with anyone she didn't know well.

On the bright side, maybe taking Tawnia to the theater might evoke another of her drawings, one that could give us some hint to where Rosemary might be.

"It's dead here, anyway," I said. "Jake and his sister can watch the place." I pulled on my coat, my own once again—smelling fresh from the dryer at my apartment building—and grabbed my phone, which should have the necessary picture of Rosemary's father before we arrived at the theater. "Let's go tell Jake."

We entered the Herb Shoppe where Jake was finishing up with a customer. "We're going for a drive," I said. "Will you watch my shop?"

"Sure. I've been kind of busy here, but Randa will be in soon. Is Thera coming in today?"

"No." We shared the two part-time employees, but I'd called Thera and asked her not to come in because we had no customers. The rest of us could handle any rush in the small Herb Shoppe. One thing I loved about Thera was how flexible she was with her hours. As a widow, she spent her time between my shop and her grandchildren, but I suspected she only worked at all to keep an eye on me. She'd been kind of sweet on Winter before he died and seemed to feel responsible for me, though as far as I knew, Winter had never looked at another woman in the twenty-odd years since Summer died.

"You can call her if you need to," I added.

"Okay. Have fun." He paused and added in a lower voice, "Can I call you later?"

I smiled. "Sure." If I wasn't fighting off black-masked attackers.

Tawnia was silent as we made our way out to her car. She strapped Destiny in, while I settled in the passenger seat debating whether or not to pull on my boots. In the end, the rain hitting against the windshield convinced me. I really dislike winters. If I didn't have so many roots here, I'd probably have upped and moved to California or Hawaii by now. I wondered if Tawnia and Bret could get jobs there.

"Where to?" Tawnia asked, pulling out her GPS.

"No need. I have it here on the phone."

"Oh, cool." She put the car in gear and pulled into the light traffic.

"So, what did you find out?" I prompted, unable to wait another second.

"Laina is excited to meet us, but she wants to come to Portland. Apparently, she has other children and grandchildren, some of whom live with her, and she—well, she didn't say it, but I got the impression she wants to meet us before she decides how much she's going to tell her family."

For some reason the idea of Laina being so cautious rankled. After all, it was essentially her fault that Kendall had been raped and conceived us. "I guess she's worried we might be kooks or have some strange gifts," I muttered.

"Oh, come on, Autumn. It's not like you to be bitter."

I sighed. "It's been a tough couple days, and the worst thing is that I'm really no closer to finding Rosemary."

"What about Mr. Taylor?"

"Well, he has a hatred of actors, but it seems a long shot to connect him with Cheyenne's death, and I can't figure out how he'd be connected to the other theater poisonings eight years ago."

"The poisonings have to be connected with Rosemary?"

"The timing of her disappearance and her connection with the theater say yes—I don't believe in coincidence—but I could be wrong."

"Don't worry. We'll find something." Tawnia sounded excited. Maybe now she'd understand why I couldn't quit investigating, even if it could be dangerous.

"So when do we meet Laina?"

"She's coming to Portland tomorrow for something, and she'd like to stop by. Will that be okay? She's not exactly sure of the time but in the morning after nine. Maybe we can take her to Smokey's for lunch if she comes at eleven or so."

"I'll ask Thera to cover for me. But isn't Bret getting home tomorrow?"

"Yes, but late, probably." She glanced at me and then back at the road. "I can't believe we're finally going to have answers about our relatives."

"Maybe."

"You're right. I don't want to get my hopes up too high. I mean, we each had parents who loved us. What are we really looking for?"

"I want to know about our abilities," I said. "Why we use a part of our brains that no one else seems able to."

She nodded. "That seems harmless enough. Not emotional. We should keep it that way."

Easy for her to say. My sister was a rock—logical, methodical, and persevering. I was none of those things.

In a lower voice, I added, "I also want to know more about Kendall."

We exchanged a look. No way not to be emotional about that. For either of us.

Seconds of silence passed between us, and then Tawnia asked, "Did you hear the way Jake asked if he could call you?" Tawnia deepened her voice. "'Can I call you tonight?' Wow, he sounds like some movie star or something. How can you resist?"

"I don't know." Maybe I shouldn't. It was easy between us, and I knew I could trust him with my life and my feelings. But now that I had become so involved in finding missing people, I wanted more.

"How far out in the boonies is this anyway?"

I looked at the map on my phone. "We're about five minutes away. Take a left at the next light."

When we arrived at the rundown theater, the front looked as dead as it had Saturday night, but the back lot was scattered with cars, presumably belonging to the actors.

"They must be rehearsing," I said.

As on Saturday night, someone had left a brick to hold the

prop room door open a crack. Either the last person in had forgotten to kick it out of the way, or they were still waiting for someone.

No one was in sight, so I shucked off my boots at the door and led the way barefoot through the dimly lit prop room and down the hall. The women's dressing room was empty, and we continued through the theater to the stage. A group of actors lounged about in the chairs behind Paxton Seaver and Carl Walsh. Everyone was staring at a young woman on the stage who was reading from a script.

As we peeked from the side, Walsh bounced to his feet, an action that looked too agile for his round body. After leaving the police station, he must have broken speed limits to get here in time for these auditions. "No, no, no. Sorry, miss. This isn't the part for you. Next!"

"Who's the chubby guy in the bad suit?" Tawnia whispered.

"Producer and stage manager, Carl Walsh. The other guy is the director, Paxton Seaver."

Another applicant moved onto the stage, her hesitant steps not boding well for her chances. Beside me, my sister's eyes gleamed as the woman started reading aloud.

"*For the Love of Juliet!*" Tawnia whispered. "You didn't tell me that was the play they were doing. It's marvelous! I saw it five times in Nevada. I even tried out for the part of Juliet at a community theater there but lost to the director's daughter." She laughed softly.

Destiny, intrigued with her mother's teeth, tried to put her hand in her mouth. Tawnia grabbed her hand and grinned.

The performance of the aspiring actress was met with utter disregard. "We'll let you know," Seaver said, waving the woman off the stage.

Carl Walsh stood and faced the actors in his company behind him. "This isn't working," he announced. "One of you will have to do it. Vera, what about you? You could do the part justice, don't you think?"

Vera. The actress with the red wig who'd told me about the bad luck revolving around this play. Walsh would never convince her to do it.

Before Vera could respond, one of the male actors I hadn't met said, "What about them?" He pointed to me and Tawnia as we edged onto the stage.

Walsh and Seaver turned, hopeful expressions on their faces. Seaver stood, and both men hurried over, Seaver smiling when he recognized me. "Come to try out?" he asked. "I told you you'd be good for the part."

Walsh harrumphed.

I opened my mouth to say no, when Tawnia shoved Destiny into my arms.

"Sure, why not?" she said. "Give me a script."

They both stared at her and then at me, puzzlement on their faces.

"My sister," I explained, not hiding the irritation in my voice.

"She wouldn't have to wear a wig," Seaver commented.

Walsh rolled his eyes. "We need someone who can act at least well enough to let the others shine. You know what it means if we don't find someone. We'll both be looking for a new job. We need the funding."

Funding? This was the first I'd heard about money being involved. I knew Walsh had important relatives on Broadway, but was there more to it than their hunt for good actors? Had they been supporting him as well? Yes, that had to be it. No wonder the small company had been able to survive all these years.

Paxton Seaver smiled. "My director's gut tells me we'll be okay." He handed Tawnia a script and indicated a marked passage. "Whenever you're ready."

I went down the stairs and followed the men back to the front row of seats. Taking her time, Tawnia read silently through the script. Then, with a quick nod of her head, she began to pace the stage as she spoke, unlike the previous applicant, who'd stood in one place like a frightened child. Tawnia was bold, brilliant, and someone I suddenly didn't know.

I stared. She'd told me about her theater experience, but it wasn't something I'd witnessed firsthand. It belonged to her old life, before Portland, Bret, and the baby. Before she'd met me. In my untrained eyes, she was good. There were rough spots that had Seaver wincing and Walsh grimacing, but when she'd finished, they looked at each other and nodded.

"We can make this work," Seaver said, in a voice that only Walsh and I could hear.

"We could still get Vera to do it, or maybe Erica."

"Vera's all wrong. She's got the witty part down but not the heart. And Erica, well, she's too strong. We need the crowd to feel more sympathetic. This girl is likeable."

Walsh pursed his lips. "You're the director."

"Have I ever let you down?"

"Plenty." The two men stared at each other in mutual dislike until I wanted to squirm.

With a shake of his head, Seaver stood, and his voice boomed out in the quiet of the theater. "You're hired. We start rehearsal today."

"Better watch her back," someone whispered to me. I turned to see Vera, whose pretty face was drawn in a spiteful grin. "You know what happened to the last four women who took the part."

I felt ill. The actress who had died in a car accident and the one who had cancer might not be connected, but the disappearing couple eight years ago and Rosemary and Cheyenne now were more than suspicious. What had I gotten my sister into?

Within minutes, Tawnia was pacing in a small alcove area awaiting her turn to go onstage. I held Destiny, while she practiced her lines.

"You can't do this," I said, keeping my voice low.

She looked up from her script. "Why not? It'll be fun. I haven't acted in forever."

"Because this isn't community theater. These people aren't in it for fun. It's their livelihood, and they mean business. The other actors in the play think this is their big Broadway break."

"Broadway? From here?" Tawnia shook her head. "Not going to happen. That's a fantasy."

"What about Destiny?" I rocked the now-sleeping baby in my arms.

"That's what you're here for. Rehearsals shouldn't last more than a few hours. They'll have to work around her."

"What if she needs to eat?"

"There's a bottle in the diaper bag in the car."

"Is it your milk?"

Tawnia rolled her eyes. "I hate to remind you that both of us grew up on formula and somehow we survived. But yes, it's my milk, and it's on ice." She gave me another placating grin.

"Look, you need someone on the inside, and I can get us the inside scoop. We'll solve the case in no time."

"Then what? You'll go off to Broadway and be an actress?"

She laughed. "No. I'll do the play, have a little fun, and while I do, you and Bret finally get your share of Emma." She put her head close to mine. "Don't worry. No one's going to hurt me. They know the police—and you—are watching."

I wasn't so sure. Tawnia didn't understand the lengths to which people would go in order to get what they wanted—poisoning, murder, hitting someone with a hammer. I barely understood it myself, and I had witnessed the events as though I'd lived them. Whoever had murdered Cheyenne was still around, I was sure of it, and at least a few people believed her death and Rosemary's disappearance were connected to this play. That meant Tawnia could be in danger.

I watched my sister's happy face, knowing I'd have to put a stop to this. Still, if everyone here understood that my sister wasn't a serious actress nor a contender for any Broadway role, maybe it would keep her safe.

I still planned to tell Bret everything as soon as he got home tomorrow night, so he could help me talk Tawnia out of playing Juliet.

Waiting until Tawnia was with Millie, the other actress in the play, I went in search of Paxton Seaver. He was standing before the stage arguing over a scene with Lucas, who was playing bad boy Alex.

"I just don't think I should use that line," Lucas was saying in his unnaturally high voice. "It sounds too feminine." His good looks still took me by surprise, especially when coupled with that odd voice.

"Not if you deepen your voice when you say it," Seaver countered.

"That's easy for you to say. You have all the good parts, and you get the girl in the end. How realistic is that, anyway? A muse getting the girl instead of a human?"

What? I blinked my surprise. Paxton Seaver was playing Romeo, the muse who was grooming Juliet for Broadway? Suddenly the whole idea of my sister playing Juliet seemed much more serious when the director had cast himself in the play. But if he was trying to shine for the aunt in New York, why would he pick Tawnia? Was she really the best available with Rosemary and Cheyenne out of the picture? Or was there some other reason?

Though the idea disturbed me, I couldn't figure out why his being in the play would make him more suspect. Would no other male actor take the part? I somehow doubted the superstition ran that deep. Maybe he was trying to get away from this two-bit outfit, hoping for a chance to make a name on Broadway. No wonder Walsh had said Seaver had as much to lose as he did.

"Do it, or we'll find someone else," Seaver growled. Lucas stalked off, tossing his wavy hair as he went. He had really good hair. Too bad brains didn't seem to come with the package.

"Look," I said to Seaver, shifting Destiny's weight to my other shoulder. "My sister's not looking to go to Broadway. You know that, don't you?"

He shrugged. "As long as she's good enough, Millie and Lucas have a chance."

"Not you?"

He rubbed a hand over his face. He seemed about to say

something, but his eyes went past me, and I turned to see that Walsh was coming toward us. "Look, we'll talk later," Seaver said. "I need to block this scene with your sister. I'm glad she's seen the play before. That really helps."

"Wait. Did you see this man come here last Thursday looking for Rosemary?" I fumbled for my phone and shoved the picture of Mr. Taylor under his nose.

"Nope. Never saw him before."

"Thanks."

He gave a quick nod and bounded onto the stage. "Tawnia," he called, "let's go through this scene."

There was a brief delay in her arrival, which had me panicking, but eventually she swept onto the stage. Seaver smiled and led her to the far side. For a moment, I stood fascinated as I watched them run through a few lines. I'd noticed before that the plain Seaver had presence, but on stage this was more apparent than ever. Even as he stopped to discuss the scene with Tawnia, he was mesmerizing.

"I would have done it!" Vera's voice interrupted my concentration. She'd come up and was speaking to Walsh while glaring at Seaver and Tawnia. "You didn't have to go and hire another outsider."

Walsh blinked at her. "Then why didn't you speak up?" He shook his head, like a dog shaking off an unwanted hand. "Anyway, I know how you feel about this play, so you're off the hook."

"Maybe I don't want to be off the hook. I deserve my chance at Broadway just as much as anyone else!" She flounced her hair as she turned and stalked away.

"Actors," Walsh grumbled under his breath.

Her outburst surprised me. Either she'd miraculously overcome her fear of the play or the fear had been an act. Maybe she'd been vying for a part all along, and now with Rosemary and Cheyenne out of the picture, she had a much better chance. Her romance with that playboy she'd been kissing in the hall might mean she had an accomplice. I'd have to ask Shannon to dig into her background.

Next to me, Walsh's breathing sounded loud in my ears. "Have you seen this man?" I asked, showing him the picture of Mr. Taylor.

He held the phone away from his face to see it better. "No. I haven't. Really, I've told you guys that none of us knows anything about what happened to Cheyenne."

"Well, someone knows. You just got back from the police, didn't you?"

He wiped his sweaty forehead with a white handkerchief. "A while ago. How'd you know that?"

"I consult with them, remember?"

"I don't think you ever said."

"Well, I do."

On the stage, Seaver was speaking, waving his hands energetically. For a moment, we both watched, mesmerized. "He's good," I said. "Maybe he should be on Broadway."

Walsh blinked and shook his head. "He's just trying to make Millie and Lucas shine. They're the best actors I've got."

I hadn't seen the two in any role, so I wasn't betting money on their abilities. "Too bad about Lucas's voice," I said, more to needle Walsh than anything.

Walsh drew his round figure up to his full, unimpressive height. "He overcomes it quite well."

"Carl!"

We turned at the harsh voice. Erica was coming down the steps between the seats, walking with a stiffness that showed annoyance, her dark eyes flashing. "Are you still going through with this play? After everything that's happened?"

"Of course," Walsh said. "You know as well as I do that the play must go on."

Erica rolled her eyes. "There are other plays. Better ones that use more actors."

"So you've said, but I feel this is our best chance."

"Ours or yours?" Her disgust was obvious, but Walsh didn't seem to notice.

"Everyone's," he said.

Ignoring him, she turned to me, her face softening. "Babysitting now, are we?"

I indicated the stage with my chin. "My sister's filling in. This is my niece."

Erica stepped closer. "She's really cute." She admired the sleeping baby for a polite space of time before turning back to Walsh. That she'd stopped in her ranting at all surprised me. I'm always amazed at the power babies have over people.

"So are we going to run through *our* play?" Erica asked, sounding less upset. "You remember that we open next week, right?"

"At five o'clock we'll work on a few scenes. And again tomorrow morning before the Juliet rehearsal."

Erica rolled her eyes. "That's going to be fun, getting these night owls here in the morning."

"They'll be here. Besides, we've done that play before. Everyone knows it well."

"Don't you have a performance tonight?" I asked.

Erica shook her head. "We're only open for the public Thursday through Saturday, except for special events." She shot a glance at Walsh. "We'll probably do some of the Juliet performances on Mondays and Wednesdays, though."

Walsh inclined his head in agreement.

"Look, Erica," I said, taking advantage of the brief lull in the conversation. "I need to ask you a few questions."

"Okay, but I have a lot to do. Can you walk with me?"

"Sure."

We went through the door and down the hall to the women's dressing room. From a cupboard she took a basketful of folded clothing and a sewing kit. "These need fixing before our next play." She frowned as she glanced toward the closet where we had found Cheyenne. Evidence tape still crisscrossed the closed door. I wondered how long it would stay there.

I brought up the picture of Mr. Taylor on my phone. "Have you seen this man?"

She tilted her head to the side. "Hmm, maybe. He might have walked through here on Thursday. I was a little busy."

"Might have?"

She shrugged. "I think I overheard him or someone else talking to Cheyenne."

"Are you sure it wasn't Rosemary?"

"Maybe. I didn't hear her voice, just his, and I caught a glimpse of her hair as I went past." She looked up at the ceiling, trying to remember. "I guess Rosemary has the same kind of hair, more or less. It could have been her."

Her comment made me wonder if maybe Rosemary or whoever had been hit by the hammer had been mistaken for Cheyenne. Maybe the killer thought the poison hadn't worked after all. No, it would have had to be the other way around since Rosemary had gone missing between Thursday night and Friday lunchtime, and the imprint on the glass said the poison had been given to Cheyenne late Saturday afternoon. Maybe the murderer realized he'd hit the wrong woman and used the poison to correct his error. The only thing that wouldn't make sense was the previous poisonings. The feelings in both poisoning imprints had been so similar that I was convinced they'd been committed by the same person, and successful murderers didn't usually change their methods so drastically. The poisoning was planned, well thought out; the hammer, a moment of passion.

"I'm going to find a window and a bit more light," Erica said. "Do you have any more questions?"

"Not right now."

She took a few steps toward the door before giving me a tight grin over her shoulder. "I really hope you find whoever did this. Things will never get back to normal here until you do. That's not good. Actors are very sensitive, you know. Stress like this can throw off their acting."

I hadn't noticed that actors were any different from regular people, except for the added drama within their group, most of which I felt was for show, but I didn't really care how Erica saw herself or her theater family.

"Thanks for your help," I told her. "I'm just going to look around a bit."

Cradling Destiny in my right arm, I reached out to a hairbrush on the vanity in front of me. Seeing it reminded me of how the imprint on Rosemary's brush had abruptly cut off when she'd looked up and seen a man enter the dressing room. Surely that wasn't when she'd been hit, because the man would have been a witness.

Unless he was a conspirator with whoever hit her. But if the man had been Rosemary's father, they would have had to talk first for her to leave the imprint on her princess rock. Maybe it wasn't the father at all on the brush imprint but Rosemary's supposed boyfriend. I wished the imprint hadn't cut off before I'd seen his face.

I toyed with different scenarios as I set down the brush. The faint imprints it held were unremarkable. Many here had used it over several years, and no one claimed ownership. I touched a few more objects as I contemplated Grady Mullins's possible involvement with someone at the theater. Maybe he'd also been hoping to win a part in the play, and therefore a shot at Broadway, and getting rid of Rosemary was the act he had to perform in order to receive his prize. Except he wasn't in the play and Shannon didn't think Grady knew where Rosemary was. My dislike and suspicion of the man might simply be a result of my bruised body.

A movement at the door to the dressing room drew my attention. Erica was still standing there, studying me with narrowed eyes. "What are you doing?" she asked me.

"Getting a feel for things."

"Are you some kind of psychic?" There it was—the hint of derision people used when they first learned of my gift. I was accustomed to that, and the old desire to convince didn't even surface.

"No."

She shrugged. "Well, whatever. I hope you find what you're looking for." Balancing her basket on one hip, she disappeared.

I chewed on my lip, staring first at the empty doorway and then at Destiny's sleeping form in my arms. She stirred, her tiny mouth searching for something to suck on. I'd probably have to go out and get the diaper bag soon. I knew from experience that she was impatient when she grew hungry.

Wait. If two people had been poisoned eight years ago, two glasses were likely used, and since one glass had been used in a second poisoning, it was possible the other glass was also still here somewhere at the theater. The glasses might have been purchased as a set. If so, the matching glass might contain imprints that could shed more light on the identity of the murderer.

I needed to get back to the kitchen. The imprints hadn't been washed away from the first glass, so there was a chance I'd be able to read the second as well. Of course, there was also the chance that the second glass had broken long ago and been thrown away.

That was when the screaming began.

Chapter 13

*H*ugging Destiny tightly, I hurried into the hall. What now? Should I run to the door and get the baby out? What about Tawnia?

Several actors ran down the hall in the direction of the kitchen, from where the sound was coming. Better that I stay with them. There was protection in numbers, though protection from what, I wasn't sure. For all I knew, someone might have only seen a mouse.

In the kitchen, Erica was on the floor in the corner, her chest heaving with frantic breaths, her basket of costume pieces scattered everywhere. I tensed and looked around. No one else was there. The window, however, had been completely removed from its frame and was now shattered on the floor.

"What happened?" I asked. Destiny wriggled in my arms, and I loosened my hold slightly.

Walsh appeared in the doorway with the cast of Juliet, including my sister, who grabbed Destiny from me. Everyone waited for an answer.

"Someone was in here," Erica said, still breathless, her voice having lost all power with her fear. "Someone wearing a black mask. He had a bag, and he hit me with it. Knocked me down." She rubbed her upper left arm to show where the blow had landed. "I think he was stealing something."

I looked around again. The ancient dishwasher and the cupboards were all open, with no glasses in sight. A sinking feeling dropped in my stomach. The hypothetical glass I'd intended to look for was likely gone—and if so, that meant the killer must know about my gift. Why else would he steal an old glass?

I met Tawnia's eyes. In them was a question about why anyone would take dishes, but I moved my head slightly, communicating almost without indication, and she didn't voice the thought aloud. I didn't want to explain the importance of the glass now, but one thing was sure: whoever took it knew about the poisoning and also what I might find. Too bad the person had rectified the mistake of leaving the glasses in the first place. I should have been quicker.

Did this mean that no one at the theater had been involved? Someone on the inside could have removed the other glass at any time after the police found traces of poisoning on the first one. If it wasn't one of the actors, my list of suspects was dwindling.

"I'd better see if they took anything from the office," Walsh said. He looked at Seaver. "Why don't you go outside and look around? Maybe Erica startled him enough that he dropped whatever it was he took."

"Or she," Tawnia said. "Since the person was wearing a mask, it might have been a woman. Just like whoever attacked Autumn in the prop room."

My stomach lurched. Maybe Rosemary wasn't missing but had left on her own. Maybe she'd stolen the glass. But eight years ago she would have been twelve or thirteen years old, and it was hard to believe she could have been involved in poisoning the other two actors.

"I suppose it could have been a woman," Erica said doubtfully. "He hit me awfully hard, though. I think it was a man."

Walsh turned to leave, but a figure loomed in the hallway. "What happened here? Did I hear someone say *mask?*"

I'd know that voice anywhere. But who had called him? I certainly hadn't.

"Glad you're here, detective," Walsh said. "We've been robbed." He motioned to the group. "They can explain. I have to check my office to see if they've taken anything important." He pushed past the crowd, hurrying much faster than his bulk should have allowed.

"Who called you?" I asked Shannon. My eyes met Paige Reed's behind him, and she shook her head, her shoulder length, ironed blond hair barely moving at the motion. Today, she wore navy suit pants and a white blouse under her police jacket, almost a matching copy of Shannon, who was in black. I'd have to remember to give him back his other coat.

"We're actually off duty," she said, "but I wanted a look at the murder scene myself."

I nodded, knowing Shannon's partner hated being kept out of anything.

"Looks like someone should have called us." Shannon's eyes went past me to Erica, who still sat on the floor rubbing her arm. With her ultrashort haircut and perfectly shaped skull, she looked young, innocent, and helpless. Beautiful, even. "Are you okay?" Shannon asked, his voice gentle.

She nodded. "It was just kind of frightening, being surprised like that."

"Tell me what happened." Shannon moved past the actors into the kitchen. He offered Erica a hand up, which she accepted, looking at him demurely from half-closed eyes.

In Tawnia's arms Destiny let out a sound. "Sorry, sweetie. I didn't mean to hold you so tight," Tawnia murmured, rocking her gently. Despite the tension in the room, Destiny's eyes drooped again.

Paige had followed Shannon into the kitchen, her attention on the window. "This glass has been cut. Must be the entry point."

Grady Mullins had carried a glass cutter when he'd tried to break into Rosemary's room. If the police had let him go already, he might be our prime suspect.

"It broke when he was climbing out," Erica said. "When I came in, he was standing at the counter. He hit me with his bag and ran over to the window." She smiled at Shannon. "I hope you'll find him. I don't know what he took, but we have some very valuable costumes here."

I looked at the open cupboards and back to Shannon, who was now staring at me. "Okay, everyone, unless you have something to add, you need to leave," he said. "This is a crime scene now."

"Come on, everyone." Seaver beckoned to his actors. "Leave them to their work. Let's run through that last scene again."

"I'll call it in," Paige said, heading to the door. "Get the guys out here for fingerprinting. I'm also going to take a peek outside to see if he left anything behind."

Tawnia touched my arm. "Maybe I should take Emma home."

"If there was a danger, it's over now," Shannon pointed out.

"That guy isn't coming back with the police here. Besides, it looks like he got what he came for."

Tawnia looked torn. "It's okay," I said. "I won't let her out of my arms. Shannon and I will both keep an eye on her until you finish."

"Okay," Tawnia said. "But you know where to find me if you need me." She kissed Destiny before placing her sleeping form in my arms and leaving with the others. Only Erica remained.

"Besides the mask, he was wearing gloves," Erica told Shannon. "The thin sock kind."

Sock gloves like the person who'd attacked me in the prop room. Had he come back for what he hadn't been able to get the other day? But why not come in the middle of the night when no one was here?

"Do you remember anything else about the bag he carried?" Shannon asked Erica.

She started to shake her head. "Wait. It might have clanked." She blinked. "You know, now that I think about it, when he hit me, it sounded like dishes banging together."

"That would explain the open cupboards."

Her forehead gathered. "But these are regular dishes. They often double as props, but there's no real value to them. Let's see, the plates are here, the bowls—" She broke off in confusion.

"There are no glasses." I stated the obvious for her.

Again Shannon's eyes fell on me, but when he spoke, it was to Erica. "That will be enough questions for now. We'll want a full inventory of what was here, if you could take care of that."

"Millie will know. She keeps track of stuff like that." Erica bent to retrieve the costumes that had been in her basket, but Shannon stopped her.

"Leave that for now. Until after we finish with the room."

She smiled at him, all soft and willing. "Okay. Thank you so much." She shuddered delicately, which I was sure was an act because it belied the tough, no-nonsense actress I'd seen on Saturday night. Unless maybe her brush with the intruder had brought out her fragile side.

"You okay?" Shannon asked.

Erica took a deep breath. "I am now."

I almost couldn't stop from rolling my eyes as she swept from the room.

"So," Shannon said to me, snapping back to business. "Sounds like your guy from the prop room."

"Is Grady still in custody?" He hadn't been wearing gloves at Rosemary's place, but that didn't mean anything.

"Should be. He hadn't made bail when I left. Apparently his actor friends don't have the funds to get him out."

"This guy used a glass cutter."

"I know."

"Two separate guys use glass cutters?"

"Or Grady Mullins made bail."

I sighed. "He must have."

"And now the second glass is gone."

I arched a brow. "So you didn't just come here to satisfy Paige's craving to go over the crime scene herself."

"No. I realized there had to be another glass. In fact, I remembered seeing at least one matching glass when they were testing. No poison, but I was hoping it contained an imprint."

I sat down at the small table, gently laying my sleeping niece on top, making sure she was tucked snugly in her blanket and keeping hold of her to make sure she stayed put. "I've been thinking. Some years after those two actors went missing, an actress died in a car accident and another of cancer—all after being cast by this company in the same play. Is it possible that poison was involved in those cases but was somehow overlooked?"

"If so, we have a serial killer on our hands."

"Or someone who has a definite agenda."

Shannon sat down in the chair next to me. "Still a serial killer, whatever the reason. When he's set off, he'll do it again."

Even if my conjecture had merit, we had no proof there had been two more poisonings, much less four.

"Could be that actress Vera," I said. "She was really upset today about not being cast in the role of Juliet."

"The superstitious one?"

"An act," I said. "At least that's what I think now. She has a boyfriend. He could have been the one to break in today, but he couldn't have attacked me in the prop room on Saturday. He was too busy making out with Vera in the hall."

"It wouldn't make sense anyway. Why break in if you're already here?"

"And why break in during the day when people are here? Do they have an alarm?"

Shannon nodded. "One of the few extra expenses Walsh splurges on."

"Well, at least that explains one thing." I sighed. "So what about the Taylors' cabin?" The police should have had time to arrive there by now and do at least a cursory search. That is, if Paige had acted immediately on my information.

"No recent trace of Rosemary in the cabin or in the woods immediately surrounding the area, and they brought a dog.

Basically, nothing amiss that they could see. You might have better luck."

"This from the man who really, really hates what I do?" I couldn't resist the jab.

"I don't hate what you do." He leaned forward. Closer. Too close. "Okay, I used to, but that was before I knew you." His warm breath had the faintest hint of mint.

"You think you know me?" My voice sounded a bit rough, even to my own ears. I knew he'd been fighting his feelings for me a long time, but what I hadn't expected was the way something in me would respond to his emotion once he allowed it to show.

"Yes."

"And what is it you know?"

His eyes held mine. "The most important thing I know is that I'm not willing to share you like Jake seems able to do."

"You're not sharing me."

"That's exactly what I just said." He was close enough that I could see the five o'clock shadow on his face. For a blond man, he could grow a nice crop of stubble.

"I mean," I said, accentuating each word, "I'm not his, and I'm not yours. No one is sharing me. I make my own decisions."

"Which is?"

Our lips were inches apart now, and I wanted to close the distance more than just about anything. "Depends. I'm not sure what all my options are yet. Some are clearer than others."

"I see." His hand covered the one of mine not holding Destiny, sending shivers up my arm. I was really, really glad I couldn't read people like I could objects, because the fire in his eyes was intense.

"I'd have to experience the options," I added.

"I can arrange that." He moved forward until his lips lightly touched mine, though he didn't actually kiss me.

"Aren't you back on duty now that there's been a crime?" I whispered.

"No. That's why Paige is calling someone else to come in."

That's right. I remembered her saying something to that effect.

Neither of us moved. I both wanted and didn't want this moment. I wasn't betraying Jake. I'd been honest with him about my feelings for Shannon, but this could change things permanently, one way or the other.

Shannon's hand left mine and slipped around to the back of my neck. My mind was screaming something, but I couldn't hear what.

Destiny let out a wail.

We drew away at the same time. On the table between us, the baby was desperately trying to take my finger to her mouth. For the first time in my aunthood, I felt frustrated with her.

Shannon sat casually back in his chair. "I think someone's hungry."

I knew how to wipe that knowing smirk from his face. Scooping up the baby, I dropped her into his arms. "I'll get her bottle. It's in the car."

I fanned my face as I hurried down the hall, through the prop room, and out to the car. The temperature had dropped at least ten degrees since we'd arrived, and my feet should have been cold without my boots, but I was still feeling flushed from my encounter with Shannon. That man could heat my blood without even touching me. Had there been a time when Jake could do that? I couldn't remember.

I returned in time to free Shannon from the baby so he could talk to the two officers Paige had called to process the scene. His eyes rested on my face, the smirk gone. This time there was only his attraction to me and his acceptance of it. That scared me far more than when he'd been hoping to prove me a charlatan.

We moved into the area outside Walsh's office so the officers could finish in the kitchen. Along with the diaper bag, I'd brought in the car seat, and after Destiny finished her bottle, I settled her in the seat and arranged a few hanging toys on the handle above her head. She couldn't exactly reach out and play with them yet, but they fascinated her.

"I'm going out to the Taylor cabin," Shannon told me.

"You and Paige?"

"No, she has plans tonight. I think she's seeing someone, though she keeps denying it."

My turn to smirk. "Maybe that's so you won't do a background check on him, his relatives, and four generations of ancestors."

He didn't take the bait. "I was hoping you'd come along."

Oh, yeah. I wanted to. But only because I still thought Mr. Taylor had something to do with his daughter's disappearance. My desire had nothing to do with wanting to be alone with Shannon.

I was never a good liar—except to myself.

"Well?" he asked.

I took a step toward him, cutting the space between us to a few inches. "I can't leave my sister yet," I said in a quiet voice. "Not with a murderer on the loose around here. Besides, I'm watching Destiny."

"We'll wait, then."

So we did, watching the actors coming as they arrived for the later rehearsal. Even after Paige joined us, the tension between Shannon and me was as alive as the electricity that flickered in the old fluorescent lights above our heads.

"This place wouldn't pass code these days," Paige commented, glancing up at the lights.

I nodded. "Hurray for grandfather clauses."

"What an interesting case." Paige flipped a page in her small notebook. "I can't wait until we break it."

I couldn't wait until we found Rosemary.

The police still hadn't finished processing the kitchen when my sister showed up, arms out for the baby.

"That was fun," she said, smothering Destiny with kisses.

"Look," I told her. "I'm going with Shannon to check something out."

Tawnia looked at me, turning her head so Shannon couldn't see her wink. "Sounds fun. Call me later?"

"Sure."

We walked out to the cars together. The rain was coming down again steadily, but none of us commented. We knew what to expect in Portland. I held Tawnia's umbrella over her and the baby, and since there wasn't much of a breeze this evening, it mostly did its job.

She glanced over to where Shannon and Paige were climbing into his white Mustang. "Look, something strange happened a few minutes ago. I'm not sure if it's important, but since the whole reason for my taking the role was to get the inside scoop, I should probably tell you."

"Well, I think the real reason you took the role is because you wanted it, not to help me with any case. I still think it's a terrible idea. What happened to my normally sensible sister?

I keep waiting for her to reemerge. Don't think I'm not going to rat you out to Bret the minute he's home."

Tawnia grimaced. "Oh, believe me, I know you'll both have a lot to say. Now do you want to know what I heard or don't you?"

"Please."

"I had to use the restroom—don't worry, it opens from the hall and has a lock. Anyway, when I was inside, I overheard an argument between two people, a man and a woman. I think it was coming through the heating vent, and it was kind of distorted. I didn't recognize their voices."

I wondered if instead of a man and a woman arguing, it could have been the actor Lucas with another man. His regular voice was high enough to be mistaken as a woman's voice, especially through a vent.

"It wasn't that an argument was strange," Tawnia went on, "it was the subject of the argument. The woman was saying something about how she should have the main role in the play—I don't know which play—and that the man owed her and should make it happen. He had all kinds of reasons why it wasn't a good idea. Mostly, it sounded to me like he didn't trust her. She was furious and said that she was the best actress in the company and that he knew it. That she would make him sorry if he didn't do what she wanted. Then they must have moved away from the vent because the only thing I heard after that was the woman saying something about her father or his father—someone's father. She sounded very, well, disgusted, and whatever she said shut the man up good."

"And you have no idea what?"

"No. But it sounded serious, you know? The woman was

furious, she could barely speak, and he was cowed but determined. Strange."

I frowned. "Doesn't make sense. I mean, the only ones who seem to have input over casting are Walsh and Seaver. Actually, Seaver told me that as the director he has final say, but I don't know how reliable that is with Walsh holding the purse strings."

"Maybe one of the male actors has something over Walsh or Seaver and the female actress wants him to use that to get her a better part."

"Could be. Let's think on it a bit more." I was leaning toward the idea that maybe Vera and her boyfriend had been plotting, but it could be any of the actors. "I don't like Walsh at all," I confessed to my sister. "In an ideal world he'd be responsible for all of it."

She shook her head. "Too much for him to lose."

"Maybe we need to look at the backgrounds of all the actors and find out about their fathers. See if there's a possible connection. The police might already have a lot of the information. Paige said she was checking everyone."

"I hope they find something soon. Poor Rosemary." Tawnia sighed. "Well, I'd better get this baby home, and if she doesn't eat enough, I'm going to have to use my pump. I have so much milk, I'm going to explode."

"Thank you for that picture," I said dryly. "And speaking of picture, do you feel like drawing any?"

She groaned. "What I feel like is getting home and feeding this baby and going to bed. I forgot how exhausting this stuff is. But don't forget, you're calling me later."

I didn't know who was in denial more, me or my sister.

"Here, take your umbrella." Waving goodbye, I went to Shannon's car where Paige was seated in the back, leaving the front passenger seat for me. "Just drop me at the precinct," she said. "It's not too far out of the way."

"You sure you don't want to come out to the cabin with us?" I asked.

"Nope. Not my idea of a double date."

"Ah, so you do have a date," Shannon said.

Paige shrugged. "Maybe. Besides, the local guys said there was nothing out there."

"She's gotta be somewhere." Shannon met her eyes in the mirror

"Maybe Autumn can find something they missed." The amusement was thick in Paige's voice, and I knew she was thinking of the months she'd gone behind Shannon's back to bring me evidence to read that eventually helped solve their cases. What she didn't know is that Shannon had been aware of her duplicity and had gone along with it because solving cases was all-important to him—even if he had to involve my questionable talent.

I took advantage of the drive to the station to tell them what Tawnia had overheard. "It might be nothing," I said.

"And it might break the case." Paige sighed. "I'll talk to the officer I assigned to do the background checks and make sure they include the father angle for everyone connected to the theater."

Shannon laughed. "Don't keep lover boy waiting."

"Shut up. We need to break this case." She looked at me. "The captain has threatened us both with forced vacations if we keep volunteering for overtime."

I laughed. That, I believed.

The hour's drive to the cabin went faster than I'd hoped. I kept going over the "father" comment Tawnia overheard and wondering how it connected to the case. Had they been referring to Rosemary's father? Maybe he'd paid someone to help him take care of Rosemary after he hurt her. Or maybe he'd somehow convinced Rosemary to help him plan for Cheyenne's murder and cover it up—though she didn't seem to have that kind of relationship with him. And why would he want Cheyenne dead anyway? Because she was a bad influence?

Wait. The women looked somewhat alike. Maybe the connection was that Cheyenne was Mr. Taylor's daughter too, born from a past relationship with an actress. That might explain why he hated the profession so much. If so, Mr. Taylor might be responsible for murdering both women.

But to murder one and maybe two girls to cover up an indiscretion? That would take a coldhearted freak of a man. Was Mr. Taylor that cold? Besides, how likely would it be that the girls would meet by chance and discover a connection—if one actually existed? Paige would have to do her research, but I didn't consider it likely at all. My entire theory was seriously flawed.

The more likely suspect was Rosemary's boyfriend. Because of that threatening note, he couldn't be discounted. He had to know more than he was telling.

"Did you ever check to see if Grady Mullins is still in custody?" I asked Shannon.

He nodded. "He made bail, but if he was out there at the theater, he'd have had to sprout wings. The officers are searching for him now to check his alibi."

The easy thing would be to pin everything on Grady. He could have hurt Rosemary and taken her somewhere and then repented of his act and killed Cheyenne to keep the part open for Rosemary. Maybe his plan backfired when Rosemary died of her hammer wound.

I didn't much care for that scenario because it didn't account for the poisonings eight years ago. Besides, I trusted Shannon when he said Grady didn't know where Rosemary was. I made a mental note to call Rosemary's grandparents when things calmed down. It was a long shot, but maybe they knew something.

We were in a wooded area now, about an hour northwest of Portland, and every so often we drove past cabins illuminating the early darkness that had fallen over the area. We were high enough in altitude that the rain had become snowflakes, but they were wispy, half-hearted things that lent themselves more to postcards than inconvenience.

"Should be right up here," Shannon said. "There. I think that's the one." He pointed to a dark A-frame cabin settled in a backdrop of trees and brush. "The officer said he left the key under the mat. We're supposed to give it back to a neighbor when we leave. Apparently, the neighbors live here most of the year and keep an eye on the place."

The cabin wasn't as large and sinister as I'd anticipated, but rather quaint and homey-looking and would be even more so in the summer. A long, covered porch ran along the front of the house, bringing to mind long lazy summer nights when darkness was the only bedtime clock one needed. It didn't have that austere, wealthy appearance of the other vacant cabins we'd passed. Not what I'd expect from Mr. Taylor, who seemed more concerned with appearance than with the welfare of his family.

Shannon found the key and let us inside. A fine layer of dust covered the furniture, but there was no trash or rodent damage. Obviously, the Taylors cared enough about the cabin to keep it up. The room was colder than outside, if possible, and I bet they had to winterize their pipes to keep them from freezing.

"Go ahead." Shannon indicated the room. "Touch whatever you like. I'm going to do a once-over myself."

"Don't trust the locals?"

He snorted. "Remember those cellars at the commune? Even we didn't find those until we knew where they were."

I shivered at the remembrance. I'd been locked in one with a dying woman and two others. Entombed alive. We'd had to dig our way out.

"I want to look at everything, just in case," he added.

I was glad for Rosemary's sake that he was taking this seriously, but my gut ached with the need. A father should take care of his daughter, not be a suspect in her disappearance.

Clenching my jaw, I went to work, holding my hands above objects to see if they radiated an imprint. Many did, but most were faint. Memories of days gone by. Of laughter. The Taylors hadn't left anything of real importance to them here, nothing except these faint memories that painted quite a different picture of Mr. Taylor from the man I knew. Apparently, this had been the one place away from it all where he had at least played the part of the loving father and husband.

Quite unlike his usual role of an austere man who would cut his in-laws from the lives of his wife and children and cause his family to live in fear.

I checked the two bedrooms, the kitchen, the single bathroom, the living area, the front porch, and the small back patio. Shannon had found a miniature door behind a dresser in one of the rooms, and that led to a child's playroom stocked with tiny chairs, a table, a plastic kitchen, and a plastic tool station. There were even two tiny beds crammed into the corners. I could imagine that Rosemary and Liam had loved playing here as children. In here the imprints were even more faint. It had been a long, long time since anyone had entered the tiny playroom.

Not all the imprints in the cabin were pleasant, as they wouldn't be in any family, but even the negative ones were fleeting and fading. Either the family hadn't imprinted anything of value on the objects or nothing out of the ordinary had happened here.

I removed a white sheet covering the love seat and sat down to consider this new information. Judging by the objects, Rosemary hadn't been here for years, and the family only once sixteen months ago. The locals were right: The cabin was a bust.

Shannon still hadn't returned. He'd searched the cabin thoroughly, including an attic that made him choke from the dust, and then gone outside with a flashlight to walk the surrounding area. I could almost imagine him shoving huge boulders aside looking for entrances to secret cellars and might have laughed if I hadn't lived through that experience. I knew Shannon still felt responsible for how I'd almost died.

Rosemary, I thought. *Think about this case.*

But I didn't want to. I wanted to think about Shannon. I wanted to finish what we'd started at the theater. I wanted to *know.*

A noise on the porch shook me from my reverie. Someone was coming inside. I hoped it was Shannon, though he'd gone out the back door and I'd expected him to return the same way. Standing, I peeked outside and saw another car.

Someone else.

The door opened slowly, and I saw the barrel of a gun. Definitely not Shannon. He knew I was here alone.

I'm not normally one to jump to conclusions, but I'd been attacked twice in the past three days, and I wasn't anxious to repeat the events—especially not with a gun-wielding murderer.

Of course, I still had my own gun, and I was a good shot.

But who was I fooling? I didn't think I'd be able to risk shooting the wrong person by accident. Better to depend on my other skills.

I stood frozen by the curtain waiting, hoping my clenched muscles were ready.

The door creaked open wider, and the gun moved forward.

ho's here?" came a deep voice. The intruder still wasn't all the way inside the door, but I could tell whoever it was didn't wear the uniform of a police officer. In fact, he was wearing a suit coat, and some of the most dangerous criminals I'd encountered cloaked themselves in expensive suits that hid a world of sins.

I rushed from the side, sprinting along the window. In a fluid motion, I chopped down on the arm with the gun, sending it to the ground. I had only a second to be grateful it didn't fire, before grabbing the man's arm, pulling him and leaning forward so I could roll him over my back and onto the floor. He was taller and heavier, but I had training and the element of surprise.

I just hoped he was alone.

I jumped on him, making a fist to deliver a blow, when I recognized the man. He lay there, eyes wide with fear.

I hesitated. "Mr. Taylor?"

Recognition dawned. "You!"

"Autumn Rain," I said.

He struggled under me. Before I'd come to the cabin tonight, I would have been safe and hit him anyway, but the imprints hadn't indicated that he was dangerous.

"Wait." I jumped off him, picked up his gun, and stepped away. "Okay, you can get up now."

He swore, his fear turning to anger. "What are you doing in my cabin?"

I couldn't answer. Grabbing the gun without a glove or using a piece of cloth hadn't been the smartest thing I'd ever done. An imprint rippled over my consciousness.

The lights were on. Who was in the cabin? The police should be long gone. She didn't have the right to allow the police to come here looking for Rosemary. I hated the idea of anyone violating a place that had been my family's haven. The memory of the children growing up here was precious. I had loved walking through the woods and talking to them, teaching them. They'd listened then. This had been the happiest place. Nothing had intruded.

Could be a burglar.

But what if it was Rosemary? Maybe she was hiding in the secret room. Careful now. I didn't want to shoot her. For all the pain she'd given me, I didn't want her hurt.

Another imprint, an older one, followed. A faint pleasure at hitting a paper target.

Taking a deep breath, I shoved the gun in my coat pocket before more imprints could come. It was a large gun, a .45, and the hilt stuck out of my pocket and would have even if I hadn't placed it on top of my Ruger.

Mr. Taylor stared at me. "Are you listening? I want to know what you're doing here. And give me back my gun."

I took another step back, prepared to defend myself if

necessary. He was bigger, but I was younger and well trained. "I'm here with the police," I said. "Detective Shannon Martin came to check out the place himself. That's his car out there. Unmarked police vehicle."

"How do I know you're telling the truth?"

"Because I have better taste in cars," I retorted. Truth was, I couldn't afford that Mustang if I'd wanted it. "Detective Martin will be back in a minute. In fact, let me give him a call." I fished in my other pocket for my phone, but it had no service.

Great. I was alone with a man who was a suspect, if not for Rosemary's disappearance, then maybe for Cheyenne's death, and I had no phone service. Some smart phone it turned out to be. At least I had the guns—for the moment.

"The question is," I said, "what are you doing here?"

"What? It's my cabin."

"That your wife gave us permission to search. You almost never come up here. Why come tonight?" It was barely seven-thirty, so he must have driven here directly after work. "We're investigating your daughter's disappearance and a murder, so anything you do is of interest."

"Judith told me she'd given the police permission to come here. Look, can we sit down? It's been a long day."

I nodded. "You take the love seat."

He obeyed reluctantly, poorly concealing irritation at being told what to do on his own property. I moved toward the window, taking out my phone again. Ah, service here. I pushed Shannon's number and sent a text: *visitor.*

Sitting down on a wooden chair that had no sheet cover, I indicated that Mr. Taylor should continue.

"I was angry at first, but then I started thinking that maybe

Rosemary had come here. She knows the cabin well. There are places she could hide."

"You're angry that she might be pulling a joke on you."

He blinked. "Maybe I was, but she's not really like that. She's always frank about things. I taught her that."

"Well, she's not here."

"There is a place here she might be."

"We found the playroom."

Disappointment registered on his face.

"The police who were here earlier didn't find it," I clarified. "But Detective Martin is thorough. By the layers of dust, no one's been in there for years."

I waited a few breaths before saying, "Tell me what happened at the theater. Please." I added this last to make it seem like a request, though truthfully, I was nearly ready to pull his own gun on him and force him to spill the information. "We need to find her. The smallest thing could be important." Sometime during my search of the cabin and experiencing the imprints on his gun, he had fallen on my list of key suspects. Not completely off the list but almost as far down as the producer Walsh.

Shannon appeared in the doorway that opened into the kitchen. He had his gun ready, but he relaxed when he saw I had the situation in hand. He stayed silent, waiting, and I was glad he knew when to keep quiet. If I needed additional pressure, he could step forward, but maybe Barry Taylor would be willing to talk with me now that he wouldn't lose face around his family—or anyone else.

"I went to that theater," Mr. Taylor began. "That *dive*. She'd told me she wanted to see me, and I agreed to meet her, but I didn't know it was there. I thought she wanted to come home and would be ready to come on my terms. But there she was, sitting at a vanity brushing her hair, and I knew right away that she had no intention of leaving."

I perked up at the mention of a brush. "Was anyone else in the room?"

"A brunette. She was standing over by the wall. I could only see part of her since half of her was hidden by the vanity. She said something like, 'Maybe you should listen to the note. Maybe it's serious.' But Rosemary exploded. She said no one was going to take this chance from her, that she was finally going to Broadway. Rosemary turned and saw me then, but before either of us said anything, the girl rushed up to her and grabbed the brush from Rosemary's hand, throwing it down on the vanity."

I leaned forward. "Did she say anything?"

"She said a lot of people had been waiting for that chance and that it wasn't fair for Rosemary to waltz in and take it away."

"Away from her?"

"That's the impression I got. Then she saw me. She told Rosemary they'd talk later and stomped from the room."

"Did Rosemary tell you about the role?"

He shook his head. "Not directly. She told me she'd seen her grandparents, that they were wonderful people, and that they'd been the ones to tell her about this company and the connection the producer had with a relative on Broadway. She said they believed she was good enough to make it."

I imagined that didn't go over well. "What did you say to that?"

"I told her what she did was an embarrassment to our family and that she should come home and get a decent education."

"And?"

He shook his head. "Nothing. She turned her back on me and started to leave the room." He hesitated.

"That was when you pulled her hair?"

He stared down into his hands. "I didn't mean to. I tried to grab her shoulder, but she was too fast."

Show some respect for once in your life—or I'll make you show it! he'd said. I remembered the scene well from the imprint on the princess rock.

"Did she stop?"

"She whirled around to face me. One hand was in the pocket of her jeans, and I remember how frightened she looked. I-I let go, and she turned and left. I followed her, but that other girl was in the hall, and she ducked behind her. She yelled at me to leave. So I did." No emotion showed on his face, but his broad shoulders drooped. "I haven't seen or heard from her since."

Shannon pushed off the door frame where he'd been resting. "Do you know who the other woman was?"

Taylor started slightly, but he met Shannon's gaze and answered. "Yes. I saw her in the newspaper. She's the one they found dead."

My mind whirled with these new developments. Because of the imprints I'd experienced here, I believed Mr. Taylor, though I still disliked him.

"Your son thinks you had something to do with Rosemary's disappearance," I said, fishing for a reaction.

He blinked. "What?"

"Maybe your wife does too."

"I had nothing to do with it! I've told you everything."

I shrugged. "We'll see." I wanted to go on, to tell him what a jerk he was for cutting his in-laws from his children's lives, from his wife's, but it wouldn't matter. His wife would have to find the same backbone Rosemary had found before things could ever be right in that family. The only way I could help them was to find Rosemary.

"Thank you for your cooperation," Shannon said. He knew how to walk the walk when he needed to, but I nearly screamed at the fake politeness. I shut my eyes to hide the emotion, feeling abruptly exhausted—and also feeling that I was missing something.

"Are you finished here?" Mr. Taylor said.

Shannon nodded and handed him the key. "We were supposed to give it to the neighbors, but since you're here, you might as well take it."

I stood and pulled my coat sleeve over my hand before retrieving Mr. Taylor's gun and giving it to him. I really needed to buy new gloves. Shannon's eyes widened at the sight of the .45, but I gave him a smile and preceded him to the door.

Back in the Mustang, Shannon drove down the road and parked. "What are we doing?" I asked.

"Just want to see what Mr. Taylor does now."

"You don't believe him?"

"I never believe anyone. Not fully."

He'd better not be talking about me. "If he's telling the truth, Cheyenne might be the last person to have seen Rosemary alive."

"How inconvenient that Cheyenne is dead."

I snorted. "Makes for a stronger argument that the cases are connected."

"We've known that was likely all along. But connected doesn't mean the same perp."

"No." I sighed. "Did the crime people find anything on Cheyenne's body? Something I might be able to get an imprint from?"

"They should be finished processing everything in the morning or after lunch at the latest, but it was pretty much just what you saw on Saturday."

"Well, she was wearing some jewelry I could read, and a costume. A lot of the costumes at the theater have some kind of an imprint. They aren't like regular clothes, though even those hold an imprint if the experience is potent enough."

Shannon scowled, and I felt my stomach clench, not at his expression but at what I'd said. We both knew dying created very strong imprints. "I was hoping you wouldn't have to do that."

I shrugged. "So was I."

Minutes ticked by as we sat in silence. I looked over to find him watching me with those eyes that stole my breath. All at once my exhaustion vanished, and my nerves hummed with anticipation.

"Autumn," he said, his voice sounding gruff and unused, though we'd just been talking. "At the theater when we were alone in the kitchen . . ."

The moment I'd been waiting for. Maybe. "Yeah?"

Another ten painful seconds passed before he reached for me and I for him. My stomach rumbled, but I ignored it. He didn't.

"Are you *always* hungry?"

"Pretty much." I grinned, my eyes going to his lips. It was time. A revving engine broke our concentration. Shannon glanced toward the cabin. "Looks like he's leaving."

"I think he's telling the truth. At least about Rosemary."

"Maybe." Shannon sighed and started his engine. "We should follow to make sure."

"I thought you weren't on duty."

He gave me a faint smile. "You'll never forgive me if we don't do everything we can to find her. Or yourself."

He was probably right. I still had nightmares over our first case together and the little girl we'd found too late. Even saving another child didn't lessen the loss of the first.

As we followed Taylor, my heartbeat eventually returned to normal, and the exhaustion crept in again. I fell into a doze and wasn't aware of anything until we pulled in front of my long-closed shop where I'd left my car.

"Welcome back to the land of the living," Shannon said.

"Taylor?"

"He went straight home. Which is what you should do."

I was awake enough to feel disappointment and exhausted enough that it must have shown in my face. He reached over and touched my chin, turning me to face him. "Unfortunately, we're not alone." His eyes went to the Herb Shoppe where the lights were still on. Through the glass front, I could see Jake walking to the door. That was enough to bring me back to my senses. I couldn't hurt Jake, not here, not like this.

"I'll see you tomorrow," I said. "I'll come to the station."

"I'll check on the vic's clothes. What time would be good?"

"I'm not sure. Can I let you know? Maybe early afternoon.

Tawnia and I have an appointment sometime tomorrow, but we're not sure exactly when. Hopefully in the morning."

He lifted a questioning brow.

"With our biological grandmother," I conceded. "But Rosemary's disappearance is more important, so let me know if they clear things early."

"Okay."

I slid from the car and into the rain. Wearily, I tugged on my hood, already missing the fluffy snowflakes at the cabin.

Shannon dipped his head toward me before driving away.

Jake emerged from his shop, locking the door behind him. "I thought that was you. I was just going to call. See if you were up for something tonight."

"What are you doing here so late?" Not waiting for me, I hoped. Knowing him as well as I did, I bet he wanted to ask about Shannon but wouldn't because he'd promised to be patient.

"Inventory. I had nothing else to do, and it's overdue. Guess what? We got a little busy this afternoon, so I called Thera in, and she had a successful hour or two in your shop."

"Good." For sure I'd have to go on another antiques hunting excursion this weekend. I'd missed last week.

"Have you been reading imprints?"

"Yeah. They weren't bad, but there were a lot. It's been a long day." I briefly ran down what I'd been doing, including the glass burglar, Tawnia's new role in the play, and what had happened at the cabin. I left out Mr. Taylor's gun because Jake was in the same club as Shannon, wanting to protect me.

Besides, I hadn't added even one more bruise to my collection tonight. I felt more guilty leaving out what had almost happened between Shannon and me. It was crazy. I'd grown to trust Shannon and at some level I wanted to be with him, but when I was with Jake, our long friendship was everything. No wonder Shannon was frustrated with me.

Not that he'd pushed.

Maybe I wanted him to. I'd meant it when I said that I needed to experience firsthand the options. I wasn't the kind to live on dreams. Actions were what I believed in.

"Well, everything's locked up now," Jake said. "Would you rather me drive you home? Wouldn't want you falling asleep at the wheel."

"No, I'm fine." Actually, I was starving since I'd missed dinner, but if I mentioned that he'd feel obligated to feed me. "Thanks for taking care of everything. I owe you." I hugged him.

"How about dinner tomorrow?"

"Can we play it by ear? I may have to be at the theater with Tawnia. No way am I leaving her there alone. Something's not right at that place."

His brow scrunched, and I could tell he was considering my being at the theater at all. I wasn't waiting around for his objections. "See you tomorrow, Jake." I put a jaunty note in my voice.

I hurried to my car, feeling his eyes on me. Part of me wanted to turn back and ask him to come home with me so we could make dinner together as we had so many times before. I wouldn't mind the company, but having him there might make my choices more difficult, especially as tired and vulnerable as I was feeling after my almost encounter with Shannon. No, being alone with Jake now was definitely not a good idea.

I was halfway home when my phone rang. I checked the caller ID before putting in my earpiece and answering. "Hello?"

"Autumn, thank heaven you picked up." Tawnia sounded frantic, which was so far from her norm that I was instantly alert.

"What's wrong? Is it Destiny?"

"Someone just called my phone. It was a threat! They told me I had to quit the play or else." "Or else what?"

"Just 'or else.' What more needs to be said? Good grief, Autumn, this is your forte, not mine. Bret won't be here until tomorrow, and I'm scared! There's no name or anything on the caller ID. Just a number."

"I'll be right there," I said. "Keep the doors locked."

Chapter 15

The smell of burnt pancakes wakened me from a sound sleep in the spare room on the main floor at Tawnia's where Tawnia, Destiny, and I had all spent the night together.

Of course I'd ended up staying with Tawnia. She'd been too unsettled after the threat to stay alone. Since the only people she'd recently given her contact information was to Walsh's acting company, I suspected one of the disgruntled actors was playing a prank.

Not a very funny one, in light of the murder.

Of course it could be the actual murderer, but since phone calls were traceable in large part, wouldn't that be stupid?

I wasn't the morning person Tawnia was, though I always opened my shop by nine, but I should have risen earlier to save the pancakes. My sister was perfect in everything except cooking and sewing and growing things. She simply didn't have the patience or the talent, which was odd, considering that she could struggle over a drawing or a painting for hours and that the inside of her cupboards resembled something from a magazine. She was the quintessential organized person. I both admired her and despaired because of it.

Yawning, I stumbled into the kitchen, wearing some of my sister's pajamas. I always kept a change of clothes here and various odds and ends like a toothbrush, but anything I didn't have, Tawnia would pull out of a drawer somewhere. I didn't understand the purpose of using pajamas when underclothes did the job, but Tawnia swore by them, so when I stayed with her, I acquiesced to her pleas.

I picked up the spatula, barely in time to rescue the most recent batch of pancakes from the griddle. My sister had obviously gone to some trouble with the pancakes, since they were homemade from whole wheat flour instead of her usual packaged mix. From someone who adored white pancakes, I recognized this as the sacrifice it was.

"Any more calls?" I asked. Tawnia glanced up briefly as I took over. She was drawing on a large pad at the table while Destiny lay on a blanket on the floor, surrounded by a mass of toys she appeared to have no interest in, her fingers being adequate entertainment.

"No." She shivered. "The one was enough."

"It had to be one of the actors." First in my mind was Vera, the brunette who'd worn the red wig. She'd supposedly fainted when I'd found Cheyenne's body, but the fit she'd thrown when she hadn't been given the Juliet role yesterday remained with me. "I wish you hadn't given them your info."

"I had to. They needed to let me know when we're doing rehearsals. They're practicing two different plays and have one more week of performing *The Comedy of Errors*, so they'll be moving rehearsals around until they find a good fit."

I tasted the pancake batter and hid a grimace as I rummaged through her cupboard for the spices I'd given her. A little organic sunflower oil would also go a long way toward making these palatable. "I really don't think you should do the play," I said as I poured the doctored mixture onto the griddle.

Tawnia's jaw tightened. "I'm not going to let some joker run me out. I'm sticking to it until we find that poor boy's sister. That is, as long as you'll watch the baby while I go. I don't want her there until we find who's behind all this."

"Well, I'm not leaving you alone, so Bret will have to watch her. Or your neighbor will. She's great with Destiny, isn't she?"

"Yeah, but Sophie's own two kids are already a handful."

"She'll handle it, or I'll get Shannon to assign an officer to you. He'll have to now that you've been threatened."

"Maybe." She sighed. "I forgot to ask last night. What did Shannon and Paige say about the father connection?"

"They added it to their list of things to check as they go through the actors' backgrounds, but it could take a while. I haven't heard anything. At least Bret will be home tonight." I was counting on him to talk sense into his wife about the play.

Her face became glum. "Actually, he called, and he has to stay until Thursday. I'm sure he won't stay longer than he has to, though. He likes to be here to oversee every bit of the rebuilding."

Rebuilding the Hawthorne Bridge, she meant. "You mean he won't stay any longer than he has to because he can't bear to be away from you any more than you like to be away from him. It's not because of the bridge."

"I do miss him." A secret little smile played on her lips.

I knew the love Tawnia felt for Bret, but was it similar to my feelings for Jake? Once I had thought so, but there is no way she'd ever consider kissing another man, so now I knew the answer was no, and if the answer was no, then pursuing my feeling for Shannon was the logical thing to do.

I still hated the idea of hurting Jake, of letting him go. He was a good man, and he'd been the best of friends. I wouldn't have made it through Winter's death without him.

"Did you tell Bret everything?" I asked.

Tawnia set down her pencil. "I told him about Laina coming today and about the play, but not about the murder or the threat, if that's what you're referring to." The sharpness in her voice said she knew that was exactly what I meant. "He'd have me layered in bubble wrap and sent home to my parents to protect me if he knew any of that. When he gets home, I'll explain everything. It'll probably all be over by then anyway."

I took off the pancakes and poured more batter on the griddle. "So what are you drawing?" I was hoping it was something that would help us solve the case.

"I'm just fiddling."

I crossed to the table and looked at the pencil drawing. A grizzled man sat on the front porch of a wide, squat house that had seen better days. The surrounding trees made the place seem isolated, but the paper was big enough that I could clearly make out his features. "You don't think this has anything to do with Rosemary or the murder, do you?" I asked.

Tawnia laughed. "No, I don't. No girl on the floor, no sign of anything weird. Just an old man sitting on his porch."

"Looks cold. He's wearing a lot of layers. You sure your advertising firm doesn't have a client who sells cold-weather clothes?"

"Not that I know of." She sighed. "Though they might actually have a new account I haven't heard about yet. I'm out of things since I started working from home. I wish the new creative director hadn't canceled the meeting yesterday."

She complained, but at the same time, I knew she wouldn't give up being home with Destiny for anything. I bent to get a closer look at the drawing. "He looks a little familiar."

"Probably based on someone I've seen around. It's hard to create a completely new character. My drawings are usually composites of many people."

I retrieved the newest batch of pancakes and poured the rest of the batter before bringing the plate to the table. There were enough good ones to give even the two of us a hearty meal. Tawnia arose and took organic raspberry jam from the fridge for me and heated maple syrup for herself.

"I hope Laina comes early," I said between ravenous bites. Tawnia had fed me leftover pork roast last night, but I felt starved. Too many imprints in one day. "I mean, if we have to go over to the theater for rehearsal."

"You could stay at the shop with the baby."

"No. I'll go. I already called Thera. She's coming in at ten. Even if we're slow, we did enough business yesterday that I won't go broke."

She sighed. "I'll make it up to you. I'll watch the store on Friday morning while you go antiques hunting, okay? Provided I don't have a meeting at work I have to go in for. Right now it's rescheduled for tomorrow morning."

We hurried through the rest of breakfast and were nearly ready for the day when Tawnia's cell phone rang. She froze and looked at me before checking the ID. "Not the same number as last night."

I'd called the number when I arrived, but it only rang and

rang. I suspected a phone booth, and I'd texted the number to Paige, who said she'd have it traced. Yes, I'd contacted Paige, not Shannon. I was half afraid he'd come barging over and half afraid he wouldn't.

"Well, answer it."

"Hello?" Tawnia said. "Oh, I see. Okay. That's fine. Thanks for calling."

"Well?"

"It was Paxton Seaver. He says they're canceling the Juliet rehearsal today, and he'll let me know what time tomorrow or Thursday. He wasn't sure which."

"That's odd after how anxious they've been to get going on it. I bet that producer Walsh is busting a vein or two with anxiety. I wonder what happened."

Tawnia grinned. "Well, at least you don't have to worry about me today. Or about watching Emma."

"Maybe a day or two with no rehearsals will calm down whoever made that call." Or give me enough time to track them down. This was my sister they'd threatened.

Tawnia glanced at the time on the clock stove. "We'd better leave if you're going to open your shop on time."

At nine sharp we were at Autumn's Antiques with the door open and ready for business.

Jake came in, looking stunning in a black-and-white shirt and white pants. He knew how to brighten up the coldest mornings. "Hey, no rain today. Might even see a bit of sun."

Tawnia laughed. "You're a bit of sun in those pants. Goodness, Jake, don't you know it isn't kosher to wear white in the winter?"

"Kosher? I hate to tell you this, but I'm not Jewish. And

I don't eat kosher foods." He reached out to Destiny, and the baby promptly latched onto his finger. She loved playing with him as long as he didn't try to hold her.

"You know what I mean." Tawnia pulled Destiny away from Jake's finger and went around the counter to sit on a stool. I glanced toward the door.

"Waiting for someone?" Jake's voice was matter-of-fact, but I suspected he thought we were waiting for Shannon.

"Our biological grandmother," I said. "We're not sure what time she's coming."

Jake smiled, his teeth very white in his dark face. "Wow. Big day. Let me know if you need to leave. I'll keep an eye on the store."

"Thanks. Thera will be in soon too."

Laina Walkling showed up twenty minutes later. There was nothing to separate her from any other customer who might walk in the door except a slight tugging in my chest that I recognized as connection. I cut off my conversation with Tawnia in mid-sentence.

Still on her stool, Tawnia froze. "What is it?" she asked in an undertone.

"I think it's her."

We waited, watching the woman approach. Her hair was dark brown like ours—probably dyed, given her age—and cut becomingly at her chin. She was built like us, too, average height and slender. Not quite as wiry as I was now, but a bit more rounded like Tawnia. Her eyes were both blue, and under her coat she wore a lavender suit that reminded me of what Tawnia had liked to wear when she worked full time. The type, but not the color. The light purple fit the woman's age well, which Mariel in Hayesville had said was around sixty-five.

She smiled, and even before the ever-collected Tawnia could speak, she said, "Yes, I can see the resemblance. Especially in the eyes."

"To Kendall?" Tawnia asked. I wanted to echo the question. The retired adoption worker we'd tracked down had been sure Kendall's eyes were blue.

"No, to your father."

That shut us both up. Disappointment flooded me. I didn't want a legacy of any kind from the man who'd hurt our mother.

"But you look like my Kendall too," Laina went on. "Which one of you is Tawnia?"

"I am," Tawnia said, bouncing Destiny, who had decided to begin fussing.

"Oh, yes, the baby. Wow, I can't believe I'm a great-grandmother."

Tawnia's lips pursed, and I knew she was thinking that this woman hadn't yet earned the right to be a great-grandmother to Destiny. She obviously hadn't been much of a mother to Kendall.

"Can you tell us about Kendall?" I asked. "We can go in the back room. There's more seating there."

"What about your customers?"

"There's a bell at the door and another on the counter if they need me."

A short while later Laina was ensconced in my ratty easy chair, looking as comfortable as Tawnia looked awkward on the wood chair next to the worktable. I was on the worktable itself, my bare feet and legs folded under me in my usual Indian-style position. After a bit more small talk, Laina launched into her story.

"I was barely sixteen when I had Kendall. I had no family,

and her father was long out of the picture. I did what I could. I lived with some girls and worked at a bar. I thought after a few years it'd get better, but it never did." She sighed. "I started drinking. Doing drugs. Dating a lot of men, who would sometimes help me with the bills. We barely scraped by. I didn't realize then what a disfavor I'd done to my daughter in keeping her. I thought the love I had for her would move mountains. I only realized my mistake when I learned how she got pregnant. That was what made me change. Oh, I didn't change right away. At first I blamed Kendall because Cody left, and I'd thought he was different from the others, that he'd stick around. But he was as caught in the life as I was. There's never an escape until you make the decision yourself, and sometimes you have to scrape bottom before that can happen. I hit that right before Kendall disappeared from the bar where she was working. I knew we couldn't keep the baby. We couldn't do that to another child. It deserved better."

She paused and looked at each of us in turn. "You had a good life, didn't you?" Her eyes begged us to say that we had. For a moment she looked much, much older.

I nodded. "We weren't raised together, but we each had a good life and parents who loved and took care of us. Adoption was the right thing. For us, anyway."

Her face relaxed. "I'm grateful for that, at least."

"Did you know about Kendall's death?" Tawnia asked.

She nodded. "I knew, but not for a year or so after. I'd been looking for her, and finally someone sent me a letter." She blinked at the tears in her eyes. "I don't suppose you can imagine what that felt like. I'd gone through all the therapy so I could be there for her, but she was never going to be there again. I almost gave up."

"But you didn't," Tawnia said.

Laina managed a smile. "No. It was touch and go for a while, but I eventually met a good man and got married. We had two kids. My husband knows about Kendall. The children don't. I never dreamed I'd get the chance to meet Kendall's child—children." She shook her head. "Twins. Who'd have dreamed?"

"They don't run in the family?"

"Not on my side." She hesitated. "Do you want to know about your father?"

Ah, so she hadn't missed the earlier tension. "He had eyes like ours?" I said in answer.

"He did. Came down from his father's side, I think. I don't know if he really knew. His mother died when he was young, and he was raised in a series of foster homes. Not good ones for the most part. He got into drugs early. Ran away. Lived on the street. I loved him so much, or thought I did. What happened just about killed us both." She swallowed hard and held her hand to her throat as if it hurt. Her eyes were once again full of tears.

Killed them both? I could imagine Laina suffering, but this man, Cody, had been the cause of the heartache.

"Would you like a little herbal tea?" I forced myself to ask, though I wanted to reject her pity for that monster. I'd put the kettle with the water and herbs on the stove when we'd entered, and the tea should be hot by now.

A tinkling signaled someone had come into the shop, and Tawnia arose. "I'll get the tea. You go see who it is."

It was Thera, tying on her customary blue apron over her blue dress. I felt a calmness just by looking at her. Maybe she was right about the color blue.

"You're early," I said. "Must have read my mind."

She smiled. "Your visitor is here already?"

"Yeah. My sister too."

"Don't worry. I'll take care of the customers." My turn to smile. "Hopefully, there'll be some."

"There will. It's not raining."

I admired her optimism. She did have a point, though. For Portland dwellers, not raining in the winter was almost like sunshine.

"Go on, dear."

In the back room, Tawnia had settled the baby in her car seat and poured everyone a cup of tea. Resuming my position on the worktable, I swirled the amber liquid around in my cup.

Laina had recovered her composure, for which I felt immense relief. She'd obviously suffered enough already. Still, I wasn't quite sure I was ready to hear anything more about my father. My father was Winter, not some animal who'd hurt a fifteen-year-old girl in her own home.

"His name is Cody Beckett," Laina began, her voice loud in the silence. "He was a gorgeous man. Blond hair, those amazing eyes, strong build. Good worker, when he wasn't drugged up—which was pretty much all the time back then. As I said, he'd had a hard life. We didn't talk about it much, but I knew there were things he was hiding from, things that had happened in his youth. He was in some abusive foster homes." She gave us a wistful smile. "I thought I was in love, but I was really just looking for someone to take care of me, and Cody couldn't even take care of himself." She grimaced. "I was pretty much wrapped up in him. I liked being with someone who could get me drugs."

"And Kendall?" Tawnia asked softly, her eyes going to her own daughter.

"She was used to me having different boyfriends, bringing them home. Cody stayed with us for several months. Then she had a birthday. Her fifteenth." Laina stopped talking and stared down at her hands. When she continued, her voice was soft. "I bought her a stuffed bear. A brown one. She loved stuffed animals, and I knew she'd love that one because it was so soft and cuddly. But when she left, she didn't take it with her."

Kendall had written about the bear in the letter she'd left us. "Because she wasn't a child anymore," I said, "not after that night." Tears started down Laina's face. "We'd had a cake. I drank too much. Cody brought the drugs. It was all a blur after that. Late the next afternoon, I awoke and found him sitting on Kendall's bed, holding that bear. His face was . . . it was horrible. I didn't know what had happened, but I think he'd realized, and he felt terrible."

"He should have." Since she'd died in childbirth, I felt he was also responsible for Kendall's death.

She nodded. "He left after that, though I begged him to stay. I didn't want to lose my supply, you know. When Kendall came back to visit, she told me what had happened, but I didn't believe her. Not right away. I was still so drunk I barely knew my own name. When it finally began penetrating, I realized it was all my fault. I'd let my baby down. That was the beginning of the change for me. I'll never forgive myself that it came too late for Kendall." She put her face in her hands and sobbed.

Tawnia and I looked at each other helplessly. "There were complications during delivery," I said. "That's nobody's fault. Kendall had medical care, the best at the time."

Laina lifted her tear-stained face. "She should have been home playing with her teddy bear." She had a point, and nothing I could say would alleviate the pain or her guilt. It was something she'd have to live with the rest of her life.

We were quiet as we waited for Laina to collect herself again. I felt numb, and Tawnia had tears in her eyes.

"Cody went to jail," Laina continued suddenly. "Not for what he did to Kendall but for beating a guy at a bar. Attempted manslaughter. Only Cody wasn't guilty of that. He wasn't even there that night, but he didn't try to defend himself. I believe he wanted to go to jail to make up for what he did to Kendall."

He'd gone to prison for a crime he didn't commit to pay for the crime he did commit. There was a strange sort of justice in the idea.

"He's still alive?" I asked.

She nodded. "Maybe. Last I heard, which was probably ten years ago, he was off the drugs—he got off them in prison—but he spent his time between jobs drunk. Back then he lived on the edge of Hayesville. Way out. Made huge sculptures from junk and giant tree logs. A guy sold them for him. Everyone in Hayesville knew about Cody, and that he never left his place. Maybe he stayed out there to make sure he didn't hurt anyone again. If he's alive, he's probably still there."

"But you got married," Tawnia said.

"Yes." Laina ran a tissue under her eyes. "My husband owns a car repair shop. That's how we met—my car broke down. He runs it now with our son. We have two children, both married, and four grandchildren. My son-in-law is studying to be a dentist, so my daughter lives with us. He only sees them on the weekends. It's tough on my daughter, but I don't know what I'll do when the grandkids move out. They're pretty much my life. Them and my husband."

Grandkids. We were also her grandkids.

I pushed away from that vein of thought. I didn't expect anything from this woman, and I didn't want her to expect anything from me. "So, did any, ah, talents run in your family?" I asked. "Or did Cody ever mention any that ran in his? Things that might have been handed down genetically to us. Particularly anything . . . uh, unusual."

Laina's brow creased at my odd question. "Well, I have a way with plants, but that's really the extent of my abilities. I love cooking and taking care of my family. I didn't always love it, but I do now. As for Cody, he once told me his mother painted. There was something odd about her, though, and she was put in a sanitarium and died when he was young. I don't know the particulars. Cody didn't like to talk about it. He was very sensitive. He paid attention to details. Sometimes he seemed to know things, and I didn't know how."

She frowned and swallowed hard. "Like when I found him holding Kendall's bear. He hadn't been any more aware than I was that night—he couldn't have been with what he'd been using—but somehow he knew what he'd done, and that's what made him leave."

I looked at Tawnia. Could it be that Kendall had left an imprint of terror on the bear? If Cody shared my ability, he would have relived his actions as though he'd been the victim. I knew for myself that such an experience changed you forever.

I had to know. That meant I'd have to visit him and hear the truth for myself. Face him as Kendall couldn't.

Later, I thought. *After this case is over. After I think about it some more.* A large part of me was relieved to have the excuse. I think I'd heard all of the past that I could stand for right now.

Laina's eyes were on Destiny. "Do you think I could hold her?"

"Sure." Tawnia didn't hesitate. "A minute is probably all she'll stand, though. She's at an age when she really only likes Autumn and me. Even my husband has to really work to get her to stay with him if I'm around."

Laina enjoyed her minute with Destiny, giving her back when she started fussing. The numbness was wearing off now, and I was glad Laina had come. She asked about our lives and what we were doing. I told her about the antiques shop, my herbs, and my love of organic foods, purposefully leaving out my work with the police. Tawnia told her about her part-time work as an artist for the advertising agency, her parents in Kansas, and her engineer husband. A peace seemed to settle over Laina, as though knowing we were content went a long way toward lessening her guilt and filling the hole Kendall's death had left in her life.

"Well," Laina said some time later, trying to arise from the chair. "I'd better get to my appointment."

I grabbed her arm and helped her up. She felt thin and frail under the long sleeve of the suit.

"You will keep in touch, won't you?" Laina asked hopefully.

"Sure." Tawnia said. "Thank you so much for coming."

"Thank you for looking me up. It helps to know what happened to Kendall's baby—babies."

We watched her leave in silence.

"Well," Tawnia said, bouncing Destiny, "I'm going to feed Emma."

I was glad she didn't want to talk about it now. I didn't either. What I wanted to do was take Shannon's gun from my coat pocket and shoot up a few targets or go to my taekwondo class and spar with someone. The punching bag there might help. Since tonight was my Tuesday class at the martial arts studio, I was at least partly in luck.

For now, I opted to clean out my glass cases. It needed to be done, and my mood couldn't grow any worse. Tawnia came to help me after a while, leaving Destiny asleep in her car seat by the counter.

We had started on the third case when my phone beeped with a text from Shannon. "They're finished processing Cheyenne's belongings," I said.

"You should go, then." Tawnia paused in her cleaning. "Thera's had only three customers all morning. She doesn't need either of us. I'll finish up this case and then go shopping. I'm practically out of food. Is there anything I should pick up for you?"

I shook my head. My organic grocery list would take her out of her way and to three more stores, which wasn't exactly a lot of fun with a baby in tow. "What then?" I asked.

"I'll head home. I have some drawings to work on. You're coming back to stay again tonight, right?"

That she asked showed she was still worried about the threat. "Sure. But you can go to my place and wait for me if you'd rather."

She shook her head. "I'll go next door to Sophie's if I get worried. Like I told you, I'm doing this play. I need to do my part to help Liam."

"I think you just want to do the play," I teased.

She grinned. "It is a lot of fun."

"See you in a bit." I hugged her. "I'll let Thera know where I'll be."

"Autumn?"

I turned back to her. "What?"

"That picture I drew of the man in front of that house. Do you think it might be Cody? I wish I'd brought it so I could have asked Laina."

A shiver rippled through me. Now I knew why he'd looked familiar. He looked like us. Not his white hair, but the shape of his eyes, and maybe his face. I nodded, and she gave me a wistful smile. "We're going to have to meet him, aren't we?"

I nodded. "But not today."

"Right."

I left her then, thinking of Cody's mother who'd died in a sanitarium, a place where people had once gone to convalesce from a long illness. She'd been an artist, like Tawnia.

Had she also shared the strange part of Tawnia's talent? Maybe we'd never know.

Chapter 16

Paige was waiting for me at the station instead of Shannon, looking official in an actual police uniform, complete with her sidearm. Her iron-straight blond hair looked freshly done, though I knew she'd been here for hours. Paige was one of those rare people who would have looked just as at home at a high society ball as in a shoot-out with drug dealers.

"I have everything waiting for you in a room," she told me. "I hope you don't mind if we record your examination. In case we need it for court later."

"Sure," I said, though I suspected it wasn't to prove I'd "seen" something but rather to prove I hadn't contaminated the evidence. "So how was your date last night?"

Paige grinned. "Better than yours, I bet."

I thought about the almost kisses and rolled my eyes. "You got that right."

"Oh, about that number you texted me last night. The call did come from a pay phone. I've sent someone to dust for prints and requested footage from a nearby security camera, but it's up in the air if it'll show anything useful. The angle isn't all that good."

"That's what I was afraid of. Thanks."

The precinct was alive with activity, as it always seemed to be. There was barely a hiccup in the action as I followed Paige through the department, though there had been a time when everyone had stopped and stared at the odd woman who claimed to do strange things. Progress.

"Hey, Autumn."

I waved at Peirce Elvey, a short, flaming-haired officer whose usual grin stood out on his freckled face. He was always ready with a smile or joke and from the beginning had treated me normally— not like someone to avoid or to use. Most of the other officers were still just faces to me, except for Paige and, of course, Shannon, but Peirce I considered a friend.

"So where's Shannon?" I asked Paige, feeling a slight heat in my face at his name. Or maybe it was because it was too hot inside the building. Too hot in the winter and too cold in the summer. They'd probably save taxpayers a bundle if they could regulate their thermostats.

"He's questioning the director of the Portland Players."

"Paxton Seaver? I thought he'd already been interviewed." At least that told me why rehearsal had been canceled. Can't practice a play without the director, who was also a main character.

Paige gave a short laugh. "Ah, but we uncovered new information about Mr. Seaver. Apparently, Seaver is not his real last name, and under his real last name we discovered he has a violent record involving an ex-wife. Two incidences of domestic violence."

"Seaver? Really?" He'd appeared so mild, so nondescript,

except when on stage. I'd guessed that he was behind any artistic success the company had, aside from Walsh's rich aunt, but domestic violence and a fake name? That didn't fit with my impression of him.

"Interestingly enough, his real last name is Earl, the same name as the director who originally started the Portland Players."

A ripple of goose bumps ran down my back. "Oh, the father connection." Tawnia would be happy to know there was some value in what she'd overheard.

"Yes, but it's not the only one we've found. It appears that the father of Rosemary's still-missing boyfriend, Grady Mullins, was at one time an actor with the Portland Players. That was before he branched off and created the company where Rosemary used to work before quitting to play Juliet. There may be a longtime grudge we've overlooked."

"And another reason why Grady could have been so upset about Rosemary taking the Juliet role. If she's as good an actress as I think she is, Grady's father wouldn't have been happy about her defection. You say Grady is still missing?"

"We've been searching for him since the break-in at the theater yesterday. Not even his father knows where he is. Or claims not to know."

"I thought Grady hadn't been released in time to have made it to the theater."

"Well, we might have the time wrong because he fits the description, and every other likely person has a solid alibi. The very fact that he's on the run might mean we let him go prematurely."

"What about the other actors? Weren't there two who were involved in the theater eight years ago as children?"

"Yes, but their roles were very limited and only part time. They didn't tour with the group, and their fathers or mothers weren't connected to the theater in any way. They were found through a local high school Walsh sometimes does free performances for."

We'd reached the room now, and Paige indicated that I should sit at the table near where an officer was already in place behind a video camera on a tripod. Two other officers were in the room, but she dismissed them. I was glad to have less of an audience. I might find absolutely nothing, but what I found could knock me out, if the imprint was strong enough.

"Wait," Paige told me. "Shannon wanted to be here. I've already let him know you've arrived."

I wasn't surprised. The guy had saved my life, and I'd saved his. It was a hard habit to break. He'd learned the hard way how imprints could affect me, and he felt responsible. Of course, there was also that other aspect of our relationship.

"What about the rest of the company?" I asked, removing my coat and placing it on the back of my chair. Paige had cleared the gun when I entered the station, so it was still there in my pocket along with my cell phone.

"No one else has parents connected to the theater that we are able to determine. There have been nine divorces and several deaths, and one actress was adopted at age ten after her mother died, though we don't have information on the biological parents. She spent some time in foster homes. She wasn't at the first one long, less than six months, and the foster parents were later convicted of child abuse. She had better luck at the second home; they ended up adopting her and two other children before they quit being foster parents."

"Who's the actress?" I wondered if it was Cheyenne, because if it was, maybe my long-shot idea about Mr. Taylor being her father had some basis after all. Except Paige was talking about suspects here, not the victim.

She looked through several papers in her hand. "Erica Tibble."

Erica? Ah, now perhaps I understood the short-haired actress's abrupt, bitter manner a little better. She'd experienced early losses, which had hardened her. At least she'd finally found a home. I hoped it had been a good one. Maybe if I had a chance, I'd ask.

"But no information on her biological parents?" That seemed a gap we shouldn't ignore.

"Well, the mother died of a drug overdose, so there's no current connection there. We have no information on what she did for a job, if anything. The father was never named."

What if the father was someone at the theater? There weren't more than two or three actors the right age, but there were some. Or maybe it was Mr. Taylor, though how that might work into the murder, I had no idea. Unless Cheyenne had found out and was blackmailing him, and that's what got her killed. A long stretch at best. "Is there any way we could find out if the father is someone connected to the case?"

"We could ask Ms. Tibble. She might know. But short of doing DNA testing on everyone involved—which would require a warrant—we're pretty much at a dead end."

I thought of that picture in Walsh's office with the dark-haired girl I'd thought at first was Erica. "What was Erica doing before she joined the Portland Players?"

"She attended a community college full time. More than

full time, actually. All drama, dancing, or singing classes. No GE. She was there two years before joining the company six years ago."

So Erica had been telling the truth about when she joined the Portland Players. Whoever the other dark-haired girl was, she didn't seem to be connected with the theater now. The police must have obtained the full list of employees eight years ago and would have researched her. I needed to let that go and find something that clicked.

"Cheyenne wasn't adopted too, by chance?" I asked to make sure.

"No. Her parents flew in from Denver on Sunday. Nice couple. It's really sad."

I frowned, glad I hadn't been around to witness their pain. I knew too well how it felt to view the body of a loved one.

So still no obvious motive for Mr. Taylor, though Paxton Seaver was looking more and more likely. My mind went over my mental list of suspects for someone we might have over-looked. "Nothing on an actress named Vera?"

"No. Why?"

I shrugged. "One minute she's talking about how the play they're doing is bad luck, and the next she's upset because she didn't respond fast enough to be in it. She has a boyfriend there, too, another actor. A playboy—you know the type."

"I'll take another look," Paige said. "You never know. Ah, here he is."

Shannon walked through the door, his sandy hair mussed on top as though he'd been running his hand through it. "Hi, Autumn."

"Hi." I hadn't felt self-conscious before, but I did now.

"You can go," Shannon told the officer behind the video camera. "I'll do this."

The officer nodded and relinquished his post. I smiled. The fewer witnesses for me, the better, though for all I knew, they would show this video to their officers as a part of training.

I hoped not.

"So what's Seaver's story?" I asked.

Shannon shook his head. "The director says his father has nothing to do with the theater now and that he'd been retired several years before Seaver took over as director."

"So the murder isn't a way of trying to get back at Walsh for somehow gaining control of the company?"

Shannon left the camera and sat down in a chair next to me. "Seaver says there really isn't anything to control. They survive month to month."

"You believe him?" Paige asked.

"I don't know. He doesn't seem to have much love for Walsh, or his father for that matter, but he's intent on doing this play. I think he thinks it's his way out. His big break."

I snorted. "He's not the only one who's thinking that way."

"There is a twist in his story. This morning Mr. Paxton Seaver, AKA Mr. Paxton Earl, claims to have received a threatening note."

I leaned forward, nearly placing my hand on the objects on the table by accident. Not a good idea where murder was involved. "What did it say?"

"Not to continue with the play or another actor in it would die." Shannon sighed. "He can't produce the note, though. Says he showed it to Walsh, who thought it was nonsense. I called Walsh, and he claims he saw it but threw it away."

"So we go through the trash," Paige said.

Shannon shook his head. "According to Walsh, today was trash day. It could be anywhere by now."

"If there really was a note," I said, "they should have called you, which means Seaver could be lying, and Walsh might be covering for him in order to save the company."

"Seaver had canceled the rehearsal before we brought him in for questioning, so I'm not quite sure he's lying." Shannon stood and walked to the small window.

"Has to be," Paige said. "He's looking more and more like a suspect to me."

"On the other hand, he might be telling the truth," I countered. "After all, Tawnia received that threatening call, and I know she's not lying."

Shannon grimaced. "Speaking of which, I wish you would have told me about that last night."

"Paige and I had it covered." Better he understand from the beginning that I was my own person. Falling for him—if that's what I was doing—wouldn't change who I was. I had a job to do every bit as much as he did, and I was growing more confident in my ability to protect myself and find leads in our cases.

"I had a patrol car sweep Tawnia's neighborhood several times," Paige said. "Nothing suspicious. It could be a prank and totally unrelated to Seaver's claim." A smile touched her lips. "Hey, I just had an idea. What if, after we're finished here, we find something on Seaver for Autumn to read? We have cause."

"We'd still need a warrant at this point." Shannon had left the window and now fiddled with something on the camera.

She shrugged. "Unless it's voluntary. Or put them in a room together. He might not even have to know."

"He's not exactly going to hand over his wallet."

I watched them go back and forth as though I weren't in the room. I'd become a simple asset again, which didn't feel as good as one might think.

"Uh, I'm ready to do this," I said. There were imprints on the objects in front of me. I could sense them. One by one, I removed my antique rings and put them into a pocket of my jeans.

I touched the costume first, but there were no imprints from Cheyenne, only fading ones from actresses who'd worn it in the past. Okay, moving to the shoes. Faint imprint signaling pride of ownership. They were fine shoes. Her own, not from the prop room.

"She liked to dress up," I said. "She favored these shoes. Thought they made her look slim."

"She was as skinny as a rail," Paige said with a grimace. "Too thin."

Nothing on the nylons, so I moved on to the small gold earrings. Jewelry was the best holder of imprints, especially fine jewelry, and these looked like white gold, or at the very least silver. The first imprint came from Saturday afternoon as she put on the earrings while dressing for rehearsal.

Who cares if he sees me wear them and reads something into it. I don't care. They go with the costume, and I'm the star now. I'm going to Broadway, not that lying sneak Rosemary. With this thought came a quiver of guilt, but I pushed it away. My day. Don't think about her.

An older imprint followed from Friday, a day before the murder. Cheyenne sitting at a vanity, the earrings in her hand, and Paxton Seaver standing behind her.

"You have to leave me alone! I don't love you, Paxton."

His face twisted, no longer nondescript but mean and dark. "So all this time you've been using me?"

I flipped my hair over her/my shoulder. "How else could I get you to give me the best parts? But it's over and has been since the minute you cast Rosemary instead of me for Juliet."

"She was good for the part! That's the only reason I did it."

"Tell yourself what you like, Paxton. The truth is you just want to keep me here under your thumb. Or maybe you thought playing opposite her would get you to Broadway. Well, I don't care what your reasons were. I have the role now, whether you like it or not, and I'm going to impress Walsh's aunt, if it takes every last breath in my body. I'm going to make all the papers!"

She'd succeeded in that last bit, at least, though not in the way she'd intended.

A third imprint came quickly on the heels of the second, but it was from nearly a year earlier.

I stood in the theater kitchen with Paxton holding the earrings. "For me? Wow, thanks. That's really nice." I laughed. "But it's not my birthday."

Seaver's eyes locked on mine. "I love you, Cheyenne. I have for months."

A wave of revulsion swept through me. But he did the casting. If I let him think I liked him, he'd give me better parts. I could endure a little attention if it got me the practice and the roles I needed to get out of this dive.

"Oh, Paxton." I let him hug me. His lips found mine, and the sensation wasn't as unpleasant as anticipated. He kissed with the same intensity he used when acting. I was the sole focus of his attention. Not bad at all.

No more imprints came, and I set down the earrings, heat rising on my face. I'd liked Paxton Seaver the first day I'd met him, but I'd never expected to share such an intimacy. That was another danger of imprints. I was lucky there had been nothing more graphic.

"Well?" Paige asked.

"Um," I hesitated, wishing I didn't have to say anything. Shannon was behind the camera but not peering into it. "Seaver and Cheyenne were involved. But from what I can tell, she was playing him to get the best roles, and it all fell apart when he put Rosemary in the role of Juliet instead of Cheyenne. She thought he was trying to make it so she had to stay at the company or that he was trying to make himself look better so he'd get his chance on Broadway instead of her. Either way, she wasn't happy. She told him exactly what she thought of him on Friday, the day before she died."

"That's motive," Shannon said.

"But not proof." Paige gestured to the remaining objects. "Maybe there's more."

I knew there was more, I could feel imprints buzzing in front of me. I reached for the ring.

Immediately, I was choking. I couldn't breathe. What was happening? Was I dying? I dragged in gulps of air, but I was still dying. I felt wrapped in plastic. My eyes couldn't focus. My heart raced. My blood burned. My fists clenched, and the ring dug into my fingers. My legs cramped.

The glass. Something had been in the glass.

"Relax," said a voice. "It'll only take a few more minutes." Distorted. But I knew who it was. Didn't I?

Oh, the agony. Everything hurt. Blackness filling the edges of the little bit I could still see. A blurred face with short hair watching. Grinning. Mocking.

Pain, going on and on. First in my chest and spreading

outward. No more thumping of my heart in my ears. Only the unending agony.

Then blessed nothing.

"Autumn! Are you okay? Wake up!"

I lay face-down on the table with my eyes closed, waiting for the scattered remains of who I was to come back to me. It took longer than I expected.

"She needs something else. I don't have my watch." Was that Shannon's voice?

Something was shoved into my hand. Paper? No time to decide as an imprint caught me.

A man laughing as he closed my hand over the tickets. "You'd better hold onto these in case we need to go out. The last time I lost them and had to rebuy tickets to see the show."

The way he's looking at me, I'll save them forever. He just might be the one. Walking into the theater, his arm around my waist. I could feel the pressure of his touch through my coat. So good-looking. Kind. Not to mention smart. My heart thumped with excitement.

I opened my eyes. Both Shannon and Paige were leaning over me, Shannon's arms keeping me on the chair while Paige kneaded my hands.

"You were right, Paige. He really is good-looking," I murmured.

She snatched the tickets from my hand, her face flushing as she shot a sidelong glance at Shannon. He didn't seem to notice. "Are you okay?" he asked.

"I'm not sure. I've never died before." Of course, I hadn't actually stayed with Cheyenne all the way to her death, just until she passed out. Probably a good thing. I didn't know what would happen if I experienced death in an imprint. Would my body believe it had died? Not something I was going to try to disprove.

"She was wearing the ring when the poison took effect," I managed. "I saw it." Experienced it, rather. "I could see a blurred face, and I heard a voice, but Cheyenne was in too much pain to record details. The murderer had short hair, though. Or maybe it was pulled back. Like I said, it was really blurry."

"Makes sense," Paige said. "The lack of air in her bloodstream affected her vision."

"The imprint didn't start until she realized she was dying and gripped her hand tightly over the ring." My head whirled as I lifted it from the table. "Hope you got all that on camera."

"Not exactly," Shannon said. "I might have been in the way of the camera when I came to see how you were."

Good. No one could say to recruits, "This is what happens when a crazy woman pretends to read emotions and experiences on objects in a murder investigation."

My knees felt weak, and I was glad to be sitting on the chair. My hands were shaking too, and I clenched them in my lap and waited for them to stop. "What now?" I said, keeping my voice steady.

"You don't want to take a break?" Paige asked. "I had to work to get the ring out of your hand, you know. And you were out a good two minutes."

I was glad it was her who said it instead of Shannon or I might have thrown something at him. Maybe a clue that I should stick with Jake. I didn't have any internal conflict about accepting his help.

"I'd rather finish." There were two objects left. A chunky turquoise-and-silver necklace and a thick silver bangle bracelet.

Of the two, the bracelet was worth more and therefore more likely to be important to Cheyenne. I made a silent vow to drop it immediately if I experienced even a hint of suffocation. Better yet, I wouldn't even pick it up. That way, if I fainted, I'd lose contact with it anyway. Provided, of course, that I didn't fall on top of the jewelry.

Paige pushed the necklace and the bangle bracelet over to me from where she must have put the objects after I passed out. But this time they weren't close to me, and I'd have to extend my entire arm to touch them. No chance of falling on top of either object.

"Wait a sec." Shannon went back to the camera and adjusted the angle. "I'm coming back over there."

He did, and I found it almost laughable the way he and Paige both stood over me, as if waiting to snatch away the jewelry if I so much as sighed.

I reached out a finger, but it went to the necklace, not to the bangle, and I almost wept with relief when all I felt was the joy of ownership and the contentment Cheyenne had experienced two years ago when she'd bought it.

I shook my head and reached for the bangle, using two fingers this time. Bold.

At once I was scrabbling at the silver bangle, trying to get it off Rosemary's wrist. She wouldn't have this. I didn't want Paxton, but I didn't want her to have him, either. She already had the role that should have been mine.

Clutching it at last in my hand, I sat staring at her prone form. Why was Rosemary lying so still? Wait, the hammer. It lay on the floor beside the fallen woman, and red stained the back of her brown hair. All at once I remembered the blackness, the hatred I'd felt. Horror swept through me at the memory.

What have I done?

"I didn't mean to hurt you, Rosemary. Not like this." My stomach twisted. Was she dead?

Wait, she was moving. I needed to get help. But what if she pressed charges? Did she see it was me? What should I do?

Oh, why had I confronted her about the Juliet role? She'd only come back tonight to watch me in The Comedy of Errors. I should have taken it up with her back at the apartment, not here where everyone would soon be arriving.

Had she really come to support me or to flirt with Seaver?

Rosemary had stopped moving. "What should I do?" I moaned.

The bangle in my hand felt heavy. If I didn't call for help, Rosemary might die. But if I called for help, she'd tell and I'd go to prison.

An arm came around me. "Don't worry. I know what to do."

The voice came from a tunnel, familiar and known to me, but my focus was the body and the part I'd just played. I pushed the bangle onto my arm, and the scene vanished.

Another imprint followed: *I was looking into the face of Grady Mullins. "It's a beautiful bracelet, Grady. Thank you."*

"Are you sure this is the right thing to do?" he asked. "That company is smaller."

"It has connections. I think I have a chance. Cheyenne says there aren't many there who have my talent. She's a good friend."

Grady frowned. "I don't like it. And I don't like her. She only hangs with you because you tell her how good she is."

"Oh, Grady. She is good. Don't be jealous. Be happy for me that I have this chance."

"Okay. Here, let me put it on. That way, even when we're not together, you can remember me."

He was silly and a bit sweet. I didn't have the heart to tell him I thought we needed time apart. We'd spent almost every moment of the past two years together, but I wasn't sure we had a future. I wanted space, a chance to find myself. Another reason for switching theater companies. Grady was a little too controlling. He reminded me of my father.

The imprint vanished and nothing followed, so I took back my hand, which now seemed to weigh fifty pounds.

I sighed, meeting Shannon and Paige's expectant gazes. "Cheyenne was the one who hit Rosemary with the hammer. Apparently after Rosemary saw her father, she went home—that must be why her princess rock was there—but she came back later to support Cheyenne in *The Comedy of Errors*. They must have had a fight. Probably because Cheyenne was angry about her getting the Juliet role but also because of this bangle. Grady Mullins gave it to Rosemary sometime earlier, before the Juliet auditions, but for some reason Cheyenne seemed to think it was from Paxton Seaver."

"But it was definitely Cheyenne who hit Rosemary?" Paige asked.

"I didn't see the actual hit, but she grabbed this bangle off Rosemary afterward. She felt guilty when she looked at the hammer."

"Obviously not guilty enough," Paige said.

"She was afraid of going to jail. That's why she didn't call for help."

"That supports the DNA testing we did on the hammer." Shannon sat on the edge of the table. "It came back two hours ago positive for Rosemary's blood. Too bad we couldn't lift any prints besides yours, but it had definitely been wiped clean."

I frowned. "The state Cheyenne was in, I don't think she

would have thought to wipe it. But I was just going to tell you that she wasn't there alone. Someone came in, someone who may have helped her hide the bo—" I'd been going to say body, but I didn't know for sure that Rosemary was dead. "Helped her hide Rosemary," I amended.

"Who?" Shannon and Paige asked together, both leaning forward eagerly.

I was suddenly all too aware of the video camera pointed in my direction, the red record button aglow. "I'm sorry," I said. "The person spoke only two short sentences and the imprint stopped before Cheyenne looked at him or mentally identified him. Or her. I can't even say if it was a man or a woman." I shrugged. "That's the drawback of imprints. I can only experience what they experience. Or see what they saw right at the moment."

In the past, I'd been able to recognize people in imprints that the person creating the imprint hadn't personally known enough to identify, and often people mentally identified people they interacted with during their imprint. But in both the ring imprint and the bangle imprint, Cheyenne had been too involved with her own pain or emotions to register anything else. That could have a lot to do with who she'd been—a self-centered person who, when it came right down to it, cared first and foremost about her own welfare—but it was more likely caused by her emotional state.

"It could come to me," I said. "If I hear the voice."

"At any rate, Cheyenne knew whoever helped her, as well as her killer," Shannon said. "That narrows it a bit. Could even be the same person."

"Cheyenne was a user," I mused, "but somehow it doesn't make her death any easier."

Shannon shook his head. "It never does."

"It could be Paxton Seaver," Paige said. "He was in love with Cheyenne, and obviously, she felt some emotion toward him if she became jealous thinking he'd given the bracelet to Rosemary."

"But why didn't Rosemary tell her it was Grady?" I asked. "They were friends, after all. Grady had met her. Wait a minute, Grady didn't like Cheyenne, and it was possible Cheyenne felt the same way about him. Maybe Rosemary was embarrassed to tell her friend that she'd accepted a gift from Grady when she planned to break up with him. Cheyenne could have assumed it was Seaver since Rosemary won the Juliet role. Maybe she couldn't believe someone actually landed the role on merit alone."

"Maybe it's time to talk to Mr. Seaver again," Shannon said. "To confront him with this new information. Crime of passion and all that." He started for the door. "Want to come along, Autumn?"

I did want to go along, except my body wasn't complying. The idea of trying to read another imprint made my stomach turn.

"Oh, no," I mumbled and barely made it to the trash receptacle against the wall before losing my pancakes from that morning. Or what was left of them. Unfortunately, I was in full sight of the video camera. *Great.*

"No more imprints for you today," Shannon said firmly.

I didn't even care that he was ordering me around. I guess dying changes you—at least for a while. Anything I might find imprinted on Seaver's belongings would have to wait until they made an arrest, or at least until tomorrow. Just the fact that he and Cheyenne had fought might be enough to get a warrant to search his car and his house.

"Imprints may not be needed," Paige said. "The information about his failed relationship with Cheyenne might drive a confession."

Except there was still the unanswered question about Grady's father, who had once worked for the Portland Players, and the identity of whoever had broken into the theater to steal that second glass. Seaver and the other actors at the theater yesterday had alibis, so that only left Grady or someone we hadn't focused on yet.

"Why don't you get some lunch?" Shannon suggested. "We'll let you know if Seaver spills anything."

"I'll come back," I said. I knew a place where they made great organic fried chicken. I'd order a double helping and the protein would get me back into shape, maybe enough to field more imprints today.

"I'll see you later, then." Shannon's eyes met mine, which would have made my heart jump if I'd been in any condition to react. Those eyes held a promise that had nothing to do with imprints or police work, and I was going to hold him to it.

Maybe.

Paige walked me out of the station. I was replacing my antique rings when she asked, "Why do you think only the ring had the death imprint? If she was also wearing the earrings and the rest when she died?"

"Maybe because she was clenching it so tightly." I really had no answer. Imprints and the way they were made often didn't follow logical patterns. I knew they had to be attached to the way different people's brains worked. Some people imprinted on things they wore, and others only on things they held in their hands or fingered often. Somewhere someone was probably doing scientific experiments about it.

I left the station and was two bites into my second chicken breast when I checked the time on my phone. It was already nearly two o'clock. If Shannon didn't need me, I had plenty of time to go back to the shop and get in a little work before my martial arts class that evening. I also had two voice messages. Not surprising since my phone had been silenced and in my coat pocket during my time at the station.

The first message was from Thera, saying she'd discounted the antique grandfather clock in order to sell both the clock and a wall table from the same era. It was a good move, and I was smiling with satisfaction and thinking I should probably stay away from the shop more if Thera did that kind of business without me, when the other message from Tawnia began.

"Autumn, it's me. Look, someone from the theater called. A woman. She said they were going ahead with rehearsal after all, so I'm heading down there. But not to practice. I thought about it while I was shopping, and I've decided to drop out of the play, and not just because of that weird phone call or because you want me to quit. Emma had a meltdown at the grocery store, and I had to take her out to the car and comfort her and feed her, and, well, I know you and Bret would like the alone time with her, but I'm just not ready to leave her for hours of practice every day and then for performances. I mean, that's why I quit working full time—I wanted to be home with her. I don't want to miss a minute of her growing up. Besides, she really needed me today, and while I know that you and Bret would do everything to make her happy, I can't bear thinking she might cry like that while I'm off practicing a lousy play with strangers. Not that it's lousy—you know what I mean.

"Anyway, you'll probably be finished at the station soon, and it's closer to the theater than the store where I am now so maybe you can meet me there and watch Emma while I run in to tell them in person. I know I'm letting them down, but my baby comes first. I can do plays later when she's in school—and I'll do it at a place where they don't have poisonings or creepy phone calls. I don't know what I was thinking getting involved. Investigating is your thing, not mine, and it's best to be on the safe side with Emma around, anyway. If you can't make it, don't worry. I'll just run in really quick and call you when I'm finished. All the cast will be there, so I won't be alone." She laughed. "I promise not to drink any lemonade. See you when I see you!"

My heart went into overdrive. When I'd left the police station, Seaver was still there. No way would they hold a practice without him. Tawnia couldn't know that. And she hadn't called back to tell me she'd finished at the theater, which meant she was still there.

"Waiter!" I called. "I need my check. Actually, pay it from this. Keep the change." I gave him two twenties, all the cash I had on me, and headed for the door, calling my sister's number as I went.

Her voice mail picked up. I tried twice more with the same result. Then I called Shannon before I knew I'd made the decision to do so.

"I was just going to call you," he said. "Seaver admits to the argument, but he doesn't know anything about the bangle, though he says Cheyenne stuck it in his face during Saturday rehear—"

I broke in. "So Seaver's still there?"

"Yeah. We'll have to release him, though. We're trying to get a warrant. Might take an hour."

"Tawnia went to a rehearsal at the theater. Someone called her. A woman."

"Seaver claims he's not holding rehearsal until we find the murderer. He's says he's afraid he's next. Could all be for show."

"I'm going to the theater. Something's not right. Tawnia's not answering her phone."

"Wait. Let me call Walsh. Maybe he scheduled the practice. Tawnia could be busy with lines or feeding the baby." The phone went dead.

I reached my car and climbed inside. Let him call—I wasn't waiting around. Because in the past two minutes, something in my chest told me my sister needed me. A feeling, my imagination, it didn't matter. I was going now.

I turned the key to my ignition. Nothing.

Desperately, I tried again and again. A sense of surrealism fell over me. *No!* my mind screamed. Of all the times for the Toyota to die on me. *What should I do?*

I jumped out and opened the hood.

"Need a jump?" a man leaving the restaurant asked.

"Yes. Would you?" *Hurry, hurry,* I thought. What would I do if we couldn't make it start? What if it wasn't the battery but something else more serious? In the movies, the good guys would pull out a gun and steal someone's car. Could I do that if it meant saving Tawnia?

The Toyota started, so I would never know what my choice would have been. I thanked the man, jumped inside, and roared away.

Long minutes ticked by as I raced through the streets of

Portland, almost hoping to be pulled over by an officer who Shannon could order to come with me. While impatiently waiting at a light, I turned on my phone's GPS, just in case I couldn't remember how to get to the theater. This was one moment I couldn't afford to be directionally impaired, especially as I went through downtown with all its one-way streets.

Why hadn't Shannon called back? What was taking so long? Maybe Walsh was behind the murders after all. On Saturday Erica had called him a womanizer, and maybe he and Vera were in this together.

I didn't remember how long ago Tawnia had left that message. What if I arrived too late? A sick feeling washed over me. I should have done more to keep her safe.

My phone finally rang. I didn't let off the gas as I answered.

"Walsh is at home with his wife," Shannon said. "He claims he doesn't know anything about a rehearsal, but he's worried now that he knows about it. I can hear it in his voice."

"I'm on my way there," I said.

"Wait for me."

"She's all the family I've got."

He hesitated a second. "Then take the gun."

"I have it."

"Rack it. I'll be there soon."

"Okay." At the next light I pulled out the gun, unzipped it from the cloth case, and racked the slide. All I had to do now was pull the trigger. The guy in the truck next to me was staring down through my window, his eyes wide at the sight of the gun.

Ignoring him, I punched the engine and sped forward, anticipating the green light. "Please," I muttered, "don't let me be too late."

Chapter 17

$\mathcal{I}$f something happened to Tawnia, it would be all my fault. Unequivocally. True, I'd let her come to the theater, never dreaming she'd end up in the fatal play, but I was still responsible. Every bit as responsible as on the day I'd let Winter go with me to hunt antiques and we'd ended up in the river when the bridge collapsed. I'd survived. He hadn't.

I could see the Willamette now, and as with every time I saw it, I remembered that horrible day. I usually avoided the river as much as possible, but that was hard since I lived and worked in downtown Portland where eight bridges spanned the Willamette.

After what seemed an eternity, I arrived at the theater. No cars out front, but that was to be expected. In the back parking lot, the only car there was Tawnia's. A chill shuddered through me. My careful sister would never have stayed if no one else had been here, so where were the other cars now? Had whoever enticed Tawnia here taken her somewhere else?

No, I'd been feeling the connection with my sister since I

pulled into the lot. She was here. Somewhere. And still alive—
for now.

I checked the car, but no one was inside. No car seat, either,
or Destiny's diaper bag. A cloud drifted over the weak sun overhead, signaling more rain and filling me with dread. I had to
find my sister and her baby.

I sprinted to the back door of the theater, planning to use
the gun to shoot my way in if I had to, but as usual, it was
propped open with the brick. Did that mean someone was
planning to return? Or was someone inside waiting for me as
he—or she—might have waited for Tawnia?

My sister had been tricked. My bet was on Vera and her
boyfriend and maybe Walsh, but Grady was also high on my
list. Seaver was the only one who couldn't be responsible.

Unless he had an accomplice.

I ducked inside, keeping low in case someone was there. I
felt relieved when the door closed again and cut out most of
the light behind me except the bit let in by the brick. Nothing
as yet had moved. Not even the normal dim lights were on in
this large room, and I was almost blinded. The only light came
from a slice near the door and two tiny windows so caked with
grime that they barely radiated a glow.

I pulled off my boots and started forward on silent bare
feet, choosing to edge my way through the prop tables and
racks instead of taking the relatively clear path I'd always used
before. Every now and then I squatted and listened. Nothing.
Absolutely nothing.

My eyes had adjusted to the dimness by the time I reached
the far side of the room. I would have several new bruises from
the tables, but those meant little to me in my hurry.

Had the killer poisoned my sister? Was she even now in a closet somewhere struggling for breath? I had to find her without alerting whoever might be here. Or would the precious seconds I was taking to go unnoticed cost my sister her life?

I nearly stumbled into Destiny's car seat before I saw it standing sentinel to the right of the door leading to the hall, the back of the seat facing the path through the props. A baby blanket had been tossed over the top sloppily, as if whoever had done it had been in a hurry. Grabbing for the blanket, I held my breath, hoping.

Destiny was lying inside, asleep, her tiny face reddened as though she'd cried for a long, long time. Her fists were still clenched on top of a second blanket that was only loosely tucked around her.

"It's okay," I whispered. "I'm here." I went around to the front and scooped her up. She barely moved at the motion, but her pulse was strong and indicated that she had simply cried herself to sleep. She was so exhausted that even as I rewrapped her in the blanket, she didn't awaken.

Instinct told me to run. To get out and get the baby to safety. That was what Tawnia would want me to do. But I couldn't leave my sister. So, should I try to hide the baby and go on? Or would her cries simply alert whoever had lured my sister here?

I decided to keep Destiny with me. She wasn't crawling yet, and in a pinch I could find a place to hide her where rolling wouldn't be an issue. Maybe. Whatever happened, she was a part of me, and I couldn't leave her any more than I could leave Tawnia.

Covering my hand with the edge of my coat to avoid imprints, I swept a few props from a table into the car seat and replaced the blanket that had been over it earlier. With luck, that would fool anyone wishing Destiny harm for at least a few minutes.

The hallway was absolutely black, and I knew Tawnia wouldn't have stayed in a dark theater, so someone had turned out the light after she arrived. Or she hadn't been in a condition to object. *I'll find you,* I thought.

Wait. I was forgetting something important.

I crept back to the car seat and, pulling off my antique rings, I slipped my hand under the blanket, touching the plastic handle. I knew there were imprints on the car seat, but they'd always been faint—feelings of satisfaction, frustration, and a number of other emotions—more from constant use than from any attachment my sister had with it. This time there was something new, something recent. Less than an hour old.

I have to get out of here. Something's wrong. Three cars outside and those people standing around talking, but where is everyone else?

Hurrying back to the outside door, only to see it opening from the outside, illuminating a figure there. Black clothes, black mask.

"Where are you going, Juliet?" A high voice. A woman? Or simply effeminate?

The figure hurtled across the prop room.

What about my Emma? I can't let him hurt her. The black figure stumbled. Must be over the diaper bag I dropped.

Running back the way I'd come, farther into the prop room. Reaching over to set down the car seat, as far as I could from the path through the room.

Abruptly, the imprint cut off. Tawnia must have tossed the

blanket over Destiny, trying to hide her. Had the person in black taken Tawnia far enough away that they hadn't heard the baby's crying?

My bare feet padded softly over the wood floor but still sounded loud in my ear. The theater was cold, the heat obviously off. I wished I dared call out for Tawnia, but that would alert whoever was with her.

The women's dressing room was first on my list of places to search, but nothing inside stirred, and the connection with my sister hadn't thickened.

Again I debated leaving Destiny, perhaps inside one of the larger cupboards, but I decided against it. I cradled her in my left arm, leaving my right hand free for the gun. I'd sworn to myself and Shannon that I could never use the gun on a person, but all that had changed, now that my sister and my niece were in danger.

I went on, peeking inside every room as I passed. I didn't have time to check the closets—yet.

The door to the backstage was open, and I headed in that direction. One look through the curtains and I'd be able to see if anyone was on stage or in the audience seats. The term *backstage door* was a little deceptive, since it really led to the right side of the stage. There was another matching door on the left side. The connection with my sister was growing stronger, and for a moment, I felt relief.

"So," a high voice was saying as I crept through the darkness. "Are you going to drink, or should I go find that baby of yours and give her a sip first?"

Fear crawled across my shoulders. I knew that voice, and it wasn't the actor Lucas with the high-pitched voice. There was no denying the bitter, sarcastic tone. And now that I'd recognized it,

I believed it was also the voice from both Cheyenne's imprints. And from Tawnia's.

Erica Tibble.

What I didn't understand was her motive.

"What's going to stop you from doing something to her even if I do drink it?" Tawnia asked.

"Well, you have a point there."

Inching up to the curtain that blocked me from view of the stage, I peered through the gap and saw a slender figure dressed in black, a knit ski mask over her face and matching gloves. The way she walked was all woman, and even with a coat partially obscuring her figure, I didn't believe she was the same person who'd attacked me in the prop room Saturday night. In fact, I'd seen her moments before in costume, and there hadn't been enough time for her to change. So why the pretense? Why the mask? Even Tawnia had to guess who she was.

My sister sat on a wooden chair, a solid, old-fashioned chair that had likely been a prop for decades. Each of her arms was tied to an armrest, and her waist and feet were tied as well. I could tell by the stiffness of her back that she was frightened, but she wasn't groveling, and I knew she hoped to talk her way out. The chair was positioned in front of a table that held a single glass full of yellow liquid and a fake lantern running on batteries.

"Even if I have to shove this lemonade down your throat, you'll still get enough to kill you." Erica paced around Tawnia's chair. "But it would be easier if you'd swallow. Easier for both of us. Faster for you in the end."

"I'm not staying in the play," Tawnia said. "I've told you that. That's what I came to tell Seaver today. I only came in the first place to help my sister with the investigation."

"Your sister." Derision laced Erica's voice. "It's because of her I have to do this. Sooner or later she was going to run into something I'd left imprints on."

"What do you know about imprints?" I could hear the defense in my sister's voice and a strength that made me proud. *Good for you,* I thought.

"I saw the way she was touching everything—it was obvious she was more than she let on. And you'd be surprised how much your average uniformed cop will tell you when you turn on the charm." She struck a dramatic pose with her hand to her heart. "Then there's the Internet. The police have kept it remarkably quiet, but there's still a journalist or two that got it right. Turns out, there's even a picture that looks just like you and your twin when they talk about an unnamed source. So I've been following your sister and talking to people. I even followed her to Rosemary's parents' house and chatted with Rosemary's brother after she left. I pretended my car broke down and that I needed to use their phone. He didn't even recognize me from when he came to the theater—I was in costume when he came. Sweet kid, though rather too trusting, if you ask me. Anyway, your sister is why I had to get rid of this glass, pretend someone else stole it. Of course, I brought it back especially for you today."

"You faked the break-in?" Tawnia asked.

Erica laughed. "I'm an actress and a good one. I can fool anyone. It was easy enough to get the information about the person who attacked your sister. Everyone wanted to believe it was the same guy. And I got rid of evidence without being suspected."

Tawnia sighed. "Look, you can walk away. You can be long gone before the police get here. I left my sister a message, and it's only a matter of time before they show up."

"Then we'd better hurry. Because it's too late to stop now.

I tried to convince them. I tried to tell my father we needed to do another play, one where I could finally have the lead role. That lying, cheating sneak owes me that much."

Father? Who was she talking about? There weren't many at the theater who had influence over what plays the company chose.

"You won't get away with this!" Tawnia said. "This isn't like Cheyenne's murder. This time everyone will know it was you."

"It'll be my grand performance before I disappear off stage and go somewhere to raise my new baby girl."

"Your baby girl?" Tawnia sounded as outraged as I felt.

"Oh yes, I've been planning this ever since you agreed to do the Juliet role." Erica pulled off her mask and leaned down, one hand on each of Tawnia's arms. A large amulet swung back and forth on a thin necklace at her throat. "Take a good look," she said. "I'll be the best mother to your baby. Don't worry. And in exchange, she'll make the perfect cover for my new life. I've been preparing for this for a long time. Father dear has trusted me with the accounting, and it's been easy enough to skim off the top. It's always been easy to fool him. He's so afraid his wife will find out about me."

She had to be talking about Walsh. Was he really her father? I remembered her comments about his being a womanizer the night we'd discovered the murder. I'd suspected she had first-hand experience, but not this kind of experience. If she was really his daughter, no wonder she'd dared say those things.

"It'll be a whole new life, and I'll be a good mommy. Not like mine, who was stupid to put her trust in a man like my father. He never cared for her, only his wife's money." She gave an uncharacteristic giggle as she pushed away from Tawnia's chair. "Guess I put a crimp in his plans. It'll all come out now.

Everything he wanted to hide. She'll leave him for sure, and he'll lose everything."

I had no doubt she was more intelligent than Walsh—and probably most of the other actors in the company, but another thing was also clear: Erica's hold on reality had completely snapped. She'd passed the line of carefully planned murders and had become careless, erratic. That made her more dangerous. Her sense of self preservation would no longer prevent her from doing whatever her crazy mind told her was necessary.

I spied a light switch and leapt for it, hoping to make Erica flee with the sudden brightness. Nothing but a soft click. So, she'd disabled the electricity. Maybe that also explained the cold.

Erica picked up the lemonade. Even from where I stood, I could see the glass was a twin to the other one I'd read. She'd had it all along, faking the intruder in the kitchen to cover her tracks.

"Bottoms up, Mommy dearest," Erica sang.

"I had nothing to do with any of this!" Tawnia shouted.

"Oh, I know." Erica sounded almost sympathetic. "But if you hadn't shown up and agreed to be Juliet, I would have won the fight to do the other play, and I would have been on my way to Broadway, despite my father's attempt to keep me here where he could control me." She snorted. "As if. The guy's an idiot. I don't know what my mother saw in him." She paused, swirling the liquid around in the glass. "Besides, if your sister hadn't interfered, no one would have connected Rosemary's disappearance with Cheyenne, and I would have had time to get rid of Cheyenne before anyone found her. It would have been another mystery."

She was too close to my sister now for my comfort. I had to act. Yet shooting her wasn't an option. Tawnia was between us, and Erica was leaning forward to give her the poison, not offering me enough of a target. I wasn't that confident of my shooting ability, natural talent or no. Not to mention that I had the use of only one hand.

"If you have a beef with me," I said, raising my voice so it would carry, "take it up with me, not my sister. Or are you too much of a coward?"

I'd hoped to startle her enough to make her drop the poison— hopefully not on my sister—but Erica only froze for a brief second before setting the glass down gently on the table. "Ah, Autumn, you joined our party."

"Run!" shouted Tawnia. "Get Emma out of here! She's in the prop room!"

I was already moving but not to the prop room. I angled around the back of the stage behind a huge white screen the theater used for projecting. If I could make it to the other side, I might be able to jump Erica. I'd have to find a place to hide the baby, though. But where was it safe to quickly hide a three-month-old from a maniac?

I stumbled into a prop, and Erica laughed. "Little hard to find your way in the dark, isn't it, sister dear?"

I wasn't the only one moving. By the time I got around to the other side of the stage, Erica had disappeared. She wasn't gone, though.

"Autumn, Autumn," she called from somewhere behind the curtains, "give it up. I have a gun, you know. How else do you think I convinced your sister to sit in that chair? Walsh keeps it locked up in his office, and you know I have access to the keys. I don't like guns—they're so messy and noisy. Impersonal. But I'll make an exception for you. You really should come out because I won't hesitate to shoot your sister. You know,

I would have liked a sister. If my mother could ever have gotten her life together, I might have had one. I had two brothers, but brothers just aren't the same."

I had to do something to draw her fire, if she really had a gun. Tawnia was helpless tied to that chair, yet with my precious cargo, I was every bit as helpless.

Then I saw it in the dim gloom. An oversized magazine rack, a prop that might work. I needed something Destiny couldn't roll out of and something sturdy enough to pull a cover over so Erica wouldn't find her. Shoving the Ruger back into my pocket, I grabbed the rack and carried it to the rear of the stage, placing it behind a solid-looking end table. Solid enough to stop a stray bullet—I hoped.

Please don't wake up. I grabbed a dress from a chair, threw it into the rack, and gently laid Destiny inside, patting her briefly as she stirred. Now what for the top? Not something the baby could pull in on herself if she awoke. I mentally kicked myself for not leaving her in the car seat back in the prop room.

There. A piece of cardboard that was a grate to a fake fireplace. That would do nicely, especially if I shoved the chair up against the edge. And if the worst happened, Erica might not find her as she would have in the car seat.

"Come out, come out, wherever you are!" Erica said in singsong. "You have thirty seconds."

I hurried to the side of the stage and moved the curtain to distract her, diving away as a bullet whizzed overhead. She really did have a gun, with a silencer attached, which meant that even if there was someone in the nearby buildings, they wouldn't hear a thing.

Gritting my teeth in resolution, I pulled out my Ruger. Erica had chosen the wrong family to mess with.

hooting my gun might alert neighbors, but it would also give away my hand and possibly cause Erica to shoot Tawnia right away. An unsilenced shot would likely wake Destiny as well, placing her in danger. I had to get Erica away from the stage area.

"Why wouldn't Walsh want you to go to Broadway?" I called, inching toward the left stage door, keeping low to the ground. "If you're really his daughter." This time she didn't let off a bullet, which made my knees weak with relief.

Erica laughed. "He was terrified his affair with my mother would come out. She was only twenty when she had me, and she couldn't make it without his help. She eventually OD'd, you know, and I blame him. I've always blamed him. If his wife found out, she'd cut him off, and he wouldn't be able to use her aunt on Broadway to entice decent actors to work for him."

"The aunt on Broadway is hers, not his?" From the importance he'd projected, I never would have guessed.

"Oh, yeah. He doesn't like to tell people that. But I know. I know all about Daddy dearest. I have since I was little. Mother told me about him, even took me to see him once. He was thin back then but still as ugly as he is now. Even after seeing me, he barely gave her any money. He threatened her, though. I remember that."

"You were adopted. They were good people, weren't they? Why would you care about a jerk like Walsh?"

"Because he killed my mother. Because acting's in my blood. Because he deserves to pay."

I couldn't see her, but her voice was coming closer. At least that meant her focus wasn't entirely on Tawnia. In the dark, neither of us could be accurate about shooting the other, so we were on equal ground—or would be if it hadn't been for Tawnia. She was a prime target tied in the middle of the stage, framed by the lantern.

As if reading my thoughts, Tawnia struggled to move her chair forward. One hop, then another. She tipped the chair forward and aimed her head toward the lantern. Not quite there, and she almost fell sideways to the ground with the effort. I had to give her more time.

If Walsh was Erica's father, that was the long-term connection we'd been searching for. Too late I remembered the eight-year-old photograph in Walsh's office of the young girl with the long black hair. The evidence had been in front of me all along.

"What about eight years ago?" I asked. "Did you poison the other actors, too?"

Erica was close enough that I heard an intake of breath. Fear arched through me, zipping to the tips of my fingers.

"He deserved it. They both did," Erica said, sounding angry and indignant. "He played with my emotions. He romanced me for months, told me how pretty I was and how talented and how much he loved me. But then he laughed at me with that girl when Walsh told me I had to finish high school and take acting classes at the junior college before he would let me join the company."

That explained why she hadn't shown up on any official employee documents until six years ago yet why she'd been in the photograph. She'd looked softer and so much younger that I'd believed her when she claimed it wasn't her. I wondered if she'd still hoped then that Walsh would be a proper father to her and that she'd find true love. Everything she'd experienced afterward had turned her into the vindictive woman she was now, and I felt pity for that young girl in spite of what she'd become.

"So the actor you loved turned out to be just like Walsh," I prompted.

"I caught him kissing that girl, the one who got the Juliet role Walsh should have given me, his own flesh and blood. When I confronted him, he mocked me. Told me to go home to play with my dolls. He didn't love me at all." She paused, and when she spoke again, the fury was gone from her voice. She could have been talking about dirty laundry for all the emotion she showed. "But don't worry. I took care of them. He was easy to get away from the theater, and when I called to tell her he wanted to meet her alone, she came running for the tryst. They didn't even question the refreshments set out for them. Their bones are probably still intertwined where they died." The horror of what she'd said didn't seem to worry her.

"You were just a teenager."

"I was never a teenager. Not with the life I'd lived. Do you know what my first foster family did to make me obey? They said they had a warehouse, a place where they took all the kids who didn't behave, where they hid their mangled bodies. They promised that's where they'd make me disappear if I wasn't good." Though her tone was still detached, the ring of truth hung on her voice.

Before I could probe further, the light on the stage crashed to the floor and went dark.

"I'm over here," I called to Erica. "Near the door. Tawnia can't go anywhere. She's tied. Come get me first, if you can."

I hurried through the door, pausing to see if she'd follow. A bullet ricocheting off the wall told me I'd succeeded. I was too exposed here in the hall, though. The walls weren't thick enough to protect me from bullets, and she could shoot around the bend with her hand only partially through the door. Unlike with Mr. Taylor when he'd come into his cabin, she knew more or less where I was and could continue to pull the trigger blindly until she got lucky. I had no idea how many shots she might have or if she had an extra magazine.

I wasn't as familiar with this backstage door as I was the other, but I remembered the hallway divided after the bend. I made a dash for it, thumping more forcefully on the ground than my bare feet liked. I had to be sure she'd follow.

Another shot ricocheted behind me. Odd for the ricochet to be louder than the actual firing of the silenced bullet itself. Spooky. Especially in the dark.

The hallway forked, and I hurried down the right side, which I hoped angled around to the men's dressing room and the main hallway. I was heading for the prop room, which would offer many places to hide—and to attack—but I had to make sure she kept following me and didn't return to the stage.

"What about Rosemary?" I said, stopping to listen to her progress. "Why did you help Cheyenne with her?"

"Poor thing did me a favor hitting Rosemary like that.

Too bad Cheyenne had to take the part afterward, though. She regretted it in the end. I used less poison with her. I wanted her to really *feel* it. What right did she have to mess with my plans?"

Good. She was still coming. Except that meant any minute she'd round the corner and I'd be in the open. Even in the dark she might be able to hit me. I sprinted down the hall past the men's dressing room, slamming my hip on the wall as I turned into the main hall. I experienced an instant of relief that I'd chosen the right path before I pushed myself to move forward again. The steady thud of Erica's feet continued behind me, sounding loud in the darkness.

The main hallway seemed to stretch forever before me.

"There's no getting away," she called. "You can't make it to the outside door before I shoot you."

She was right, but I didn't plan on trying to make it to the door, just into the prop room.

"We really must get this over with," she continued in what might pass as a normal tone in any other situation. Now it was eerie. "I have things I need to do. Give yourself up, or maybe I'll just go back to your sister and finish the job. How would you like that?"

I hesitated. I couldn't let her do that. "What about the baby?" I taunted. "You don't think I'd leave her here, do you? You'll never be a mother, not to her or anyone else. Not when you're in jail."

"Okay, let's play it your way." Her steps quickened to a run.

I either had to turn around and shoot it out with her now, or lead her to the prop room where I could shoot from cover.

I kept running.

The prop room, then. It had always been meant to end there.

I ran past the office and the women's dressing room. Another shot, but I was already going around the final bend. The prop room door stood open. I hurried inside.

Whap! I collided with the figure before I saw him. For an instant I dared hope it was Shannon, but instead it was someone wearing another mask. A sense of déjà vu came over me.

As we tumbled to the ground, my hand hit a table. The Ruger skittered away. The masked person fell on me, and I grunted with the impact.

I blocked a punch with one hand and grabbed for the mask with the other. I pulled hard, feeling it come loose.

"Grady Mullins?" I said.

His eyes widened as he recognized me in the dim light. "You!" He glanced at the outside door, as though calculating his chances of escape.

"Hit her!" Erica said, moving through the door. "Don't be a wimp. Or move so I can shoot her."

"What?" The word came out as a yelp.

"Do it! You owe me. If you hadn't screwed up on Saturday, she wouldn't even be here."

"What are you talking about? I was here. But you said to let no one see me, and someone did, so I left."

Not without trying to hit me with a hammer first.

"You were late!" Erica's voice had risen to a scream. "Now hit her or move!"

Grady pulled back his fist. I was faster. Grabbing my right hand with my left, I pulled hard, slamming my right elbow into Grady's head. He rolled off me with the impact. I rolled the other way, under a table of props. Flipping to my knees, I scurried to the next table as a shot splintered the first. Now the darkness worked to my advantage. There was no way she could target me accurately.

She might, however, get lucky.

I crawled on as shots punctured the props and table behind me. How many shots did she have? She'd fired at least nine, hadn't she? The typical 9 mil Glock, a favorite gun among many gun owners, could hold anywhere from ten to seventeen rounds, depending on the model, and larger magazines were often purchased by enthusiasts, which I didn't think included Walsh. So that meant she could have up to eight bullets left.

I didn't know if I could survive eight.

That's when Erica got lucky. I gasped as agony ripped through the flesh of my upper left arm. Dizziness threatened to take me.

Don't faint, I ordered myself. *You have to save Tawnia and Destiny.*

I forced myself onward, pain lacing every inch. Wetness seeped inside the sleeve of my coat. It was all I could do not to curl into a ball and scream with the pain. *Tawnia,* I reminded myself.

My hand touched a cloth of some type that had fallen from one of the tables. Wadding it, I shoved the entire thing inside my coat, packing it to staunch the flow of blood.

Then I heard what I'd been waiting for: silence, followed by a muffled curse. It was now or never. I leapt to my feet, jumped on the table in front of me, and launched myself at Erica. She was scrambling to put in another magazine, but her inexperience slowed her down. I slammed into her hard and felt satisfaction as her gun and the new magazine clattered to the ground. She hit the floor with a grunt.

She bounced up the next second, surprisingly resilient. Her swing went wide, leaving her open to a perfect right uppercut, followed by a left punch to her face, which sent her stumbling backward and lances of pain through my wounded arm. For a second I thought I would faint, but I held on.

That's for Tawnia, I thought. A few more punches and a kick or two would have her subdued. Even one-handed I could take her.

Except I'd forgotten about Grady. He was a spineless, rather ineffectual fighter, so I'd dismissed him. Big mistake.

"You stupid!" Erica yelled, scrambling away from me. "Shoot her! Shoot her!"

Risking a glance behind me, I saw Grady with my Ruger in his hand. "Don't do it," I said. "The police are already looking for you."

"I'll tell them you killed Cheyenne," Erica screamed. "I'll tell them it was all your idea. That you forced me to go along so you could get the main role in the new play I was going to force Walsh to do instead of that insipid Juliet one."

"That was your idea," he shouted. "You said if I helped hide the body, you'd get me the chance that I'd never get with my father's company. That you'd tell me where Rosemary went."

"You think they're going to believe you? Never! If I go down, you go down with me."

"And how do you think she knows where Rosemary is?" I said. "She's killed her just like Cheyenne."

"Don't listen to her!" Erica shouted. "Shoot her and I'll say you were defending me. That she attacked me! No one will blame you."

I could see her words were having an effect on the spineless idiot, but before I could say anymore, Erica dived for a vase on a table, bringing it up to crash over me.

I sidestepped and sent a roundhouse into her side, following up with a right hook to her shoulder.

"Now!" she screamed.

Two seconds to decide. Did I knock her out and save my sister, or did I dive for the tables and seek protection from the hollow points in my own gun, hoping I found another chance to beat them later?

There was no real choice. I couldn't leave my sister exposed. Besides, it was dark, and I bet Grady didn't have a lot of experience with guns unless they were props. I let my fist slam into Erica's chest, feeling satisfaction at the shock on her face.

"Shoot!" she wailed. I fired another right punch, this time at her head.

A shot rang out. Or were there two? So close together, I couldn't tell. My ears were deafened with the blast. I felt no new pain, no hot slicing through my skin that I'd just experienced under the table, though I'd heard that sometimes fatal shots take a minute to register with your brain, depending on where you're hit.

With my last blow, Erica fell, bounced off a table, crashed to the ground, and lay there unmoving. I stumbled forward, fighting for balance.

The next thing I registered were voices, light from outside, and officers rushing all around. Grady grabbing his shoulder, and red spouting underneath his fingers. Shannon roughly pushing him against a table and cuffing him.

"Take it easy," Grady whined. "I'm shot."

"Yeah?" Shannon said. "That was me. Sorry, I was aiming for your head. If you don't shut up, I'll rectify my mistake."

Next to Shannon, Officer Peirce Elvey pulled on a glove, bent down, and retrieved my Ruger, showing it to Shannon. He sniffed it before Peirce put it in a plastic bag. I knew from the expression on his face that it had been fired. Grady had tried to kill me.

Paige touched my arm. "Are there any more?" Assailants, she meant.

I looked down at Erica, sprawled on the ground where an officer was checking her pulse. Bile rose in my throat.

"Not that I saw." It was hard to focus, but I didn't know if that was from blood loss, the adrenaline seeping from my body, or the simple lack of light. "But Tawnia's on the stage. Tied up. Destiny's there too. I hid her in the props behind the curtains." I wished I could go for them myself, but at the moment I doubted I could walk across the room. I had to trust Paige.

Paige and two uniformed officers rushed from the room, guns drawn.

"Someone get these lights working!" Shannon yelled. So far he'd avoided my gaze, but I could feel his attention riveted on me. He shoved Grady to a seated position on the ground. "Don't move," he ordered.

"I need medical attention," whined Grady.

Ignoring him, Shannon crossed the distance between us. "You okay?" Gruffly spoken, but the intentness in his eyes momentarily stole my breath.

"You shot him?" I asked.

"Not fast enough."

I still owed him my life—again. Because Grady might have fired a second time and gotten lucky. I might not have moved away fast enough. "Thanks."

He nodded, his face stern.

"Of course," I couldn't resist saying, "if I hadn't been carrying the Ruger, he couldn't have tried to shoot me with it."

A shadow crossed his face, and I realized he'd already had that thought all on his own. Which meant he would blame himself for my near death. Sometimes my mouth didn't know when to quit.

"I didn't mean that," I said. "It was me. If I hadn't been afraid to use it earlier, maybe things would have been different." When you were trained, a gun was all kinds of useful—I knew that. I should have fired at Erica in the hallway before Grady showed up.

Carefully, I put my left hand in my pocket where it could rest without putting pressure on the wound in my arm. There was no new wetness and the dizziness wasn't any worse, so it could wait until I saw Tawnia. And until Shannon calmed down.

The lights went on but didn't affect our eyes much in the prop room because they were so weak. A paramedic had arrived and was treating Grady. The actor was playing it up as much as possible, and I wondered if he thought it would get him less time.

"He knew about Cheyenne's death," I said. "I don't think he helped Erica kill her, but he was going to move the body for her. That's why he was here that night."

"Your attacker."

I nodded. "Erica faked the other incident in the kitchen, to cover the fact that the second glass was missing. She found out about my ability and was worried I'd identify her."

We looked up as Tawnia and an officer came in. She smiled at me but her attention went immediately to the car seat. Her face paled and her scream reverberated throughout the entire room. "No!"

I followed her gaze to the two bullet holes that punctured the back of the seat. One larger than the other. Probably from two different guns. Maybe one had been mine.

Tawnia was crying, trying to reach the seat as the officer held her back.

I rushed to my sister's side. "She's not there. I moved her. She's safe." I hoped.

Paige appeared in the hallway behind us. "You looking for this? We were securing the crime scene when I heard her fussing. Took me a while to find her, but she was patient once she heard my voice." In her arms, Paige held Destiny.

Tawnia lunged for her daughter, and Destiny gave a glad cry to see her mother. Her lashes looked wet, but her face was less red than when I'd found her earlier. Tawnia hugged the baby to her chest. Her eyes met mine. "Thank you."

I nodded, but inside I felt sick. I'd almost left Destiny in the car seat, thinking it was the safest place. What if the bullets had gone astray on the stage instead of here? Destiny could have been killed. My sister could have been killed. Would have been.

It was all my fault.

"Erica?"

We turned to see Walsh pushing his way through the officers. "Where is she?" he demanded. Spying Erica on the ground, he hurried over. "What have you done?" he asked, falling heavily to his knees. "Why would you do this?"

To my surprise, her eyes opened. "Because of you. It's all because of you. I *hate* you." She held her hand to her small chest, as if her heart hurt.

Walsh placed a fleshy hand on her black-clad arm. "I didn't believe you could do something like this, not until I saw the note you sent Seaver. I recognized your handwriting. I still couldn't believe."

She laughed. "You got rid of the note, didn't you? Couldn't risk your precious play or your wife finding out about me."

I took a step toward her. "Where's Rosemary? You were there after Cheyenne hit her with the hammer. Is she still alive? What did you do with her?"

Erica looked up at me, her face that had once reminded me of a delicate faerie now looked sharp and devilish. "Maybe you should look in the Willamette."

My stomach twisted. *Not the river.*

"Tell them, Erica," Walsh urged.

Her attention shifted to him. "You can't tell me what to do," she sneered. "You'll never get Rosemary—or do your precious play. You should have listened to me and done the other play instead. I would have been great as the lead, and once I was in New York, I would have been out of your hair forever. But no, you wanted to make sure I stayed hidden. Well, now your wife will know all your dirty little secrets." With a quick motion, she took her hand from her heart, twisted something, and brought it to her mouth, gagging as it went down.

She smiled with triumph. "I've carried this with me for eight years, just in case." She gave a sharp laugh. "A tragedy. That's what this is. Everyone dies or is destroyed. And this"— she lifted the amulet I'd seen earlier on her necklace—"is beautifully ironic."

Shannon turned and snapped his fingers at the medic. "Get over here! She's ingested poison."

I turned, feeling sick. Already Erica was gasping for breath, her hands clinging to the front of Walsh's shirt as he cradled her in his arms. She could be acting, like she had in the kitchen. Regardless, I didn't want to watch. I had my own demons to deal with. Tawnia had also turned away and was cradling Destiny, talking softly to her.

I'd almost killed them.

With stumbling steps, I pushed my aching self to the bathroom as fast as I could go. Only when the door was shut behind me did I let myself cry, dragging in huge gulps of air between sobs, my right fist shoved against my face to muffle the noise. I couldn't do this anymore. It was one thing to put myself in danger in order to save people, but the last time Jake had been in danger and this time Tawnia had come too close. They hadn't chosen this life, as Shannon and Paige had, and I wouldn't endanger them anymore.

I was through. I'd wear gloves all the time, even in the summer, and I'd forget I'd ever had such a miserable talent.

"Autumn."

I hadn't heard anyone come in, but arms went around me. Shannon's arms. I recognized the feel from my dreams. I recognized his smell. Though I'd dreamed of this moment, it had never felt so good—or so painful as the pressure of his hug exacerbated the pain of my wound. I didn't care. It was less than I deserved.

He held me as my shoulders shook, my body convulsing with sobs.

"I'm finished," I told him when I could finally speak.

The pain in my arm faded to a dull throb, and his hold lessened. "If I had a dollar for every time I've thought that—"

"I mean it. My sister and Destiny—they could have died."

"But they didn't. And now you've learned why you'll never

let them come along on any investigation, no matter how innocent it seems."

I shook my head. "It doesn't matter. Trouble finds me."

"You'll feel differently later. Believe me. Give it some time before you decide."

I kept silent, my tears suddenly gone. I wasn't going to change my mind. If this is what my talent led to, I absolutely didn't want it.

"We still need to find Rosemary," he said. "You care about that, don't you?"

I wanted to scream that I didn't care, that I didn't want to ever hear her name again. But it would be a lie. I still wanted to help Liam and his mother—and even the controlling Mr. Taylor.

"Grady might know where she is," Shannon continued. "Since he was going to help Erica hide Cheyenne's body. But if they dumped Rosemary in the Willamette, we might never find her."

I shook my head. "Grady doesn't know where Rosemary is, but—" I stopped. "Wait a minute. Erica said something about a warehouse that belonged to her first foster family. She claims they kept bodies there—or told her that to make her obey. Maybe that's what she had in mind for Cheyenne. Maybe that's where she and Cheyenne took Rosemary."

Leaving her to die? Or had she already been dead?

Chapter 19

Shannon was already drawing out his phone and barking orders. He was good at that. In no time, they would track down the warehouse, whether or not it still belonged to the foster family.

Despite my resolve, I felt a stirring of interest. "Grady might know more than he's told us," I said.

"Paige's talking to him now. We'll move as soon as we get word."

"Not me. I'm finished, remember?"

"You don't want to be there when we find her?"

"What if she's dead?" That was something I couldn't deal with right now—or did I owe it to Liam to represent him when they found her?

"Then we tell the family. But trust me. You'll change your mind about quitting. I actually wish you wouldn't, but I know you too well."

"Do not." Something about him always brought out my contrariness.

His arms went around my waist, and that look was back in his eyes.

"What are you doing?" I asked, my voice scarcely audible.

"What I should have done six months ago." His lips met mine, jumping past gentle and plunging into urgency and demand. I answered him back with equal emotion. His arms tightened, pulling me closer. My skin tingled, and my heart jumped into overdrive. Time stopped. The world ceased to rotate. All the fear and worry of the past hours disappeared. I couldn't even feel the throbbing in my arm. It was just the two of us, alone, finally getting to the point we'd both been fighting since the day we'd first met.

It was more than worth the wait.

We might never have pulled away if Shannon's phone hadn't started vibrating. We ignored it as long as possible, but he finally brought it to his ear. "What is it? Okay. We're on our way." He looked at me. "They've found the warehouse. You want to come?"

I nodded, though I still meant what I said about quitting. One world-shattering kiss didn't change that.

It only changed everything else.

In the prop room, everyone was busy taking samples, pictures, or roping off the area with tape. Two officers were leading Grady outside. Erica and Walsh were nowhere to be seen.

"You coming?" Paige called to us impatiently from the outside door.

Shannon and I hurried to meet her. Or rather, he hurried, and I struggled to keep up.

"Autumn!" Tawnia said. "What's going on? Where're you going?"

"We might have found Rosemary."

"I'm coming with you."

I whirled. "No. Please. Just go home."

"What's wrong with you?" She stared at me blankly.

"I almost got you killed. And Destiny, too."

"You?" She shook her head. "You told me not to do the play. I should have listened. It was my fault, my choice. In case you haven't noticed, I'm a big girl now." She'd struck exactly the right mixture of indignance and reassurance, and the tight grip on my heart lessened slightly. "*I'm* Emma's mother," she said. "*I* should have been more careful."

"Then start now," I said. "Go home."

She shook her head. "I'm not going anywhere alone. I'm going to stay with Shannon and Paige until I know they've arrested everyone involved. Until then, the safest place is with them."

"Enough talk," Paige groaned. "Come on, already. This isn't going to be dangerous. Trust me."

I relented. Not because I was worried there were more accomplices, or because I thought my sister would be in further danger, but because I really, really wanted to feel her near, to feel the connection between us thick and strong.

We went to Shannon's car. "Guess I'll need another car seat," Tawnia said, strapping the ruined one between us. "But this will have to do for right now." Destiny, looking no worse for wear, grinned up at us.

Shannon used the siren, and the blocks passed in a blur. I soon recognized the area where we were heading. Lovely. The lousy warehouse just had to be down by the Willamette. Silently, I prayed Rosemary would be okay, that by some miracle she would be found alive.

We arrived as officers emerged from the building. An ambulance was already there, and as we climbed from the car, two EMTs came from the building with a figure on a stretcher. Shannon strode over, and I hurried after him, leaving Tawnia in the police car. I held my breath, releasing it as I saw that the figure was actually Rosemary.

"She okay?" Shannon asked.

I held my breath for the answer. Rosemary had been missing since Thursday night and that meant almost five full days lying there injured and without water.

One of the EMTs, a bulky blond with a flushed face, nodded. "She's badly dehydrated, and she's lost a lot of blood, but she's stable for now. We hope that big gash on the back of her head has released enough pressure that the swelling won't have caused permanent brain damage. The doctors will know more once they examine her, but already she's responding."

Even as he spoke, Rosemary's eyelids fluttered. The paramedic bent down to talk to her, and she nodded faintly at his question.

"What hospital are you taking her to?" I asked, struggling to pull out my phone to call Liam. It just happened to be in my left pocket, and my arm was back to that incessant throbbing.

"Detective Martin, can I talk to you?" An officer who'd come from the building appeared at Shannon's side. He glanced at me, indicating that it was official business.

"You can talk freely," Shannon said.

The officer nodded. "We found her in the attic here, more a storage loft, really. Wrapped in a heavy quilt. Fortunately for her since it's been so cold. It was a long, steep flight of stairs to get her up there. Must have been a strong man or two people."

Erica and Cheyenne, I thought.

"And that's not all," the officer continued. "We found more human remains. Skeletal. A male and a female, we think."

"Better call it in," Shannon said.

So the actors who had missed final call on their opening night eight years ago would finally be put to rest. Their families would have closure. I wondered how much comfort it would be to them.

At least one family would have good news. I pushed the button on my phone to call Liam, only to see Shannon staring at me.

"What happened to your arm?" Barely concealed anger threatened to slice through the warm cocoon of denial I'd been building. "Is that a bullet hole?"

I scowled at the hole in my coat and the bloodstains that had blended so well with its fabric inside the dim theater. "Just a scratch. It's packed. Probably not even bleeding anymore." Our standard joke, but he didn't look happy. Not my fault he wasn't as good at detection as I was at denial.

"One of these days," he growled.

"Is that you, Autumn?" a voice said in my ear.

I turned my back on Shannon. "Hey, Liam. I have good news. We found Rosemary. They're taking her to the hospital now."

The hospital was also our next stop, and it would be our last before home since Shannon had officers drive our cars from the theater to my apartment building. I had no idea how they got my car started—probably had to jump it again—but I was grateful. I never wanted to see the theater again. In fact, I doubted I'd ever go to another play. At least not for a very, very long time.

Of course, my life was far more entertaining and complicated than any play.

Or used to be. I was still quitting.

Liam and his parents showed up at the hospital, but they weren't the only ones. As Liam had requested when I talked to him, I'd called his grandparents, and even now they were here, hugging Mrs. Taylor and Liam. Mr. Taylor had a scowl on his face, but he wasn't interfering, and I even saw him shaking his father-in-law's hand. What they made of the future was up to them. I was out of it.

My newly wrapped arm was feeling nicely numb from an injection the doctor had given me before stitching me up. The bullet had gone clear through the fleshy part of my arm, in a downward angle after passing through the table, and though it had hurt like crazy, he assured me I wouldn't have any permanent damage. I didn't even have to receive a blood transfusion or stay for observation, thanks to the support of my coat and how tightly I'd shoved in that cloth from the theater—which turned out to be men's pantaloons used in the theater's rendition of Peter Pan. I would have to buy a new coat, however, which was far more pleasant to think about than how close it had been for me in that prop room.

Information filtered in as I was treated and as we waited to hear about Rosemary. We learned some college students who'd seen the police at the theater and come to investigate claimed that Erica had found them down the street playing paintball and paid them to leave their cars in the theater parking lot and to loiter about until another car drove up. She was playing a prank on her sister, she told them. They'd been there half an hour before the car arrived. They watched Tawnia go inside and then drove their cars away. Erica's own vehicle was found one street over.

"Do you think Erica was also responsible for the other times they had to cancel the play?" Paige asked. "I mean, someone with cancer might not have had an autopsy. The actress could have been poisoned. And the woman in the car accident might have ingested just enough to make her crash. Could it really be a coincidence?"

Shannon shook his head. "At least one of the bodies was cremated, so we may never know."

I chose to believe it was coincidence. Sometimes you do what you have to do to stay sane.

Which was why I was quitting.

The most shocking thing we heard while waiting was that doctors had been able to save Erica. Barely. Either the poison she'd carried had lost potency over the years, or she hadn't ingested enough. She might have to use a wheelchair and oxygen for the rest of her life, but she would live to pay for her crimes. Walsh would pay too, once his wife learned the entire story.

At last the doctor came to talk to Liam's family, who shared the good news: Rosemary's skull had needed to be opened to reduce pressure, she'd had two blood transfusions, and she would eventually have a head full of stitches, but she was going to be all right.

"Okay. Let's go home." I was sitting in the waiting room, hands in my lap, careful to touch absolutely nothing.

"Wait," Tawnia said. "I almost forgot. We have another case." When she saw my expression, she amended carefully, "I mean *you* have another case."

I shook my head. "I'm done. I really mean it." I could feel Shannon's eyes on me, but I didn't look his way. The only effect I wanted him to have on me was the one where the world stopped. No one was going to convince me to use my ability again, especially not him.

"I thought that was what you've been wanting," I said to Tawnia. "For me to quit doing anything dangerous."

"Well, yeah, but I know how much you care about using your gift to help people." Tawnia pulled out a newspaper. "Take a look at this before you say no. I was reading it at the store while I was waiting my turn at the counter. You know, just skimming. I didn't get the chance to read the paper this morning like I usually do. Then I saw this." She opened it to the middle and shoved it under my nose. Shannon and Paige both leaned in for a better look.

For a full minute I was speechless. No. It couldn't be. But there it was, the exact picture Tawnia had drawn this morning of the grizzled man sitting on the porch of his squat house. The man we suspected was our birth father.

"Read the article," she said. "It's not really even about him. A young girl from Hayesville has gone missing. Here, let me read this bit: 'She was last seen in the area of Cody Beckett's house. In light of his police record, Mr. Beckett has been questioned and named a person of interest, but as yet no charges have been filed.'" Tawnia's eyes lifted to mine. "We have to help them find her. If Laina's right and he's living there precisely so he won't hurt anyone, we can't let them pin this on him."

"He may have fathered us, but we don't owe him anything," I retorted.

"Maybe he didn't do it."

"Maybe he did." The coldness was back in my heart.

"Then you put him away." This from Shannon. I looked up at him, feeling exposed. He did know me too well. How had that happened?

"Okay," I said to my sister. "Maybe I can go see him. But

only if you'll promise to stay out of it completely." Tears stung my eyes, but I blinked them away.

"Don't worry. I want to meet him, of course, but I'll stay well away from any investigation." She gave me a wistful smile. "I'll trust you to take care of yourself." That was a huge leap—both her urging me not to quit and her trusting me to defend myself.

"If you want company," Shannon said, "I've been meaning to see a bit more of our beautiful state of Oregon. I hear down that way there's a lot of nice land."

I looked up at him. "Speaking of land, I don't believe you've ever shown me your acre." I needed to see it, to know more of the real him.

"I could have you over for dinner sometime. I make a mean pasta."

Paige groaned. "Watch out. He's nuts about pasta—soggy, horrible junk. Thank heaven he's finally stopped trying to force it down my throat."

"Is it organic pasta?" I asked, coming to my feet. "Only certain whole wheat pastas are even any good, and I don't eat white pasta. Or white anything."

My sister laughed. "She really means it. Curse of my life."

Shannon sighed. "Maybe you should make it, then. Or we could go out. We have a lot to talk about." This last was said in an undertone so the others couldn't hear.

I was more interested in repeating the experience we'd shared in the bathroom at the theater, though I wasn't looking forward to talking to Jake, and I was sure there would be other challenges down the road. Shannon and I had been combating each other too long for a smooth transition. He was too stubborn. I was too.

"All that will have to wait until we check in at the precinct," Paige said, holding up her phone. "I already have three messages from the chief, and I'm betting so do you."

Shannon grimaced. "I have four. So I guess we have to go in, but I've called an officer to take you two home." He motioned to Peirce, who had at some point appeared in the waiting room. "Can you make sure they get home in one piece tonight?"

Peirce laughed. "Of course. Glad to do it."

Shannon didn't even look around to see who might be watching before he put his arms around me, being altogether too careful of my hurt arm. "I'll call you later." His whispered breath was warm on my cheek. I wanted to say something sarcastic to cut the tension, but I couldn't think of a single thing.

"So," Tawnia whispered as we followed Peirce from the hospital, "when are you going to tell me what happened in that bathroom?"

"You saw Shannon go in?"

She shrugged. "I was worried about you."

Again, the memory of her near death threatened to reduce me to a bowl of gelatin, but I shoved the thoughts away. Shannon was right. Maybe I needed to let a little time pass before I made a final decision about my future and my gift.

"Let's have Peirce drive us to my place," I said. "That's where our cars are anyway. I'll make you something to eat."

"No, I'll make it while you rest your arm. You can tell me what to do. But it'd better be good organic whatever, not the yucky stuff, cuz I'm starved."

I was starving too. And food could solve a world of problems.

But maybe on the way home I would have Peirce stop so I could buy a new pair of gloves to replace those I'd lost. You never knew when they might come in handy. Especially if I decided to go see our biological father.

TEYLA BRANTON has worked in publishing for over twenty years. She loves writing women's fiction and traveling, and she hopes to write and travel a lot more. As a mother of seven, it's not easy to find time to write, but the semi-ordered chaos gives her a constant source of writing material. She's been known to wear pajamas all day when working on a deadline, and is often distracted enough to burn dinner. (Okay, pretty much 90% of the time.) A sign on her office door reads: Danger. Enter at Your Own Risk. Writer at Work.

Under the name Teyla Branton, she writes urban fantasy, paranormal romance, and science fiction. She also writes romance, romantic suspense, and women's fiction under the name Rachel Branton. For more information or to sign up to hear about new releases, please visit www.TeylaBranton.com.